The Courtesan Countess

by

JoMarie DeGioia

PUBLISHED BY:

Bailey Park Publishing

I0653969

ISBN: 978-1-944181-32-1

The Courtesan Countess

Book One of the
Secret Hearts Series

by

JoMarie DeGioia

Chapter 1

London, England 1823

Marianne Ellsworth closed her eyes and held her arms at her sides. She forced her mind away from the act to come, instead focusing on almost anything else. The nightdress she wore was her finest, gossamer-thin and worth more than they had spent on food this week. Her hair was simply dressed, the long blond curls left loose as gentlemen seemed to prefer in such situations. Scrubbed and scented, she was surely a fitting ornament to the room's appointments.

The sheets beneath her were butter-soft. The very air in the chamber was sweet with the scevery airnts of cleanliness and flowers. The fire in the grate was banked, which was well-suited to this May evening. Several branches of candles lit the space as well, giving a soft glow to the pretty chamber.

The lodgings she shared with her aunt and younger sister were more than adequate, though a far cry from this residence in comparison. No, this particular townhouse was set precisely in Mayfair. Comfortable, rich, and nearly perfect. She should take pride that she had gained entry to such a home, if only she could set aside the way she had achieved it this evening. She tamped down the shame that threatened to swamp her.

The gentleman who had purchased her for the evening stepped into the room. "You are so beautiful, little dove."

Marianne absently murmured something or other as she watched him with some trepidation.

He loosened his cravat. "Fresh and sweet, I would wager."

He was young and darkly handsome, and appeared even-tempered. Surely she could divert her attention from the act until she had fulfilled her duty and was once more safely home in her bed.

In the weeks since starting on this course she had focused on nothing beyond the promise of comfort in any man's embrace once the encounter was over. Comfort and security. That was what drove her. Keeping that in her mind was all she could do. It had worked in the previous two encounters and she was certain it would in this one as well.

"I am grateful my friend refused his gift this

evening, though not wholly surprised." He unbuttoned and removed his shirt. "I daresay it shall still be money well spent."

He sat in a chair set near one window and tugged off his boots, pausing in between to flash a smile at her. She feigned an expression of anticipation as he climbed onto the bed with her. He seemed to notice her reticence, however.

"I shall be gentle, dove." He reached out to stroke a hand over her hair. "Just lovely."

He began to kiss her cheek, her neck, as sounds of rising ardor came from him. She squeezed her eyes shut and moaned. She was certain that the sounds she herself made seemed authentic. She had become quite skilled at feigning her own responses in so short a time.

Yes, she had been meant as a gift for the gentleman in the next chamber, bought and paid for by the man currently seeking a return on his investment. She was almost relieved, really. The man next door was big and strong, with a face so handsome he was just this side of pretty. He was like a golden god. She had watched him sleep for a few minutes there in his big bed before tentatively stroking him awake. And more than his eyelids had risen there in that large bed. A man so well-endowed would surely be outside her scant experience.

A current of something shivered across her skin, though she did not believe her body reacted to what her would-be paramour was doing. It was as if the air in the room had changed somehow. They were no longer alone in the chamber. Of that, she was certain.

A noise drew her attention then. Her eyes popped open and she gasped in surprise. There, framed in the doorway, was the man from the next chamber. Tall and broad, filling the space, with a magnificent dressing gown of burgundy draping his body. He watched her, his eyes a stormy green. *Those eyes…*

To her astonishment her breath caught. She let out a gasp, the sound more authentic than any she had made this evening. Her heartbeat quickened in spite of any effort to the contrary.

His robe was open, she saw. His chest was sculpted, dusted with golden hairs which led down his taut belly. He was perfectly formed and she blinked as he stepped closer.

The gentleman holding her lifted his head with a groan. "So sweet," he said, pausing to pat her hip. "I am afraid I am in dire need of your particular services directly."

"Yes, my lord," she said absently.

He rolled onto his back on the bed beside her, closing his eyes. She saw through his taut breeches that he was eager for release and knew there was nothing else for it.

She rose up on her elbows, stilling as she glanced again at the man in the doorway. His eyes were fastened on her, darkening as his lips parted. Her heart began to pound anew, her body coming alive as it never had before. She slowly ran her gaze over his finely-chiseled face.

"Will you take me, my lord?" she asked him. She was purchased for him, after all. That surely explained the hungry expression stamped on his countenance.

He gave a short nod and took a step forward.

"In a few minutes, dove," the man beside her said, clearly thinking she had spoken to him. "Employ that pretty mouth of yours now, and I promise I will ride you all night."

She was bought and paid for, and would have to deliver on the promised service. She eased herself to a sitting position, her skin tingling due to the continued perusal from the golden gentleman. Her nightdress slipped off one shoulder, and she flicked her long curls back from her face to regard him before letting her hair fall to shield herself from those eyes.

Shame threatened again as she began to fulfill her employer's request, but she set it aside as she once more attempted to occupy her mind elsewhere. Kneeling on the bed, she began to unfasten his breeches.

"Yes, dove." He stroked her hair gently. "That is the way."

She did not mind the task, really. He was clean and undemanding. Besides that, she knew just what to do to have this over with quickly. She had discovered quite by accident that the mere offer to perform this act could cause a man to nearly climax. Would that it would be over quickly. Then she could end this encounter and return to the safety of her aunt's home.

Before she had unfastened more than one button he

shifted beneath her, letting out a laugh. "I believe this will have to wait, dove. It seems that my good friend could not resist after all. Is that not so, Lacey?"

The golden one, Lacey, murmured in answer, his voice holding a wonderful deep timbre. The sound set a startling stab of wanting through her.

"She is all yours, then," her employer said as he walked away from the bed, laughter in his voice.

A rustling to her left drew her focus, soft footfalls as the golden gentleman crossed the room. She could scarcely move as the other man left the chamber. She slowly lifted her hair again and risked a glance at him.

"My lord?" she managed to squeak out.

"As you see, miss." She began to sit back on her heels but he stilled her with his next words. "Pray, keep that position. You have quite a lovely backside."

Her pulse jumped in response. She closed her eyes, breathing slowly to calm her racing pulse. What was it about this gentleman?

She felt Lacey step closer still, shivering as he lifted the hem of her costly nightdress up to expose her bottom. He ran his large hands over her, kneading and

11

teasing her skin. His touch moved between her thighs and she let out a whimper. It was a sound she barely recognized, one of fear and something else.

The golden one caressed her, deep inside, starting a rhythm that was impossible to ignore. A low moan escaped her. Lacey eased her legs apart, stroking her bottom as his finger kept up its pressure. The bed dipped beneath her, first to the right then to the left, as he climbed up behind her.

Spreading her legs gently, he grasped her hips and lifted her as he pressed his manhood up against her delicate flesh.

"Oh!" she gasped.

The friction teased and taunted her with a hint of the pleasure she sensed he could give her. It was not fear she had felt earlier, then. It was anticipation.

Lacey's grip tightened as he shifted. He entered her and she arched back. She let out a cry as he began to thrust. Long, deep movements that had her clutching the sheets beneath her in an attempt to hold on and let go at the same time. There was no separating her mind from this.

Again and again he drove inside of her, his hands gripping her hips as he skillfully brought her to her very first climax. She shuddered against him, lost to everything but the splendid friction. The sounds they both made echoed off the coffered ceiling as her passion crested again.

With one last thrust he poured himself inside her, bending close to bring his face near hers. "My God," he groaned. He dropped a kiss on her cheek and she blinked back a rush of stinging tears. "That exceeded my expectations."

He withdrew and she sank down onto the bed. The other gentleman was still absent, thank goodness. She was grateful for the bit of privacy he had given them. She settled back on the soft pillows and let out a sigh. So that was pleasure? It was heavenly. And dangerous.

She opened her eyes to find Lord Lacey staring down at her, an inscrutable look on his features. He tied his dressing gown tightly closed then raked his fingers through his hair.

He cleared his throat. "I trust you have been paid, miss?"

There was no censure in his tone, to her immense relief. Just politeness. "Yes, my lord."

He began to bend toward her and she lifted her head to meet him. The other men had never kissed her, but she craved this man's kiss. It was quick, a soft brush of his beautiful mouth against hers before he stood once more.

"Good night."

With that, he quit the chamber. She blinked back the tears when they came anew. The other gentleman reentered a few moments later, a smile on his face. He gazed down at her with apparent fondness as she attempted to hide a yawn behind her hand.

"Well, I see that Lacey has ruined you for the night," he said. "No worries, dove. Perhaps I shall purchase another night with you in the near future." She began to rise but he waved a hand. "Keep to this chamber. Lacey has plenty of rooms. I shall find one of my own."

After the door shut quietly, she thought once more about how she had come to this. The machinations, the shock of betrayal after so painful a loss. The decided lack of any other recourse for her family to survive. She had done what she had to, to augment the meager funds they had scraped together to afford them the use of a townhouse for the Season and the trappings necessary for circulating among polite society.

Another thought intruded, equally troubling. She had reveled in the touch of the golden Lord Lacey as he had brought them both to completion. The two times before she had put the encounter out of her mind as an act of self-preservation. Tonight, however? She suspected she would keep the memory of Lord Lacey and his own particular brand of passion long after this life was behind her.

She rose and went behind the screen, finding a clean bowl of water and several soft towels. She washed herself with scented soaps there, a floral scent much like that which dressed the linens on the bed. Apparently Lord Lacey's staff was quite attentive, even to his guests. No footman hung about, however. Lacey must value his privacy, then. That would surely save her any embarrassment come the morning, not that she would linger much after sunrise.

She ran the towel over the tender flesh between her legs, feeling an echo of the heat he had stirred within her. Gripping the cloth, she froze. He had spilled his seed inside of her!

She had been so lost to her own desires. Thank goodness her aunt had learned of several remedies to make certain that nothing untoward occurred.

It would not do for her to work so hard to secure their place in Society only to find herself in far worse circumstances than those which plagued her now.

Chapter 2

Marcus Lacey stretched out on the bed, one arm thrown over his brow. He gazed up at the canopy above his head, his mind on the girl in the next chamber. He had sent her from his room not more than an hour earlier, shunning the gift Rob had so thoughtfully provided. He believed Marcus needed the release. Needed to forget about his ex-fiancé and her defection to Gretna Green a week ago with Marcus' man-of-affairs. What did it matter to Marcus if the woman preferred a simpler life to that of countess to the wealthy Earl of Lacey?

In parting she had told him he was cold. There was more than a little truth to her words, harsh though they had been. His heart had not been involved at all. Joan had simply been the best candidate in a field of debutantes he had considered to fill the role of his wife. Now he would have to begin his search anew. Luckily the Season was in full-swing.

He thought of the little ladybird once more. She had been so tight. So hot. And her kiss had been sweeter than any he had ever tasted. She was too beautiful to waste away as a courtesan for a night's pleasure. No, she deserved to be set up in style. Perhaps that was what Rob was considering right now. A pang of jealously stabbed at him.

He let out a grunt. What did he care if Rob set up the girl as his mistress? Marcus needed to wed and before his thirtieth birthday, a ludicrous stipulation of his father's will. If he did not find a bride before the Season was out, he had little hope of meeting that demand. He needed a Christmas bride at the latest, for his birthday fell on the last day of the year.

Though seeking pleasure with the girl now and again could be worth the expense of keeping her for himself in the coming months. A smile broke out, unfamiliar and a tad uncomfortable. He could surely see availing himself of her when the need required. The need and the desire, for he had never felt such acute attraction before. There was a freshness about her. A graceful beauty he had seen in the candlelight.

Surely she was experienced, yet she had seemed surprised as her climax took her. She had pressed tightly to him, her perfect bottom flush against his belly. He turned his head to regard the wall separating them. What was she about now?

He had heard Rob take his leave soon after he had returned, no doubt to check on her. She was alone, then. His body hardened at the possibilities that brought to mind. She was bought and paid for. Meant for him tonight. Why not make the most of Rob's thoughtful gift? He rose and crossed the room.

He wanted the girl with a fierceness that surprised him. He was never one to let his baser urges rule his mind. This night was different, however. An aberration. He would indulge himself tonight then return to being the stodgy Earl of Lacey he was known to be. Straight-laced Lacey, was what they called him.

He entered the guest chamber and quietly shut the door. His blood pounded, low and deep, as he turned to the bed. He found it empty and let out a curse, a first in his memory. He heard a feminine gasp of surprise from behind the screen and the girl peeked around it in the next moment. Her glorious hair was a riot of curls, her pretty nightdress clutched in front of her. He could see she was naked behind it, and the curve of her hip led his eyes down one shapely leg to a dainty foot.

"I thought you were…" She waved one hand, a look of relief on her exquisite face. "Never mind. Did you need something, my lord?"

You. "Yes, miss." He stepped closer, reading the answering heat that soon entered her blue eyes. They appeared almost black in the light of the candles, dark and deep and as inviting as her luscious body. "Let me have a look at you."

Far from the rebuff he might expect such an imperious demand to elicit, she lifted her chin and lowered the nightdress. She was not a tall girl, nor filled out with ample curves. She was perfectly formed, her breasts round and high, her waist tiny. Smooth muscles were evident in her arms and legs, and her body looked supple as she moved toward him.

She draped the nightdress over a chair and slowly climbed up onto the bed. "I admit I had hoped you would return, my lord."

Her words sent a lick of desire to his groin. "Oh?"

She nodded, her hair brushing forward to cover one breast. Its pink nipple peeped out at him and he found his gaze riveted to the spot. He finally moved toward her, shucking off his robe as he did so. She stared at his shaft, her eyes round.

"You are so big, my lord."

A flicker of unease struck him. "Did I hurt you? Before? I admit I lost control."

She shook her head, a smile lifting one corner of her mouth. "I have never felt anything like it."

He suspected from the sincerity in those deep blue eyes that she meant it. Those eyes held no guile that he could see, and he was inclined to believe her artless words. "And I have never felt such a release," he admitted.

She leaned back to recline on her elbows, the position in which he had found her earlier.

"Do you desire me again, my lord?" she asked. "The gentleman paid for the whole night."

He nearly crowed his thanks to Rob and his misplaced generosity. "Yes." He licked his lips and brought his gaze to her face. "Open your legs."

Heat flared in her eyes as she complied with his request. He lowered his gaze then, to the flesh she exposed. He hardened painfully and let out another curse.

"Christ, you are beautiful."

At his words her flesh seemed to swell. He joined her on the bed. He lifted a lock of silken hair shielding her nipple and brought it to his nose as he stretched out on top of her. She smelled so sweet, like flowers and exotic vanilla. He buried his face in her hair, breathing deeply and rubbing his chest against her breasts. Her nipples pebbled as she arched upward. One quick kiss to her lush lips, and then he brought his mouth to her breast.

Stroking his tongue over her, he marveled at her taste. More sweetness. Her moans filled his ears. It spoke to something primal in him, the notion that he could bring her pleasure.

She clutched at his head as he suckled, sighing as he aroused her. His fingers stroked the delicate skin on her inner thighs, nearing her pussy. Giving a soft sob of wanting, she arched toward his hand.

He lifted his head, staring at her face as she closed her eyes. Her hair was a wild mane, her neck long and graceful as she sought the release he silently vowed to give her. Without wasting another moment, he buried his face in the treasure between her legs.

Her unique taste was here as well, mingling with the subtle salt of her skin. He licked and suckled and stroked her, rasping his tongue against the taut little nub nestled in those damp curls. She started to tremble beneath his tongue, wriggling and bucking as her climax began. He had never tasted a woman's release, never sought to give anything but a touch of arousal before finding his own pleasure. With this girl however, he wanted to bring her there first. To taste the crest of her passion before giving in to his own.

"Oh!" She writhed against him as she came.

He held her thighs gently but firmly, wringing every last spasm from her until she was replete. With his own breath coming as fast as hers, he moved up to drive deep inside her. She cried out, clutching at him as she lifted her legs high around his waist. Bracing himself on his arms, he closed his eyes as he thrust into her again and again.

Nothing had ever felt so right, so strong, as their bodies made one. Unable to hold himself upright a moment longer, he pulled her close as he found his release deep inside her. She was a limp bundle beneath him, her fingers trailing over his back as his heart at last began to slow.

He kissed her. Her hair, her neck, her lips. A troubling fact struck him. He had spilled his seed in her. Again.

He rolled onto his back, bringing her close against his side. "It seems I forgot myself again, miss."

"No matter, my lord." She shifted to rest her head on his chest, letting out a breath. "I have taken precautions."

He did not ask her what they were, but he did not sense any artifice in her tone or posture. She seemed to be precisely what she appeared: a sweet armful meant to light an otherwise dark night. "Very well."

She laughed softly then, the sound touching something inside him.

"May I ask what amuses you so?" he asked.

She turned, resting her chin on her folded hands as she regarded him with those deep blue eyes. "Still so formal, my lord? Even in these environs?"

He blinked. Her speech was proper and well-modulated. That seemed at odds with her profession.

"How long have you been about this occupation?"

She pulled back, her brow creasing. "Long enough, I daresay." Alarm flickered in her eyes. "Did I not please you?"

"Please me? You nearly killed me." He ran a hand over her hair, smoothing the curls between his fingers. "I was merely curious."

She lost that worried expression, to his relief. "For but a few weeks now, my lord."

He thought about that for a moment. "Do you enjoy your work?" Her eyes widened and he offered her a smile. "That is not quite what I meant. Would you consider another arrangement?"

Her long lashes fluttered as she obviously sought to make sense of what he was only starting to realize. He wanted her for himself. To keep her passion for him alone.

"I can provide for you," he said. "Give you a place to live."

"I have a place to live." Her tone was chilly now, nearly as cold as his was often to his own ears. "Do not worry about me."

"Forget I said that," he rushed out. "Perhaps we can discuss another arrangement?"

She came to her knees, clutching the sheets in front of her as she settled back on her heels. "What type of arrangement?"

He sat up, giving her a bit of space as he considered the best approach to take. She was obviously proud, which pleased him. She valued herself, which eased his mind as well.

"Keep yourself to me alone, miss." He smiled, the expression feeling nearly natural now. "I feel I should know your name."

"Annie," she provided.

"Annie, then." He nodded. "Keep yourself to me and I will pay you handsomely."

"I do not understand."

"I will send word to you when I want your company." He reached out to stroke her cheek. Her skin was almost unbearably smooth. "You will come to me." She opened her mouth to protest and he held up his hand. "If you are available, of course. I will not make demands, but you must promise not to gift any other gentlemen with your favors."

She nibbled her lower lip, the expression adorable. "This will only be for the length of the Season."

"As you wish."

She nodded. "I will get word to you on the mode of communication, if that suits."

Again, he was struck by her obvious breeding. There was more to this girl than met the eye. It was of no consequence tonight, however. Tonight he had her agreement.

"Capital," he said. He yawned, the strength of his release at last catching up with him. He saw the shadows beneath her eyes then and shifted to allow her to once more recline on the pillows. Though loath to leave her, he eased away and stood at the side of the bed. "Sleep, Annie." He kissed her again, their lips clinging for a moment before he straightened. "I shall await your contact."

She blinked at him again, then nodded. He left the chamber, feeling a smile stretch his face once more. She would be his, for now at least. No other would taste her again. He might have to fulfill the demands of his title and inheritance before the Season was out, but for the next few months he would have her.

He would worry about the rest of it when the time came.

Chapter 3

Marianne rose before the sun and washed in chilled water from the basin behind the screen. She had managed to sleep a bit after Lord Lacey had taken his leave. That fact alone amazed her, as had his offer. She had ample time to consider the ramifications this morning, however.

For all intents and purposes she would be his plaything. His alone, until her family's troubles were behind them. It was a superior arrangement compared to the way she had gone on for the past few weeks. Aunt Hattie would be relieved. Despite George's care with selection and secrecy, they all knew there was an inherent danger to this particular path.

George, their trusted butler, driver and footman, the only servant left to them from their previous life, arranged for the liaisons. A new housekeeper, a cook and a maid for the ladies to share had to be engaged upon their securing the townhouse, but those women were kept in the dark regarding Marianne's nocturnal activities. No one would be able to trace any untoward actions to their family. No one would connect "Annie" with her, and her sister Brianna would never be touched by this sordid business.

Marianne carefully folded the fancy nightdress and placed it in her small satchel. After donning her serviceable dress of brown and stepping into her slippers, she coiled her hair at the back of her head and secured it with a few pins. Her dark, simple cloak would keep her from attracting any undue notice during her escape.

She walked toward the door, turning to glance once more at the sumptuous bed. She had nurtured the skill of being able to keep her mind blessedly absent from the act. To feign pleasure with a smile. Last night with Lord Lacey, however?

The man knew how to give pleasure. True, she had only lain with two men since the surrender of her virtue but she suspected he was in a category all of his own. Not only had he forced her attention to his every movement despite her intentions to the contrary, but he had wrung such piercing pleasure out of her body that she still trembled to think of it.

Shaking her head, she eased the door open. A quick glance confirmed what she had expected last night. The hallway was empty of any staff. The sky lightened swiftly however, and she guessed that vacancy would not continue for much longer. George would be waiting for her in the mews, a few houses away from here where he had let her off last night. She had best go. There would be plenty of time to consider the surprising turn of events when she was safely home.

George said nothing as she stepped toward the waiting carriage, his expression beneath his crumpled hat the combination of worry and resignation she had come to expect even after so few occurrences. The ride was not overlong. Their leased townhouse was nowhere near Park Avenue or Mayfair, but it was in a decent area of Town. The neighborhood was occupied by minor gentry and others of respectability, and close enough for calls to be paid and received now that they circulated among the Fashionable.

The carriage pulled to a stop in front of their house and Marianne alighted before its aged springs quit creaking. "Thank you, George."

That look of concern was on the man's face again, but was swiftly wiped away as he nodded in answer. She hesitated, then turned to him. "George, there will be a change to the nocturnal adventures."

"Oh, miss!" His watery eyes went round. "I been hopin' and prayin' it'd soon be so."

She smiled sadly at him and shook her head. "It is only a slight change, I am afraid. I will only visit one gentleman going forward."

"The one from this evenin'?"

Once more Lord Lacey's image filled her mind. "Yes. We will discuss the details later."

He blinked, then nodded in that stoic fashion he had. "As you wish it, miss."

As she entered the townhouse, she could hear sounds coming from the back of the house as the servants moved about. She hurried up the stairs to her chamber. Sweeping off her cloak, she regarded the room.

It was clean and pleasant, if lacking the luxury of Lord Lacey's rooms. He had offered to give her a place to live and she had all but snapped at him. Well, she had paid for these accommodations. She thought of John and his rough taking of her that first time. She had paid dearly.

She rang for water and within a half an hour she

was dressed in a pretty day gown and sitting at her vanity as the maid tended to her hair. Gone were the loose curls that had so captivated Lord Lacey. In their place was a simple, respectable style which held all but a few curls in control. Miss Marianne Ellsworth was once more present.

"Thank you, Suzie."

The maid dipped a curtsey and left to see to Brianna's needs. Marianne regarded herself in the mirror for a long moment, her eyes filling with tears.

"Just until the end of the Season," she murmured.

"I pray our luck will hold until then," her aunt said from the doorway.

Marianne dashed her hands over her tear-streaked cheeks and turned to her. "Good morning, Aunt."

The older woman smiled and closed the door against any prying ears. "And a third night, safely done." She narrowed her eyes, apparently seeing the tears clinging to Marianne's lashes. "Was it as bad as that, dear?"

Marianne gave a quick shake of her head. "No. Lord Lacey was… surprising."

Her aunt's brows rose. The slender woman bustled over, placing a hand on her shoulder. "You were not hurt? George learned of the man's reputation and assured us the rendezvous would be safe."

"And it was." She took in a breath and let it out slowly. "Lord Lacey offered to keep me."

"Absolutely not!" Her aunt's eyes widened and she covered her mouth. "Forgive me. It pains me to see you give away what is so valuable. I shall not condemn you to a longer sentence than necessary."

"It is not precisely what you think," Marianne assured her. "He wants me to be available to meet him at his home. And to keep myself only to him."

"Oh." Her aunt settled on the edge of the narrow bed. "Oh, that is not so terrible. And far safer."

"I am worried that prolonged contact might put my masquerade in jeopardy, however."

"How so? You make certain to use that false name. You look nothing but respectable in any other environ. Like the earl's great-granddaughter you are."

"Yes, if only the old earl's estate had not been entailed."

Aunt Hattie simply nodded, an expression of lifelong resignation fixed on her countenance. Marianne's mother and aunt had grown up in relative comfort nonetheless, though any true wealth was all but a memory by the time Marianne and Brianna's parents had wed. It was something that was a fact however, and wishing it away was of no good purpose today.

Marianne thought of those eyes of Lord Lacey's again. "He is sharp, Aunt. He asked how long I have been in this occupation, as if he sensed my unease."

Her aunt scowled. "He did not force you to do something abhorrent?"

Marianne could not guess what her aunt meant, but she shook her head. "No. He was quite attentive, however."

"Little wonder, that." She offered Marianne a smile. "You are a beautiful girl. And in your dishabille? How could he resist you?"

Marianne waved a hand. "I will let George arrange matters, as before."

"With the boys in the mews, yes. It has worked so far."

"But there have only been a handful of liaisons. I do not know how often Lord Lacey will send for me."

"Then you must set a price worth such dedicated attention."

Marianne thought for a moment. "I suppose."

Her aunt wrung her hands, her face wearing a frown once more. "I so wish you could end this business, Marianne."

"I cannot. I do not wish to discuss this again. You know there is no other way. Bree and I have nothing left of our inheritance. There is no money left to the three of us after Uncle's death, thanks to John."

Aunt Hattie blinked back her own tears, shaking her head. "That stepson of mine. He is nothing like your uncle was. He believed John would see to our welfare. Hah." She fell silent for a moment, then sniffed. "Keeping to one gentleman may increase your risk of discovery but it far lessens the other dangers."

"True." Marianne stood. "And in less than two months we have set up a household and begun to circulate. Attention is coming, and from the right directions."

"Oh, how I wish you could share that attention. Brianna is pretty and vivacious, but you are beautiful."

Marianne shook her head. "That does not signify. There is not enough money to outfit myself as finely as Bree. She will be the one to marry well and secure our future. As long as I keep my own comments to a minimum and let her take center stage, we can keep to our course."

"And keep anyone from equating Miss Marianne Ellsworth with Annie."

A rapid knock came at the door and both women turned in alarm.

"Marianne!" Bree called through the panel.

Letting out a breath, her aunt opened the door to Bree's entrance. "Good morning."

"Good morning, Aunt." She ran up to Marianne and took her hands in hers. Her face was flushed, her blue eyes sparkling. She was dressed though her brown hair had yet to be styled. "A note arrived, Marianne." She waved the crumpled missive in her hand. "From Mister Stilling. He wants to ride in the park. Today!"

"Mister Stilling," Marianne mused aloud. "Third

son of the Earl of Taunton. Does he have any property of his own?"

Bree waved a hand in answer. "Who knows? He is lively and he makes me laugh. He has the prettiest smile."

Marianne bit her tongue. If only Bree knew how important it was that she land a wealthy husband, she would care about more than smiles and laughter. The girl was eighteen and eager for adventure, and blessedly ignorant of any but the most blatant changes in their circumstances. Marianne and her aunt made certain of that. There were times, while accompanying her sister to the parties and fielding gentlemen's requests to call at the townhouse, when Marianne felt much older than her own twenty-one years.

"What time can we expect him, Bree?" Marianne asked.

"Oh!" Bree's brow puckered and she withdrew the note from her clenched hand. "Eleven o'clock."

Their aunt nodded. "Then go have Suzie see to your hair." She ran her gaze over Bree's dress, a lovely walking gown of rose and cream. "Your dress will do nicely. We shall discuss our strategy over breakfast."

"Strategy?" Bree laughed. "Oh, Aunt. It is simply a ride in the park."

Marianne and their aunt exchanged a long look.

Aunt Hattie waved the younger girl out of the room. "Off with you, then."

Bree beamed in Marianne's direction and hurried back to her own chamber.

Marianne turned to her aunt with a smile. "The calls begin in earnest, Aunt. Bree is on her way."

"And hopefully even this new arrangement with Lord Lacey will not have to last as long as we fear."

After her aunt left her alone once again, Marianne thought of her new role as Lord Lacey's personal ladybird. It was far safer. Physically, at least. Emotionally? That worried her. He had broken through her newly-won withdrawal and forced her attention fully on the act. On him. He had wrung wants and desires from her that she had not known she possessed.

How long before her heart became engaged? That was something she could never risk.

* * *

"You look almost genial this morning, Lacey," Rob drawled from his seat at the wide dining table.

Marcus nodded in answer and crossed to the sideboard. He chose a larger breakfast than was his usual, finding his appetite as roused this morning as his passions had been last night. He settled across from Rob, then drank deeply of his tea as he watched his friend eye his plate. He lowered his cup. "Is something amiss?"

Rob laughed, his brown eyes crinkling at the corners. "Seems you made good use of my gift last night. More than once, if I heard correctly."

Marcus felt his cheeks heat and focused on his food. He consumed his breakfast as Rob drank his tea. "Where are you off to?"

"So eager to be rid of me?"

Marcus wiped his mouth on a napkin, deliberately folding it before placing it beside his empty plate. "I appreciate your gift, Rob."

"Any time." He leaned back, folding his hands over his abdomen. "I believe I shall make some arrangements for myself, and soon."

"Not with her."

Rob arched a dark brow at his vehemence. "Indeed?"

Marcus had not thought to stake such a claim, not to anyone but himself and Annie. There was nothing for it this morning, however. "She is to keep herself to me now."

"Hmm? Seems the girl managed to do more for you than I had hoped."

Marcus scowled at him. "Explain your meaning."

Rob grinned and stood. "She loosened the laces."

Marcus eased in his chair and bid his friend farewell. His plate was removed and his cup refilled and still he sat at the table. Rob knew Annie was no longer available for any other gentleman's pleasure. *Good.* As for himself, this was new territory. He had never kept a woman, choosing instead to take his pleasure now and again with a tavern girl and never the same one twice. Now he could not think of taking any other than sweet Annie.

He stood and went into his study. Work awaited him. The tangled estate left to him by his father, which would remain his once he wed. He settled behind his desk and withdrew one worn ledger and began to pore over the numbers. It would serve his sire's ghost right if he let the property slip away at the end of the year. He was the second son. The spare. If his brother had not died of what had seemed a piddling cold, this task would have fallen on his shoulders when their drunken father had fallen from his horse.

His brother Matthew had been cut from the same cloth as their father. Wild and raucous. The two of them would drink and carouse and diddle every wench and widow within an hour's ride. Not Marcus. Stoic and cold, he was. Like their late mother. That was his father's opinion of him, and Marcus had done nothing to disabuse him of the notion. Straight-laced Lacey, he had been dubbed. So he remained to this day. Save for the astounding time spent with his ladybird last night.

She was to let him know the mode of communication. Then he would call her to his bed, and she would be his again. Yes, he would have to dance attendance on the debutantes. He would have to seek out a lady worthy of being his countess. There was still time, however.

He would spend his days at his club or in his study with his ledgers. He would spend his evenings at the parties as he sought his future bride. Later, after the work of the day and the tedium of the evening's festivities, he could have Annie again. That was as clear as the desire she fired in him. As right as the smile he could not seem to wipe from his face.

Loosened laces, indeed.

Chapter 4

Marianne adjusted her bonnet as the well-sprung carriage bounced over the cobblestones. Mister Stilling had been on time, a point in his favor, and she and Bree had been spirited away from their townhouse into the bright May sunshine. The landau was open to the elements and she tipped her head back for a long moment, relishing the warmth on her cheeks as she kept her ears attuned to the couple sitting with her in the carriage.

Bree's laughter reached her, a light carefree sound she herself had not made in what felt like ages. Marianne turned her head and studied her sister, seeing the pampered life stretching ahead of her. It was the life Bree deserved and Marianne sorely hoped to arrange. Now, with Lord Lacey's exclusivity, she should be able to gain the funds to see the Season through entertaining and gowns and the like. She had to devise a mode of communication soon, however. Before he attempted to contact her somehow. That would never do.

"Think you not, Marianne?" Bree asked her.

She shook her head and faced Bree. "Hmm?"

Bree laughed. "The crowds, sister. Have you ever seen the park bustle so?"

"No, I have not."

Bree turned to Mister Stilling. "It seems the population doubles each week we are in Town."

"Well, I have never seen the park so beautiful," Mister Stilling offered, his gaze on Bree.

Marianne hid her smile. It was clumsy, but a compliment from a third son was nothing to sneeze at.

"Indeed, Mister Stilling," she agreed.

She settled back once more, keeping herself quiet as the two others continued their inane conversation about crowds and beauty.

"Ho, Stilling!" a masculine voice called.

A gentleman approached on horseback, finely dressed and wearing a grin. Marianne's heart dropped to her stomach. She recognized that crooked smile. It was Lord Something-or-other from last night. The one who had purchased her for Lord Lacey. To her growing alarm he drew his horse alongside the carriage as Mister Stilling slowed to a stop.

"Good morning, Devlin," Mister Stilling said.

"Escorting two lovely ladies this morning, Stilling?" Devlin winked at Bree, who giggled in response. "Not very sporting of you, keeping all the beauty for yourself."

Marianne stiffened in her seat and schooled her expression, holding her lips tightly closed and affecting a look of detachment. As she lowered her head to shield her face, she watched him out of the corner of her eye.

"May I bother you for an introduction?" he asked Stilling.

Mister Stilling bristled visibly, but complied. "Miss Marianne Ellsworth, Miss Brianna Ellsworth, may I present Robert Pierce, Viscount Devlin."

"Charmed, ladies," Lord Devlin said with a bow of his head. "New to Town, are you?"

"Just six weeks, my lord," Bree provided. "Marianne, myself and our aunt are quite enjoying Town thus far."

"Six weeks?" Lord Devlin's eyes rounded in feigned surprise. "And yet I have never seen you about?"

"We have been about, my lord," Bree said.

Lord Devlin held one hand over his chest. "Then I

have been remiss. It appears I should attend more parties, eh Stilling?"

Mister Stilling glowered in his direction, looking much like a petulant boy. Marianne reasoned that she may have to mentally scratch him off the list of Bree's potential suitors. No man with ill-humor would suit her sister's carefree personality.

"And what of you, Miss Ellsworth?" Lord Devlin asked. "Are you enjoying London as your sister is?"

Marianne stiffened, slanting him a look from beneath her bonnet. "Yes, my lord," she answered in a chilly tone.

Devlin's smile faltered for a moment. "Right." His brow puckered and she prayed he would not recognize her. He stared at her lips as she attempted to keep them pursed.

To her relief, his smile resurfaced. "Well, I shall leave you to your ride, then." He nodded to them once more. "Miss Ellsworth. Miss Brianna. Stilling."

With that, he rode away from them. Marianne watched, refraining from sinking further in her seat as he turned to glance at her over his shoulder.

"He seems like a friendly sort," Bree said.

Mister Stilling grunted, still obviously put out by Lord Devlin's charming ways. Marianne could not blame him. She only hoped the man's affability did not hide shrewdness. He appeared carefree and fun loving, even last night he had been so, but there was something more behind those brown eyes.

She would have to stay away from his company, especially now that he had indicated an interest in the parties. It would not do to have Brianna's potential suitor recall that her sister had been in bed with him and had nearly… She could not finish the thought.

She must maintain the façade she had erected upon coming to Town. That of the cool, detached older sister uninterested in courtship or marriage.

No one must ever connect Annie to Marianne Ellsworth.

* * *

Marcus closed the ledger with a sense of accomplishment. He'd had to bring the figures up to date, a week's worth to be exact, but he had managed. He needed to hire another man-of-affairs and soon, however.

Perhaps Rob could recommend someone. He could not afford to let the finances tangle themselves. Not again.

It had taken most of the three years since his father's death to straighten out the mess the man had left behind. The estate was profitable now, the grounds and tenants well-cared for. At least he could count on his steward at Lacey Manor to take care of business and not run off with a lady betrothed to another. He would not be in this position if Mr. Allen had not taken a shining to Joan. Then again, if Joan and Allen had not run off he would not have been jilted and Rob would not have engaged the lovely Annie for the evening.

A Season spent with the beautiful girl was worth far more than a lifetime with a miserable wife. And Joan would have been miserable. He cared nothing for her, and most likely would have abandoned her to Lacey Manor as his father had his mother.

He tried to set aside the thought of his poor mother, always so lonely and withdrawn. She had given no affection to him or his brother, and there were times when Marcus feared he was cut from the same cloth. It was what his father had accused him of time and again, and the reason behind the ridiculous stipulation in his will. Evidently his father had believed Marcus would never marry otherwise.

Marcus could recite verbatim the litany the previous earl had rung over his head whenever he was deep in his cups, accusations of possessing no bullocks or worse. More than once Marcus had had to retrieve him or his brother, or sometimes both of them, from the village tavern. Ribald comments and shouting usually accompanied the task, as one wench or another cried over their abandonment. Just the thought made his skin crawl.

Marcus was not a eunuch, as his family declared. And he was not without a man's needs. He had never joined his father and brother on their exploits, however. There was little appeal for him in a well-used woman who had been used by either of them.

He thought of Annie again. She was worlds away from the women in that tavern. Hell, she was in a class by herself. But a few weeks, she had been at her occupation. He would not think about how many men may have paid for her favors in that short time. She was sweet and fresh, and his for the next few months.

"Mine," he murmured.

He had not yet heard from her regarding their communication, and now it was evening. He felt like a randy boy, eager to have her beneath him again. Or above him. He smiled to himself. Or in front of him. He had never been adventurous in his sexual exploits, but he could easily envision any and every position he wanted to explore with Annie. When would she contact him?

A knock on the study door brought him out of his reverie. "Yes."

His butler opened the door, bowing. "Viscount Devlin, my lord."

"Thank you, Parks."

Rob entered behind the servant, quirking a brow at the man's retreating back. "Wouldn't allow me in without an announcement."

"All of my staff know that I value my privacy." He leaned back in his chair, waving Rob into the one across from him. "What brings you by?"

"Just checking on you." He smiled. "I had to see if your good humor of this morning continues now that the sun has set."

Marcus grunted. "I am afraid it did not last, not through the hours spent working on these ledgers. I must engage a new man. Care to recommend someone?"

"Why don't you try my solicitor, Grimes? The firm is respectable." Rob was quiet for a moment. "Circumspect."

Marcus waved away his friend's concerns. "I am an open book." He nudged at one of the ledgers. "Financially, at least."

Rob smiled. "And that is why you are the catch of the Season."

"Hardly. If you recommend the firm, I shall contact them directly."

Rob nodded. "Have you given any thought about your renewed pursuit?" he asked. It was not an unwelcome changing of the subject.

"Of a bride? Not today, I haven't."

"Not surprising." Rob slanted him a look. "I am amazed you can think at all, after last night."

Marcus' lips thinned. "Never mind. What occupied you after you finally took your leave this morning?"

"Went for a ride in the park. I was surprised to see

Stilling, escorting two of the prettiest girls I have seen all Season. Insolent pup."

"I trust you forced an introduction?"

"Naturally. Couldn't rightly refuse me, not in front of the ladies, without looking like the complete ass he is. Lovely sisters, really."

"Do you know their name?"

"Ellsworth. Does that name mean anything to you?"

Marcus thought for a moment. "Property to the north, perhaps?" He shook his head. "I am not certain."

"Well, the younger one is quite pretty. But the older one is downright beautiful, if a bit cold." Rob grinned. "She would be perfect for you."

He ignored the barb. "I am sure I shall come across them at the parties."

"It is inevitable. If Stinky Stilling made their acquaintance they must be making the rounds."

Another knock came at the door and Marcus started. "Yes?"

Parks opened the door again, a missive in his hand. "This was just delivered for you, my lord."

Marcus came to his feet and only just stopped himself from running around the desk. "Oh?" He walked toward the door and took the letter from Parks. It was smudged on the outside and its corners were creased. "Who brought it?"

"A boy, my lord. One I've never seen before."

Marcus turned it over, reading the feminine script beneath the dirty fingerprints. "Thank you, Parks." As the door was closing, he called the butler again. "Have him await my reply. Take him to the kitchens and get him something to eat if he likes."

The butler nodded, then closed the door. Marcus broke the unmarked seal and unfolded the outer sheet of paper. The inside sheet was in far better condition, and held the light scent of the girl. Unconsciously he took in a breath, then opened it and read.

In a few words she spelled out the procedure for contact. He was to send a calling card, with the time of the rendezvous he desired on the back, by folding it in a piece of foolscap and setting it behind the planter nearest his servants' entrance. This area would be checked throughout the day, and when the missive was gone he could assume it had been taken to her.

He thought for a moment. He did not know how Rob had brought her into the house but she must have left through the servants' entrance this morning. It was a sound arrangement. He read the amount she had decided upon for his exclusive service and blinked. Rob let out a low whistle from over his shoulder.

"What?" Marcus asked, turning to him.

"The dove values herself highly." Marcus' face must have shown his irritation for Rob held up his hands and stepped back. "As she should."

"That is her weekly fee," Marcus clarified. He smiled and returned to his desk to sit. "Clever girl. She knows I might just call for her company every night of the week."

He withdrew a slip of foolscap and wrote a reply accepting her fee, plus a bit more additionally, and the mode of communication. Taking up one of his calling cards, he turned it over and wrote the day's date and the time he wanted her there. Half-past eleven. He added the notation "if you are available" and slipped it within the paper, folded it and waxed it sealed.

"Not wasting any time?" Rob teased.

Marcus shook his head. "I shall give the parties until eleven o'clock. That will give me enough time to make an appearance, make it be known that I am back in circulation as it were, and get the hell out of there."

Rob laughed. "So much for the lovely Ellsworth sisters."

Chapter 5

"What if he refuses, Aunt?"

Marianne paced the length of her chamber, her hands clasped in front of her. "The amount we came to seems excessive."

"Not for what he desires, dear."

"But it is ten times the amount we charged for a single night with any of the other gentleman."

"Well, he will definitely call you to him more than once a week. Perhaps every night."

Marianne blanched. The thought of being with him so often should have frightened her witless. It did, in a fashion. She could not deny that it caused her heart to race as well. She recalled that second time he had taken her, when he had braced himself above her. So strong, so focused. She blinked to clear the image from her mind.

"Oh, I know he will think me unreasonable."

Aunt Hattie took her hands, stilling her. She looked into her eyes. "You are giving something away of great value, Marianne. Not to mention your future happiness. You deserve every penny you asked for and more."

She managed a nod. "You are right. I just hope—"

A knock came at the door and Aunt Hattie crossed the room to pull it open. George stood there, wearing his butler's attire and holding a letter toward Marianne. "This come, miss. From one of the lads."

"Thank you, George." Aunt Hattie took the missive. "We will let you know if you are needed for more than one trip tonight."

He nodded and left them. Marianne took the letter from her aunt. She held her breath as she broke the seal, faintly registering the fancy crest there, and swiftly read the contents. A breath escaped her and she smiled at her aunt. "He agreed to the terms. Although he increased the amount."

Her aunt's mouth gaped but then she gave a sharp nod.

Marianne picked up the calling card that had been tucked within. "And he wants me to come to him at half-past eleven tonight."

"He is eager." Her aunt looked as if she wished to renew her objections, then grew quiet for a moment. "Will you go?"

Marianne nodded.

"We will tell Brianna you have a headache," her aunt said. "She and I will attend tonight's round of parties without you."

"Thank you, Aunt. I know I agreed to his request last night but now, with the prospect clear as the ink on this card? Now I am not so certain."

"It will be all right, dear. He took care with you, did he not?"

Marianne thought of the way he had held her afterwards, of the soft look in his eyes after his release.

"Yes."

"Then no worries. You have enough of that balm?"

Her cheeks heated as she thought of the herbal mixture purported to prevent conception, and where she would have to put it again. "Yes."

"Still, you must encourage him to keep from… you know, again."

She just nodded again.

"You will be fine, dear. I have to believe that." Aunt Hattie brushed a kiss on her cheek and patted her hand. "I will advise Brianna of our slight change of plans and tell George to have the carriage ready for you later."

"Thank you, Aunt."

Her aunt left her alone to prepare herself for the long night. She would have a few hours to her own counsel, which was preferable to the alternative of joining Bree and their aunt at the parties. Feigning cool detachment at the functions held little appeal, especially tonight. She was to go to Lord Lacey in just a few hours. She was to become his mistress.

This was far outside the realm of anything she had done since taking up this sordid occupation. Goodness knew he made her feel things. Made her experience every nuance of his touch. He gave her so much passion that she had welcomed his release deep inside of her. Twice.

He had told her he had forgotten himself. If she could not count on him to withdraw from her then she would have to make certain she kept her wits at climax.

What of afterward? When he had held her close and stroked her hair in that tender manner he possessed? Her wits would no doubt scatter to the four winds then.

She heard footsteps in the hallway and a bustling commotion as her aunt and sister took their leave. Settling down in the chair beside the bed, she picked up the book she had left on the bedstand and opened it to the marked page. It was adventurous and a little titillating, this novel, and she relished losing herself in the pages until she had to begin to ready for her visit to Lord Lacey's townhouse. She was not the remote, older sister. She was not the courtesan who sold herself to wealthy gentlemen. Not at the moment.

For the next two hours she could be simply Marianne Ellsworth.

* * *

Marcus dismissed his valet and regarded himself in the cheval glass. "I cannot believe I have to start this all over again."

He loathed the parties, with the false smiles and calculating looks. Rob had said he was a catch, and he knew it to be true. He had his mother's looks and coloring. He had his father's build, before the consequences of a life dedicated to dissipation had taken its toll. He rode and boxed and assisted the laborers now and again on his estate. He knew he was as pleasing a masculine specimen as was available this Season. That did not mean he had to enjoy being ensnared, however.

Turning from the glass, he went in search of Parks.

He found the trusted butler seeing to the staff setting the dining room to rights after his solitary meal. "Parks."

The butler joined him in the doorway. "Yes, my lord?"

He motioned the man into his study. "Shut the door." Parks did so, curiosity flitting over his face before his usual unflappable expression returned. "There will be a lady visiting tonight, Parks. At half-past eleven. You are to meet her at the servants' entrance at the appointed hour, and see to her comfort."

"A, that is, a...?"

"A companion," Marcus clarified. "The same one as last night."

"Last night?" The butler coughed. "I am certain I do not know of whom you speak."

Marcus held up a hand. "There is no need to dissemble. You are well-aware of all that transpires in this house, Parks. As you should be. You know full-well of whom I speak."

Parks hesitated. "Is Lord Devlin also expected?"

Marcus barked out a laugh. "Hardly. She will be a frequent visitor through the Season. I shall advise you on the time to expect her going forward."

"Yes, my lord. Rest assured, the staff will pay her no mind and pass no tales."

Marcus nodded. "I trust you to see to it."

Parks bowed his head in thanks.

"I have left a packet of notes for the lady. In my study," Marcus went on. "Please see to it that she gets it after she is safely ensconced abovestairs."

"Yes, my lord. Shall I call for your carriage?"

Marcus let out a breath. "Yes. I find the urgent need to get on with the evening's festivities if only to put them behind me all the sooner."

With that, Parks left to see to his master's requests. Marcus had no doubt that the man would protect his reputation as well as Annie's sensibilities. Marcus did not tolerate footmen hanging about or maids constantly underfoot, and Parks ran the residence precisely as his employer preferred it. There would be no gossip belowstairs regarding the earl and his new paramour. Not among the staff nor circulated outside this house.

Marcus boarded his waiting carriage. In what he deemed too short a time, he arrived at the first party. It was the Winslow's, whose hosts seemed overjoyed as he greeted them before stepping down into the ballroom. He felt the air shift as he looked about, noting the match-making mammas and girls of marriageable age eyeing him. How he hated this ritualistic pairing. Perhaps he had chosen Joan for the sole reason of having done with this business. He had offered for her before Easter, for God's sake! It should be of little surprise that he found himself once more on the hunt. Though tonight he felt more like the prey than the hunter.

After sharing a dance with a pale stick of a girl, Lord Withers' niece or something, he spied Rob across the room. He stood talking to a couple of men from their club, Bottom and Erlington. From the flush on both men's faces they had indulged in spirits stronger than what would surely be offered here. No doubt they would say something to offend someone in attendance, and soon. Erlington was practically swaying on his feet. As much as Marcus sometimes enjoyed his own spirits, he knew better than to be found in this arena with less than his full wits about him.

Rob lifted his chin in Marcus' direction. Bottom caught the motion and swiveled toward Marcus. His florid face broke out in a grin and he waved him over.

Marcus reluctantly joined them. "Good evening, gentleman."

"Straight-laced!" Bottom crowed, slapping him on the back. "Say, didn't think you'd be out and about so soon."

"What are you prattling on about?" Marcus asked.

"Only been a week since the fair Joan took off for parts unknown."

"Not unknown, Bottom," Rob put in. "Gretna Green."

"I wish them happiness," Marcus said, a bit startled to realize as he said it that he did.

"She was a ripe one, was Joan," Erlington slurred. "Great big—"

"Eyes," Rob quipped.

Marcus shook his head. "Have you gentlemen been here long?"

"No, no," Bottom said. "Drank our share at the

club, we did."

"Oh?" Marcus asked. "I would not have guessed."

Rob arched a brow at his jab. "The boys were asking about my gift."

"We was wondering if we could get the particulars. Maybe engage the girl for ourselves," Erlington said.

Trepidation flooded Marcus before Rob shrugged. "I told them I have no idea how to contact the gent who made the arrangement."

Bottom sighed. "Bet she was a hot piece, eh Straight-laced?"

"Not that the esteemed earl would be able to take full advantage of the girl's particular talents," Erlington added.

The two of them began to make ribald comments and suppositions of just what those talents might be and how often and in how many different ways they would make use of them.

Marcus refrained from punching them both in their ruddy faces. "I have to make the rounds."

"I as well," Rob said. "See you gents."

Bottom and Erlington still had their heads together,

laughing and poking each other, but they both waved their hands in farewell as Marcus and Rob left them.

"Bloody fools," Marcus grumbled.

"They know nothing of her, Lacey," Rob said.

Marcus hesitated for a moment. "How did you learn of her availability?"

"I had heard of a new dove in Town, one who—" He paused to smile a greeting at a group of ladies who passed by. When they were out of earshot Rob leaned closer. "She would gift a gentleman with her favors for one night," he finished in a low voice.

"Where did you hear of her?"

"At the club."

Marcus froze. "Pray, tell me no one there has…"

"Not to my knowledge," Rob said quickly. "It was one of those 'heard from a gent who had it on good authority that another gent who had learned of it' kind of thing."

Marcus nodded. It was enough to know that Rob had touched his girl. He did not want to think of anyone else he knew taking their pleasure with her delectable body.

"Thank you."

Rob shrugged again. "You are my friend, Lacey. Always have been."

Marcus grew quiet. He was not like his brother, who had many bosom chums and merrymakers at school and in Town. Rob had first run in Matthew's circle, back when they were all quite young. Almost without Marcus' notice Rob had insinuated himself over the three years since his brother's death, joining him at the club and at Lacey Manor, and proving to be a sound companion. He did not have many of those, and Rob's easy manners and ready smiles were a welcome counterpoint to his own shuttered personality.

"So, show me these paragons of femininity that caused such flutters of your heart this morning," he said.

Rob laughed and tilted his head toward chairs set in a corner not far from where they stood. "Miss Brianna Ellsworth sits over there with her aunt."

Marcus glanced in the direction of a pretty girl beside a handsome older woman. "The aunt is dressed rather somberly for such a party."

"She is recently widowed. A few months ago, I

believe."

Marcus turned his attention to the girl then. She had brown hair and a bright smile, but that was his only impression from this distance. "The girl is pretty, but surely that is not the beauty who so entranced you."

"Her eldest sister is not in attendance tonight, more's the pity." He nudged Marcus with his elbow. "Come, I shall make the introductions."

Marcus grunted an answer. "I suppose the hunt must commence sometime."

Rob just shook his head. They approached the two women and he bowed his head. "Ladies, my friend has asked for an introduction. May we indulge him?"

Both women smiled at Rob's words.

"Of course, Lord Devlin," the older one said.

"Mrs. Filbrick, may I present the Earl of Lacey," Rob said.

Her eyes widened for a moment, before she gave him a nod.

Marcus inclined his head. "A pleasure, madam."

"Lord Lacey," she said slowly. "How nice to meet you." She stared at him a moment longer before turning to the girl beside her. "This is my niece, Miss Brianna Ellsworth."

The girl giggled as Marcus took her gloved hand in his. "Miss Brianna."

"Lord Lacey."

"Miss Brianna and her sister had a very nice ride in the park this morning, is that not so?" Rob asked.

"Yes," the girl said with a vigorous nod. "There were so many people about! Marianne told me that was to be expected when we first came to Town, but it was quite a crush."

"Marianne?" Marcus asked.

"My older sister, my lord." The girl pouted for a moment, looking quite young. "She could not attend this evening."

"Nothing serious, I hope?" Rob asked.

The aunt shook her head. "Not at all, Lord Devlin."

Marcus once more found the woman's eyes on him. Was she considering him as a possible suitor for one of her nieces? He glanced at the girl again. She was quite pretty. If Rob was to believed, and Marcus knew him to be a good judge of ladies' attributes, it was indeed a shame that the older sister was absent.

"Pleasure meeting you both," Marcus said with a bow before turning away from them.

He left Rob in conversation with the chit while he retrieved a glass of weak punch from a passing servant. He checked his pocket watch. It was a quarter-past ten o'clock. He would bid farewell to Rob and head out to the next party and within the hour Marcus would be on his way home, hopefully to find Annie waiting for him.

Tamping down the lust that thought induced, he called for his carriage.

Chapter 6

Marianne looked about the sumptuous guest chamber, seeing more of the comfort and luxury she had noticed last evening. The butler, Parks, had been kind to her when he had met her at the servants' entrance and brought her swiftly to this room. Once again, no other servants seemed to be about. Before she'd had the chance to do more than remove her cloak, the butler had come back with a thick packet for her. Now she regarded the notes within. It was more money than she had ever seen at one time.

"Bought and paid for," she murmured.

She refused to feel shame. This was for her family, and she would earn every pound and subsequent payments in the coming weeks. Still, she tucked it deep within her satchel before she began to disrobe.

Unpinning her hair from the simple knot at the back of her head, she ran her fingers through the long curls. She knew Lord Lacey liked her hair, he had touched it almost reverently, so she left it loose. Before donning her pretty nightdress, she withdrew the jar of balm from her bag. She opened the jar and sniffed its clean warm scent.

Taking a large dollop of balm on one finger, she placed it deep inside of her. It did not feel sticky or cause her any discomfort, and the scent was pleasant. Vanilla was so soothing, and long her favorite. The other herbs, some she had never heard of, would hopefully do their work tonight.

She would do hers, she thought as she wiped her fingers on a towel. She would make certain that Lord Lacey knew he was not to spill his seed inside her again. It was enough to know that she would live with the memory of this for the rest of her life. She did not want there to be an innocent child to share her burden.

Glancing at the small clock on the bedstand, she saw it was ten minutes past the appointed time. Surely Lord Lacey would arrive home soon. She pulled her nightdress on over her head, plucking at the sleeves to settle the soft fabric on her body. Climbing up onto the bed, she slipped beneath the counterpane to await his lordship.

Faint noises reached her from below, footsteps on the stairs, and her pulse began to race. A door opened further down the hall, perhaps his lordship's room if she remembered correctly, and then more footsteps before the door opposite her was opened.

He stood there for a moment, his green eyes dark on her as they had been last night, and smiled. "Here you are."

He still wore his formals, and if she had thought him handsome last night in his dressing gown she now found him devastatingly so.

She ran her palms over the counterpane and shrugged one shoulder. "Where else would I be, my lord?"

He glanced in the direction of his own room before stepping inside. Surely he had not wanted her to await him in his own bed!

"No matter." He closed the door and removed his jacket. "You are here." He sat and removed his boots before standing once more to unbutton his waistcoat.

She turned back the counterpane and eased off the bed, walking over to him. "Allow me."

His hands stilled as he once more ran those beautiful eyes over her. "What?"

She took over for him, easing first one then another

button free. "Let me play valet."

"I do not let my valet undress me, Annie."

She shrugged and removed his waistcoat. "Oh?"

He grasped her shoulders and pulled her toward him. "I have thought of you all night."

In the next moment he kissed her. Hard, then soft, pulling a moan from her. His tongue tangled with hers and she found herself kissing him back. She had never been kissed before, save for that fleeting brush of his lips once, and certainly she could never imagine a kiss like this.

Grabbing his linen-clad shoulders, she held on as he wrapped his arms around her and held her close. She could feel his manhood through his breeches and it caused a fluttering her belly. Last night was not an aberration, then. He still warmed her like no one ever had.

Lifting his head, he smiled. "You taste so good." He kneaded her bottom as he had done last night. "And you feel incredible."

His words touched something deep within her, a pulsing need she had never felt before.

"You can certainly kiss, my lord."

He smiled, that expression she rarely saw on his face, and kissed the tip of her nose. "I have my hands on your delectable bottom, Annie. Please call me 'Marcus.'"

She could not deny the intimacy that would encourage, but she could not deny him either. "Marcus."

His eyes sparkled as he bent his head to kiss her once more.

She eased out of his arms and tugged him toward the bed. "Sit, Marcus. Let us get you out of those clothes."

He did as she instructed and she removed his shirt. His skin was so warm, so smooth, as she ran her hands over his shoulders. Stroking her fingers over his chest, his belly, she settled her palm over his rigid manhood.

"Christ, Annie," he rasped.

She knelt down and grasped him, feeling every beat of his heart as he throbbed beneath her touch. Unbuttoning the flap, she freed him from his smalls. He was huge in her hand, ridged and hard as she had noted last night as he had pressed close to her from behind. The memory caused her to clench inside in anticipation. She was surely turning into a wanton.

"You are in a bad way, Marcus," she said, hearing that husky note in her voice once more.

"You put me there, fair Annie."

She looked at his face, at the seriousness there, and bent her head to him.

"You do not have to do that," he said. From his tone she knew he would very much like her to.

"I know," she answered.

She resumed her task. She felt no shame tonight, just the surprising need to give him pleasure. Stroking his length, she licked and nibbled at the head until he was groaning. He leaned on his elbows, his head thrown back as his neck worked. He was beautiful in his passion. That was certain. She took him fully in her mouth then, something she had never done before.

"Annie!"

He began to buck beneath her and she lifted her head and held him as he spilled on his belly.

Sitting back on her heels, she smiled up at him. "I take it that was to your satisfaction, my lord?"

"Marcus," he panted. "And yes. God, yes."

She stood. "I will get a towel."

He opened his eyes and shook his head. "No need." He grabbed a handkerchief out of his pocket and wiped his belly. It was amazing, that belly. Flat and ridged and she bent her head to dip her tongue into his navel.

"Annie," he laughed softly.

He stood and quickly removed his breeches. In an instant he grabbed her to him and turned, tucking her beneath him on the big bed. "I cannot wait to taste you, love."

She ignored the endearment, having been called it or something akin to it by more than one man over the past weeks. If she liked the way it sounded coming from him, in that wonderful deep voice, that was of no consequence. "I am yours for the night, Marcus."

He brought his face to hers. "For the Season."

When she nodded he kissed her again. He removed her nightdress and ran his big hands all over her body. Grasping one breast, he brought his mouth to its nipple. Like last night, sparks seemed to strike her flesh. His hand was soon stroking her legs, her inner thighs. He neared her nether petals, teasing her as he eased her legs further apart.

"You have the prettiest pussy," he said, gazing down at her.

She could not think of anything but his touch on her skin. "Marcus…"

"What is it you want, love?" He kissed her lips, her neck, her breasts. "Do you want me to put my mouth on you again?"

Marianne recalled the pleasure he had given her last night, so different from anything she had ever experienced. "Yes," she breathed.

He stroked a finger deep inside of her. "Or would you like my fingers?"

"Yes, yes," she heard herself beg.

He circled that spot he had found last night and she squeezed her eyes shut. "Ooh…"

"What of my cock, love?" He shifted, settling between her legs to rub his manhood against her tender flesh. "Do you want my cock inside you?"

She murmured an answer, so close to release. He lifted away from her for a moment, then slid deep inside her.

"Ah, Annie…"

He rode her, driving hard again and again as she climaxed around him. He kept up the pressure, no doubt empowered by his earlier release. She found herself cresting toward pleasure once more as his breath began to hitch. Summoning a bit of sanity, she braced a hand on his chest. "Marcus, wait!"

He stopped moving, his breath coming fast as he stared down at her with bleary eyes. "What?"

"Do not spill inside of me."

He blinked, then gave a shaky nod. "Y-yes. Of course."

Resuming his thrusts, she soon found herself lost again. She felt him pull from her, vaguely heard him shout his release, and after a bit she found herself settled against his side.

He gazed down at her as she opened her eyes, smiling as he used his handkerchief to wipe his seed from her belly. "I believe I will have to invest in more of these." He tossed it to the side and drew her close. "Thank you for the reminder. I was nearly out of my head there for a moment."

She trailed a finger over his arm. "You are not put out? I know I am in no position to make demands."

"Not in the least. And sharing your concerns is not making demands, love."

There was that word again. She would not think it meant anything, just as she would not take his care upon release as anything but a cautious man making certain he would not be blessed with a child from the wrong side of the blanket.

He dropped a very comforting kiss on the top of her head and she suddenly felt quite sleepy. Closing her eyes, she cuddled closer and let his touch, his scent, ease her into slumber.

* * *

Marcus awoke a few hours later, smiling to find Annie still sleeping in his arms. He had thought she would leave soon after their liaison, but perhaps she wanted their arrangement to be for the whole night. He certainly was in agreement on that count.

When she had reminded him to be cautious, there as he was about to come deep inside of her, it confirmed his suspicions that she was not after him or his money.

He would gladly pay, of course. However, as innocent as she appeared while sleeping, he would not want to burden her with a child.

A child. He had to think about marriage and heirs soon. The miserable time he had spent at the parties, short though it had been tonight, increased his urgency to find his bride. Perhaps if he settled on a woman he could focus more of his attention on Annie until the Season concluded in August. He would not have to pay his intended more than a modicum of attention throughout the autumn, and once the banns were read they could settle on a wedding date close to Christmas.

Lacey Manor and its grounds were lovely in the winter. Far enough north to get the thick flakes of snow that blanketed everything yet temperate enough that the livestock would not suffer from the cold. He could see himself sitting in front of the fire come January, both his birthday and his wedding behind him, sipping brandy and watching the flames dance behind the grate. Pity he could not picture the woman sitting beside him in that tableau. No, he merely had a fuzzy image of a pleasant-looking woman of marriageable age.

He glanced at the windows, seeing light begin to peek through between the drapes. As if she sensed it, Annie stirred beside him.

"Good morning, love," he said.

She blinked up at him, her fair brows drawn. In the next instant she gasped. "My lord!"

"Marcus." He arched a brow. "Were you expecting someone else?"

Instead of the smile he had hoped the teasing comment would elicit, her eyes clouded. "I was merely surprised."

He cursed to himself. "I meant nothing by that. I am not one for making jests, and that one certainly fell flat."

She gave a nod and glanced at the windows. "I must get home."

He did not know where that home might be or whom might be waiting for her, but from the resolve on her features he would not attempt to keep her with him.

"As you wish." He stood and went about the room collecting his discarded clothing. Pulling on his breeches, he smiled in her direction. "My valet will be quite put out, I'm sure."

She returned the expression absently, wrapping the sheet around herself as she obviously waited for him to take his leave. He crossed to her and dropped a kiss on her lips.

"Good day, Annie." He went to the door and began to pull it open.

"Marcus?"

"Yes?"

"Will you have need of my company tonight?"

Tonight and every night. "I am not certain. I have been neglectful of my social obligations and no doubt will be otherwise occupied."

She kept her face impassive, but he flattered himself that she would miss him as well. "The area specified will be checked throughout the daylight hours, should you want to make other plans."

In other words, someone or other would look in the planter near the servants' entrance for any communication from him. It was a strange arrangement, but he supposed it was practical.

"I take it Parks gave you the packet, then?"

"Yes." Her gaze slid away from his, her cheeks turning pink. "Thank you for the additional notes."

It was a fair price in his mind. He would not add to her embarrassment, not this morning with her hair a tumbling mass of curls and her lips still red from his kisses of last night. Talk of money was considered vulgar among his contemporaries, yet the value of a man was measured by almost nothing else.

"Good day," he said again, leaving her to dress in private.

He returned to his room and climbed back into bed, then closed his eyes and pulled in a breath. He could smell her scent on him, fresh and hot. Sweet and alluring. She was a puzzle, his Annie. Uninhibited sexually yet refined in manners. Trying to figure her out would be like unwrapping his Christmas presents before the holiday.

Matthew had always outfoxed their parents regarding their gifts when they had been children, and delighted in boasting to Marcus. Marcus had chosen to wait until Christmas morn each year. He would puzzle over the prettily-wrapped packages which, until he opened them, could contain almost anything. He would treat Annie in the same manner. Anticipation was often far more intriguing than what was found out upon investigation.

He would enjoy his pretty package and leave her secrets be for the time-being.

Chapter 7

By the time Marianne arrived home, the household was beginning to rise. She requested a bath and busied herself changing out of the nondescript costume she wore and letting her hair down once more. She unpacked her bag and set the clothes aside to be cleaned. The packet at the bottom of the bag fairly burned her fingers as she withdrew it. She hid it and the jar of balm in the drawer of the vanity, and then took a deep breath to free her mind from the import of both items.

She recalled when Lord Lacey had asked about the money, and the shame she had felt then threatened to resurface now. She deserved that money, if she herself thought it was a little exorbitant. He, however, had not seemed anything but pleased to know that she had been paid.

Once settled in the tub, she scrubbed herself clean and washed her hair. Though she was surprised to remain in solitude until well after her bath, she enjoyed the peace and quiet. Before long, their lady's maid visited. Then Annie was Marianne Ellsworth again, earl's great-granddaughter and beloved niece and sister. Dressed, coifed and ready to face her day.

"Good morning," her aunt said as Marianne joined her in the dining room.

"Good morning, Aunt."

A glance at the sideboard showed more food than it had held any morning since arriving in Town. She helped herself to eggs and some ham and joined her aunt.

"Hungry, I see. Good."

"Not to worry." Marianne tilted her head toward the sideboard. "Breakfast is more than adequate this morning."

"Do we have the wherewithal to afford such this morning?"

Marianne nodded. "Yes."

"And you are well?"

"Yes."

Her aunt's shoulders visibly relaxed.

"Oh, that is good news!" Bree said as she joined them.

"Good morning, Bree."

The younger girl kissed Marianne's cheek before helping herself to breakfast. "Oh, everything looks scrumptious. I admit I am famished after all that dancing last night."

"I take it you had a nice time at the parties?" Marianne asked.

"Oh, yes." Bree settled down beside her and sipped at her tea. "I was worried about you, however. Aunt Hattie would not let me check on you when we arrived home last night, either. She said you needed your rest."

Marianne gave her aunt a look of gratitude. "That I did."

"And you are well today?" Bree's brow was creased with worry. "Truly?"

"Yes, dear. Do not fret about me." Marianne wiped her lips and smiled. "Now, tell me about the parties."

"What a crush! I should have supposed after seeing how crowded the park was that the parties would be as well. I drank more of that punch than I ought."

"Was it that awful?" Marianne laughed.

"Weak, was what it was. Sugar water, really."

"And what of the dancing? I believe you said there was much of it?"

Bree's face lit as she began to recount her evening.

The girl used so much detail, Marianne almost felt as though she had been there with them.

"Mister Stilling seemed quite put out, however," Bree concluded.

Marianne had seen his petulance yesterday, and was not surprised.

"There will be other suitors, Bree."

"So it seems." She faced their aunt. "Tell Marianne how gracious and handsome Lord Devlin was, Aunt."

Marianne stiffened at the mention of the name but held her expression. "You saw him again, did you?"

"He was quite attentive to Brianna." Her aunt's eyes held something there, and Marianne felt a shiver of trepidation. "He introduced us to his friend."

Bree's next declaration confirmed her unease.

"The Earl of Lacey, Marianne. An earl! He is quite handsome, even more so than Lord Devlin. He is as fair as Lord Devlin is dark."

Marianne took up her teacup and drank deeply before setting it down. "Is that so?"

Her aunt had not lost that worried expression and Marianne gave her a quick shake of her head.

"He is quite dull, however," Bree said. "He did not smile or flirt or ask me to dance."

"He had only just been introduced, Brianna," Aunt Hattie said.

"Oh, I know," Bree said, waving a hand. "And I did not truly wish to dance with him but it would be a feather in my cap to have him ask me." She leaned forward, her eyes alight. "I did hear something about him in the retiring room."

"A lady does not carry tales," Marianne said.

"I am not really carrying tales, sister. Just relating tales I heard carried."

Marianne rolled her eyes.

"What did you hear of Lord Lacey?" their aunt asked.

"He is considered exceedingly cold and dull," Bree said. "'Straight-laced Lacey,' he is called."

Marianne thought of the relaxed, uninhibited man with whom she had spent the night. Lord Lacey—Marcus—was anything but cold. "Is that so?" she asked again.

"Yes, and he is on the hunt for a wife." Bree's eyes

sparked. "He was betrothed before Easter, to a Jane or Ramona or something, and she jilted him for his butler not a week ago!"

Marianne thought for a moment. Surely not Parks, the circumspect and respectful older servant. "You must have heard incorrectly, Bree."

"Well, if not his butler than his attorney or something. It caused a bit of a scandal and now the earl must begin his search anew."

Marianne thought of the regret she had seen on Marcus' face when he told her about his social obligations. Now she knew that he meant to secure a bride. Lord Devlin had said she was to cheer him up two evenings past. Perhaps she had been purchased to ease the sting of rejection. He had not seemed particularly heartbroken over the loss of his previous betrothed, however. Not then and not this morning.

"Why the rush, I wonder?" their aunt said.

Bree shrugged. "He is considered quite eligible. He has both money and property."

"I wonder if he will attend the parties tonight?" their aunt mused aloud.

Marianne's stomach dropped to her feet. Of course he would. He had said as much not two hours ago. She would have to take much care in her appearance and manner tonight.

"You will attend tonight, Marianne?" Bree asked, her brow furrowed.

"It seems unavoidable," she answered.

"Please wear something more stylish than your usual party attire," Bree went on. "You received only a few dresses when we went to the modiste last month."

"Are you not happy with your wardrobe?" Marianne asked.

"Of course! But…" She glanced at their aunt and sighed. "I wish that uncle's money had been enough to treat Marianne to such pretty dresses as well as me."

Aunt Hattie looked down at her plate. "It was not."

"My dresses are pretty enough, Bree." Marianne saw the tears misting their aunt's eyes. "Uncle was a good man who cared for us very much."

"I miss him. Perhaps we should have waited for a Season," Bree mused aloud. "Uncle Filbrick is not gone three months and here we are, attending parties and taking calls."

Marianne and her aunt knew full well that they'd had no choice. It was the money she'd made on her back that allowed for the clothes and there was no way they could delay Bree's introduction a year to allow for full mourning. They would be destitute if the girl did not marry soon and well.

"Your uncle loved you girls," their aunt said. "I know his wishes. He would want you both to take every opportunity of enjoying yourselves." She plucked at the somber dress she wore. "If it seems that I am only in half-mourning, he would understand. He still knows my heart."

Marianne swallowed her own tears. Uncle Filbrick would turn over in his grave if he knew what they were about, or the role his own son had played in setting all of this in motion.

"I promise to attend the parties with you, Bree," Marianne said at last. "I shall attempt to make myself as presentable as possible."

Bree laughed, easing the gloom that had settled on the three of them. "Oh, you are quite beautiful! Though why you are so dull in company is beyond me."

"I have never been one for crowds," she fibbed.

"We attended assemblies and parties in Shropshire, Marianne," Bree pointed out. "Do not tell me that you did not visibly enjoy yourself at those functions."

She could not lie, not to her sister. Not about this, in any event. "Being here in Town is not quite what I expected, is all. I shall endeavor to be more lively this evening."

A smile flitted over Aunt Hattie's face, and Marianne once more realized all of this was taking a toll on her as well. Marianne would not take an active part in the festivities tonight, but perhaps she would not have to be such a block of ice.

"About time, I daresay," Bree said with a nod as she began to eat.

Marianne drank her tea as Bree and Aunt Hattie discussed several other gentlemen who had shown her sister particular notice. Perhaps it would do her good to loosen up her own laces tonight, so to speak. She would not truly be herself. She could not risk it, especially if she ran into Marcus or Lord Devlin.

She had seen one of the other gentlemen who had paid for her favors before, at one function three weeks earlier. Her manner and dress had been so altered from whatever he might have remembered from his night with her, and that seemed to save her from any scandal. The gentleman had not given her a second glance.

Lord Devlin's eyes were sharp however, despite his charm and teasing manner. As for Lord Lacey? He'd had the opportunity to study her while she had slept, let alone in complete dishabille.

Dull or not, she had to keep the mask in place when they inevitably met socially.

* * *

Marcus stood in a ballroom once more, eyeing every passing girl as a potential countess. Thus far he had found none to fill his requirements.

"Such a dark scowl, my lord?" a feminine voice said.

He turned to find Lasking's widow eyeing him. She was a pretty woman, though she wore too much rouge and perfume for his taste. "Lady Lasking," he said.

She smiled up at him. "I heard about Joan. Silly

girl. I don't know why you offered for her in the first place."

He grunted in answer. He would not discuss the subject with anyone, especially this woman. His brother and his father had both sampled what she blatantly displayed in her low-cut gown.

"Dare I say you're in need of consoling?" she asked.

"Hardly," he bit out. "Good evening."

He turned and sought out Rob, standing in the doorway to the supper room. "I take it Lady Lasking is on the prowl again?"

Rob glanced around him then nodded. "Seems her most recent gentleman cast her aside."

"God save the next one."

Rob visibly shivered. "I fear I would not retain my manly parts."

Marcus smiled, earning a comical raise of Rob's eyebrows.

"Lacey, do not tell me that you are enjoying the festivities?"

"No, though your company makes them tolerable."

Rob pressed a hand to his chest. "Ah, such flattery." He nudged Marcus with his shoulder. "Let us go mingle with the assembled ladies. The elder Ellsworth girl is in attendance tonight."

Marcus followed Rob's lead to the two ladies he had met last evening. Miss Brianna's face lit and she came to her feet as she saw them, no doubt as she was expecting more of Rob's charm. The man doled it out in buckets, it seemed. The aunt's head was bent close to another girl's, certainly the esteemed elder Ellsworth, and he saw her startled reaction to something the older woman said as they both rose to greet them.

"Ladies, how lovely to see you this evening," Rob said with a bow. "You remember Lord Lacey?"

Marcus bowed over Miss Brianna's hand, then her aunt's. "A pleasure to see you both again."

"Miss Marianne, may I present his lordship?" Rob added.

The third woman nodded in his direction, though she kept her face averted from his. "Miss Ellsworth," he said with a bow of his head as he grasped her gloved hand.

She was indeed beautiful, from what he could see of her. Her smooth skin was touched with rose. Her head was bowed, her fair hair catching the light of the candles above. Her dress was on the plain side in comparison to her sister's, but perhaps that was due to their uncle's passing. As she turned from him he saw that her profile was exquisite, though her lips seemed pursed as though the hostess had not put any sugar in the lemonade.

She leaned toward their aunt and whispered something in her ear before turning toward him, her eyes downcast. "Pleasure to meet you," she said in a soft, flat tone. She eased her hand from his grasp. "I must be excused."

With that, she went in direction of the ladies' retiring room. Marcus watched her go. *Strange little thing.* He soon dismissed her from his mind as he turned his attention to Rob and Miss Brianna's conversation about nothing. He watched the girl as they conversed, finding her joviality a pleasant counterpoint to her sister's prickly nature. Perhaps the older girl was ill.

"What do you say, Lord Lacey?" the girl asked.

Marcus blinked, and looked to Rob for

clarification.

"Miss Brianna was just extolling the pleasures of a ride in the park of a morning, Lacey. She wondered if you ever indulged."

The girl was obviously angling for an invitation, though he could not fault her for seizing the opportunity. There did not seem to be any predatory gleam in those wide blue eyes, however. There was something familiar about those eyes…

"I do not usually ride in the mornings, Miss Brianna."

She pouted for a moment, reminding him once more that she was quite young, then shrugged. "Perhaps one morning you and Lord Devlin might wish to escort my sister and me."

He gave her a nod without verbally encouraging her.

"I say, that is a lovely notion, isn't it Lacey?" Rob asked. "Perhaps on the morrow?"

Marcus kept his expression even. "If the ladies are free, perhaps it can be arranged."

"Are you, Miss Brianna?" Rob asked, turning back

to her. "Free, that is?"

The girl nodded with enthusiasm.

"Consider it done!" Rob said. "We shall be by to pick both of you up at eleven o'clock, if that suits. Mrs. Filbrick?"

"I suppose it will do," the aunt answered.

Marcus saw trepidation on the older woman's face where he had expected satisfaction. Having her nieces squired about Town by two eligible gentlemen should have put her at ease yet she was clearly agitated. The fan in her hands was nearly torn from her fiddling with it, and she repeatedly shot worried glances in the direction her other niece had fled.

Marcus watched the spot as well, eager for another glimpse of the beautiful Miss Ellsworth. If she was playing a game by appearing aloof, it seemed to him it was most effective. He was not eagerly anticipating an hour spent in her company tomorrow, however.

"I look forward to it," he said with a bow. "If you will excuse me?"

Miss Brianna and her aunt both dropped curtseys and he took his leave. Partaking of a glass of lemonade, which he surprisingly found more than sweet enough, he let his mind work. Now he was committed to ride on the morrow. Granted, it was with two lovely girls, either of whom might turn out to be an adequate countess. He glanced at his watch. He could not duck out of the parties, not so soon in any event. Why should he bother?

Any chance to summon Annie was well past, and he did not relish the idea of passing an evening alone after the incredible time he had spent last night with her in his arms.

Chapter 8

Marianne willed her heartbeat to slow as she sat on the upholstered bench in the retiring room. Women came and went as she sat there biding her time, until enough had passed that she could be certain Marcus was gone. Had he recognized her? She did not think so. He had greeted her like the gentlewoman she was, and all she could do was stare at their joined hands and think of where those graceful fingers had been last evening. How she had managed to choke out any sort of greeting was beyond her.

Lord Devlin did not seem to pay her much attention, instead basking in Bree's obvious rapture. She prayed he did not have any designs on her sister. The man had come very close to knowing her carnally, after all. And for Bree to consider him a possible match? She shivered. *Horrid.*

By her calculations, the niceties should be over. Another ten minutes should guarantee it.

"Lacey is so cold, Elise. Whyever would you consider him?"

"He is rich."

Marianne glanced around the screen at the dark-haired woman, Elise. The woman looked to be about ten years older than she, though the careful application of makeup was no doubt intended to mask that fact.

"What of Lord Bottom?"

"He hasn't the resources Lacey does. Besides, I've experienced the earl's pleasures."

Her words made Marianne's stomach clench.

"Not the current earl?" her friend asked in a harsh whisper.

"No. His father." A sly laugh followed. "And his brother."

"Elise, you are incorrigible."

"I have to keep myself entertained, do I not? And a wealthy man in need of physical release would be easy to manipulate."

Her friend snorted. "I doubt Lord Lacey has carnal appetites. He is such a cold fish."

"But a wealthy one," Elise pointed out. "Perhaps I can arouse his interest?"

Both ladies laughed as they trailed out of the retiring room. Marianne sat back. Then what Bree had overheard was true. Marcus was considered cold. Dull. A smile teased her lips. Let the *ton* believe what they will. She knew precisely how passionate Straight-laced Lacey could be.

Shaking her head, she came to her feet and peered out the doorway. Her aunt sat alone, and a quick scan of the dance floor showed Bree enjoying the attentions of a young, red-headed gentleman. She hurried over to her aunt.

"Thank goodness," Aunt Hattie sighed. "You were wise to leave when you did."

"You saw him as we were introduced, Aunt. How did he seem?"

"From what I observed, he has no notion of making your acquaintance anywhere else."

Marianne scoffed. "Hardly 'making my acquaintance,' Aunt. I am relieved to know he did not recognize me."

Aunt Hattie wore a frown and Marianne took in a breath. "What is it?"

"You and Brianna are to go for a ride in the park tomorrow, Marianne. With Lord Devlin." She paused.

"And Lord Lacey."

"Impossible!" Marianne hissed. "How am I to manage a ruse for that length of time?"

"He already thinks you aloof. Play that role in his company and wear a large bonnet."

Marianne squeezed her eyes shut. "Oh, why did it have to be him?"

"I do not know where you get your strength," her aunt whispered, placing her hand over hers.

Marianne gazed at her aunt. "From you."

They shared a smile and Marianne set aside a little of her worry as she watched Bree make her way through the steps. She was so graceful, so lovely. Surely a gentleman would offer for her soon.

"May I beg a dance, Miss Ellsworth?"

She looked up in alarm, relaxing a bit as she spied Mister Stilling before her. "Of course, Mister Stilling."

As he took her hand she saw him shoot a glance at Brianna before smiling in her direction. So he thought to raise Bree's interest by dancing attendance on her sister? He had no notion how close the two of them were. There was not a touch of jealousy between them, but she would allow him to keep to his illusion.

Smiling, Marianne let him lead her on the dance floor.

* * *

Marcus watched the elder Miss Ellsworth dance with the pup Stilling. She seemed to take some enjoyment from the exercise, he was surprised to note.

"Thinking about the morrow?" Rob asked to his left.

"My thanks for including me in your pursuit," he said flatly.

"I thought to aid *your* cause, Lacey. I am not the one on a quest to get leg-shackled any time soon."

Marcus flicked a piece of lint off his sleeve. "How fortunate for you."

Rob grinned. "My father continues in health, thank the good Lord. My mother has begun to hint about grandchildren, however."

Marcus thought about Rob's parents, so different from his own had been. Warm and demonstrative, and obviously taken with each other. "How are your parents?"

"Quite well. Fortunately for me they prefer to keep to the country, sparing me from any overt machinations to see me wed."

"Pray, give them my best when next you correspond?"

Rob nodded. "Of course. Perhaps after the Season you can join us in the country."

"Yes." Marcus thought for a moment, suddenly dreading the end of the Season more than he might have imagined a week ago. "I am certain I shall be betrothed by then. No doubt an escape would be most advantageous."

Rob tilted his head in Miss Ellsworth's direction. Marcus brooded as he watched her depart from the dance floor. He had seen a flash of her smile in the pup's direction, gone as quickly as if she had remembered that she must not enjoy herself overmuch. Now she once more wore that chilly expression he had seen earlier.

"She does not seem very lively," he observed.

Rob barked out a laugh. "You cannot blame the girl. You can be most intimidating."

Marcus shot him a look. "The last thing I need is a

timid wife. She is clearly not the one for me. And now, thanks to you, I have to pass more time in her company."

"Come, Lacey. We're to spend an hour or two with lovely ladies in a pleasant pursuit."

He thought again about the sisters, the older one in particular. "Lovely, yes." How could she breathe through such a pinched expression? "Pleasant, highly doubtful."

* * *

"I cannot wait for the gentlemen to arrive!" Bree said for the third time since breakfast, leaning close to the window to peer down at the street.

Marianne took a breath and nodded, focusing her attention on the book in her lap. "They will be here soon, Bree." Both of them, Lord Devlin and Marcus, and God help them all if Marcus recognized her.

"Have they arrived?" their aunt asked as she entered the parlor.

Marianne stifled a cry of exasperation. Her nerves were on edge as it was. She did not need her sister and Aunt Hattie adding to her unease.

George soon stood in the doorway of the parlor. "Lord Devlin's carriage has arrived, madam."

Marianne quelled the skip her heartbeat gave and stood, grabbing up her bonnet. It was not as large as she had hoped, but the deep brim should provide her some safeguard from disclosure. By the time George returned to announce the two gentlemen, she had donned the bonnet and her pelisse. The garment was finely made but quite simple in comparison to Bree's deep blue velvet spencer. That should help keep the attention on her sister where it belonged.

"The Earl of Lacey and Viscount Devlin," George announced.

Bree gushed over their arrival, extolling the brightness of the day and how perfect it was for a ride in the park. Marianne said nothing, maintaining a rigid stance with her feet rooted to the floor and her head down. She listened as the two men exchanged greetings with her aunt and sister, breathing slowly through her nose to slow her pulse. She prayed again that they would not recognize her.

"Miss Ellsworth?" she heard Marcus call.

She nodded, still saying nothing. A glance from underneath her bonnet showed her he held his elbow out to her. Resting her gloved hand on his sleeve, she allowed him to lead her out of the room. His arm was strong, and rigid beneath her fingertips. She resisted the urge to squeeze the muscles she felt there, keeping her touch as light as she could manage as they walked from the room.

"Enjoy yourselves," their aunt called as they walked through the open front door and descended to the street.

"Oh, I daresay we shall!" Bree laughed in return.

They boarded an elegant open carriage, with Bree and Lord Devlin seating themselves facing backward. Marcus assisted her into the carriage and indicated the forward-facing seat. She settled on the cushions and he sat beside her, stiff and obviously uncomfortable. Well, it was fitting. Why should she be the only one in misery this morning?

The ride to the park seemed to take an interminable amount of time. That time was mostly taken up with Bree and Lord Devlin conversing, augmented with Marcus' occasional comment to punctuate the discussion in his wonderful deep voice. She restricted herself to nods and murmurs of agreement, thinning her lips and holding her hands tightly in her lap to discourage any undue attention in her direction. Her neck was fairly aching from the angle she maintained. She could smell Marcus' masculine scent, soap and sandalwood, and after some time had passed she could not refrain from looking at him now and again out of one corner of her eye.

He had fallen silent as well, leaning back and fisting his hands on his thighs. His face was turned away from her, the muscle in his jaw visibly ticking as he clenched it tightly. She ran her gaze over him surreptitiously, drinking in the incredible picture he made in the handsome carriage. He was beautifully-dressed, appearing precisely like the wealthy earl he was. She had spent so much time in his company of late, his gorgeous form as naked as he had been born, that it was a little startling that he still affected her.

The clothes he wore today could have been picked solely for the way they showcased his physique. His legs looked strong in his breeches, his shoulders so broad she was forced to endure the fleeting brush of his body against hers now and again as the carriage rocked slightly back and forth. Each touch sent her nerves skittering from the point of contact to the entire surface of her skin.

How could she not remember what those shoulders felt like bare, so smooth and warm beneath her hands? So strong when she grasped them to pull herself closer to him as her climax took her. She could not help but recall the way his broad chest covered her as he found his own release, and shivered at the recollections.

"Miss Ellsworth, are you chilled?" Marcus asked.

Her cheeks flooded with heat and she shook her head vigorously. "No, my lord," she whispered, casting him a glance.

His brows drew together, then he blinked those deep green eyes. "Are you certain?"

She could not answer him, afraid to give herself away. No doubt her voice would hold that telltale husky tone she seemed to possess only in his company. Nodding, she returned her gaze to her hands.

She knew he still watched her. His gaze seemed to touch her everywhere as she sensed his close regard. Oh, this was a mistake! Why had she believed that she could be in such close proximity to Marcus without betraying herself? She'd never had to maintain her falsehood for such a length of time, let alone one in the presence of a man with whom she had engaged in the most intimate of physical contact.

He shifted in his seat, muttering something under his breath as he turned from her once more. Relief flooded her, mixed with the merest touch of regret. She would endeavor to ignore it.

This was what she had wanted. What was necessary to maintain her ruse. Why, then, did it sting a bit that he could simply dismiss her?

Due to Bree's gregarious nature, Marianne was spared any more discourse with either Lord Devlin or Marcus as they arrived at the park. It was as crowded as it had been when they had ridden with Mister Stilling, and a surprising number of people demanded an introduction to Bree and, by extension, to her. Lord Devlin's easy manner smoothed any awkwardness she felt conversing in front of Marcus with the gentlemen and ladies who stopped them, but she could not risk a glance in his direction during the exchanges.

She noted that his attention was diverted from her

during the discourse as well, and by the time they left the park and headed for home she was able to relax a bit on the cushions. Her back ached from maintaining such a stiff posture in the moving carriage, and she longed to lean back fully and take advantage of the comfort of the fine equipage.

She made herself the silent promise that upon arriving back safely at home she would take some time to stretch out on the bed and relax every muscle. She would close her eyes and breathe slowly in and out, finally free of the tension that had gripped her since the moment Marcus had entered their parlor.

This was far above her abilities at deception. A few moments of contact now and again at the parties was one matter. She doubted she would be able to maintain her ruse for any sort of extended dealings. Not after the uninhibited manner she displayed as Annie.

Marcus was bound to guess she was one and the same if he ever had the opportunity to see her often and up close. She would have to keep out of his company going forward, at least among society. Aunt Hattie could play chaperone from now on, should he and Lord Devlin come to call. Though loath to admit it, she simply did not possess the fortitude.

As soon as she arrived safely home, she would instruct George to tell his boys not to check the planter near the servants' entrance of Marcus' townhouse today. She could not risk going to Marcus' bed so soon after she had spent this time in his company. He would certainly request her attention tomorrow evening, and hopefully by then he would have dismissed the prickly Marianne Ellsworth from his mind and turn his focus on his temporary mistress.

Chapter 9

The evening was a crush, and this party was as crowded as the three he had attended already. Marcus stood on the fringes of the ballroom, scanning the crowd for the ladies he would consider to be his bride. Yesterday's ride in the park with the Ellsworth sisters had done little to shorten his hunt. That was certain. Disappointment had dogged him throughout last evening, as well. Annie had not come to him. He had left the communication in the appointed spot but there it had remained throughout the day. Despite the implication that elicited, he had longed for her in the hours before dawn.

Tonight, however, was a different matter altogether. He had seen to it that Parks put the card in the planter shortly after breakfast and the butler had reported by the afternoon that the note had been retrieved. According to their arrangement, and by the time he had specified, Marcus could expect her in his bed no later than one in the morning.

It had been three days since he had last held her. To his amazement he could not stop thinking about her skin, her hair. The way she touched him and the way she purred when he touched her. He took a breath to clear his mind of the memories. He was in a bad way.

Rob joined him, a grin plastered on his face.

"Good Lord, Lacey. Do lose that frown or none of the chits will consider you."

Marcus blew out a breath. "Would that any in attendance this evening would remotely do so."

"You are a catch, or so you would have me believe. Whom have you considered?"

Marcus looked about the room again. "Stilling's sister might suit."

"A bluestocking," Rob replied. "Nicely-fashioned, but the chit likes her books."

"Smarter than her brother, then," Marcus said. "No doubt she would be able to keep herself entertained in the country if left to her own devices. I would not want to be tied to her fool of a brother, however."

"I should say not. What other possibilities have arisen?"

Marcus glanced over at four plump, pretty and pleasant girls gathered near the refreshment table. "Perhaps one of the Prestwick sisters."

Rob squinted in their direction. "Which one?"

Marcus glanced over at him. "Does it matter?"

Rob laughed lightly. "Not at all, that I can see. Any of them might suit, but there is no money there."

Marcus shook his head. "I have no pressing need. My marriage will secure my estate and my inheritance, Rob. I have no desire for a dowry a desperate father might scrape together to rid himself of one of his daughters."

Rob was quiet for a moment. "Have you decided to engage my solicitor?"

"Yes, we have a meeting tomorrow. Why do you ask?"

"I tell you what you do, Lacey. Compile a list of your potential brides and have Grimes do some discreet investigation."

"I told you I care little about the finances, Rob."

"I am thinking of other matters. Delve a bit into the family background, for example."

It was a sound suggestion. "Perhaps."

"Have him search for any impediments. Check for a wastrel father, a drunken uncle." Rob cast an eye toward the Prestwick sisters again. "A horde of destitute siblings dependent upon you for their every comfort."

The thought brought him up short. The last thing Marcus wanted was his wife's relatives constantly underfoot. It would be deuced difficult to maintain his own life under those conditions. "Excellent point."

"Have him look for anything that might adversely affect the Lacey lineage." Rob winked. "And perhaps he can make certain that none of the girls you are considering harbor any tender regard for another gentleman?"

That would have saved him had he thought to do so with Joan. "Indeed."

Rob glanced across the room, and Marcus could guess his target as his eyes sparkled.

"Will you add the Ellsworth sisters to your list?" Rob asked, proving him correct.

"I suppose I should," Marcus allowed. "The younger one might suit. She is pretty and pleasant."

Rob smirked and turned back to him. "What of the eldest?"

Marcus thought about the distant blond girl again.

He saw she sat with her sister and aunt as usual at the moment, her back rigid even from this distance. "I am not at all certain. She is stiff and prickly. She is pretty enough, though I did not catch a glimpse on our ride yesterday of the beauty you extoled. I could hardly see her face with that blasted bonnet on her head."

"Then you missed a delightful display, take my word for it."

Marcus thought for a moment. "She is put together quite well, from what I was able to ascertain. Her hands appeared graceful when not clenched in her lap in displeasure. I cannot decipher her age, even now. She carries herself like a woman of an age with her aunt."

Rob shook his head. "I have it from Miss Brianna that Miss Marianne is but twenty-one."

That surprised him. He shook his head. "Not too old, then. But the girl showed no partiality to me."

"You were not seated where I was. The girl's eyes lit on you more than once. Her gaze appeared quite warm."

Marcus doubted that but said nothing more on the subject. "I shall think on this more on the morrow. Just another hour and my time will be my own once again."

Rob's brows rose. "The little dove?"

"At long last," Marcus admitted.

"Lacey, you astound me. I have never known you to be overly…"

Rob did not need to finish his thought for Marcus to grasp his meaning. "Never mind."

Marcus took a breath and refrained from counting the hours until he could hold Annie in his arms and put this tedious business behind him.

* * *

Marianne gazed at Marcus across the throng of merrymakers. He seemed ill-at-ease, his eyes scanning the room repeatedly since his arrival not thirty minutes ago. She had fully expected she would see him here, but not so close to the time set for their rendezvous. When she saw him check his pocket watch, a look of impatience stamped on his face, her heart tripped.

He was eager to get to her, even mired in the social whirl as he was at present. She should be unaffected by that notion, as theirs was a business arrangement, but the woman inside her was thrilled to her toes that she had somehow managed to work her way beneath that cool exterior he displayed in polite company. Once more, the wanton fought to come to the surface. Her cheeks heated and she fanned herself vigorously.

"It is nearly half-past twelve," Aunt Hattie whispered in her ear.

Marianne jumped. "Gather Bree and let us return home, Aunt. I have scarce little time to ready and have George take me to Lord Lacey's."

As the three of them made their way out of the house she was forced to come very close to Marcus. It seemed he was talking to the host, no doubt readying for his own departure. Thank goodness Sir Frederick was notoriously long-winded.

She kept her head down and held her arms stiffly at her sides, though as she passed him she could feel his heat and smell his scent. She had never been so aware of a gentlemen, even before in her other life in Shropshire. Perhaps it was the knowledge that he would soon make love to her. That she would once again find in his strong arms the pleasure she had not known existed.

She halted as a group of chattering girls, the

Prestwicks, clambered past her. Jostled, she brushed against Marcus and a short sound of surprise escaped her.

"Miss Ellsworth?" she heard him ask, his hand on his arm to steady her. "Are you all right?"

She could not answer him, not now. She could not look at him, knowing that soon he would see all of her in his very home!

Cursing herself for a coward, she gave a shaky nod and he dropped his hold.

"Come dears," Aunt Hattie said, the overly-cheerful tone masking her alarm.

She sensed Marcus' regard again, as she had in Lord Devlin's carriage yesterday, and all but flew out of the ballroom. Soon they were safely in the carriage, and George deftly led their way through the traffic. She tapped her toes and peered out the window at the scenery as they slowly passed by. *Hurry, hurry, hurry.*

"What has you in such a state, Marianne?" Bree asked. "Pray, do not tell me your headache is back."

Marianne looked up to meet her sister's worried gaze, guilt frothing up inside of her. First the lies about her health over the past week and now the deception she could never divulge.

"I am quite well, Bree. Please do not fret. I am just eager to be home."

"I agree." Bree yawned, one dainty hand held in front of her mouth. "Just the thought of bed is so tempting."

At her sister's innocent words Marianne's cheeks heated anew. "Yes."

She once more peered through the window, ticking off the moments until she could keep her promise to Marcus. He might have paid her for the week but if she continued to keep herself from him, even through no fault of her own, he might decide she was simply too much bother.

Aunt Hattie took Bree in hand when they finally arrived home, leaving Marianne to her ablutions. She knew she could count on her aunt to keep Bree from the hallway, thus allowing for her escape.

She hurriedly changed out of her fancy gown and donned her serviceable brown dress. "No time to take off the stays," she muttered as she employed the special balm. Unpinning her hair, she raked her fingers through it then plaited it in a simple braid and stepped into her slippers. Her cloak finished her dress and she hurried down to the street. George drove her to the Lacey townhouse, leaving her off several doors away as was their custom.

Marcus' butler met her at the servants' entrance, a calm expression on his features despite the fact that she was nearly a quarter-hour late. He silently escorted her up the stairs and past the room in which she had twice entertained Marcus. Her surprise must have shown on her face because the butler tipped his head to her.

"His Lordship requested that from now on you are to await him in his chambers."

"Th-thank you," she murmured.

Parks closed the door and she stood and looked about the chamber for a long moment. That first night she had hurried to his bed as Lord Devlin had instructed, giving little notice to the surroundings in the dark. Now she could see that absolute comfort was clearly the goal here, from the plush carpet beneath her feet to the sumptuous curtains hung at the tall windows. The sitting room was lovely, with a wide mantle flanked by two of the most comfortable-looking chairs done in rich fabric to match the deep green of the drapes and shot through with gold threads. Beyond that area was a pass-through to the bedchamber.

Once stepping through, she saw nothing but the largest bed she had ever encountered. It was tall and wide, and draped with the same cloth as the windows in the sitting room. Brocade in subtle shades of green and gold draped the bed. The counterpane was folded back and the many pillows fluffed for the night's comfort.

She imagined Marcus on the big bed as she had found him that first night, his magnificent body as naked as it had been clothed at the ball. His face, however. She imagined no dourness or dismissal there. No, in her mind his beautiful smile stretched his features as he anticipated their coupling. Her heart raced at the image.

There was a screen set to one side, as in the guest chamber. She removed her cloak and stowed it behind the screen along with her small bag and slippers. She had barely had time to loosen her braid when she heard the door open in the sitting room.

"Annie?" Marcus called.

His voice did things to her insides. Things that should shame her. She shoved her misgivings aside and became his Annie for the rest of the night.

"In here," she answered, coming out from behind the screen.

He stepped into the chamber, a smile of relief on his face. "At last."

In a heartbeat she was in his arms, welcoming his lips on hers. She opened beneath him, taking his tongue deep in her mouth. His taste was richer than the wine she'd had in the supper room. He moaned in the back of his throat and she felt his arousal press into her belly.

"It feels like an eternity since I last held you," he rasped, his face buried in her hair. He kissed her throat. "I have been thinking about you for hours."

She knew he exaggerated, as she had seen him talk with and dance attendance upon several young ladies at the party. She had seen him check his watch repeatedly, however. There was at least a bit of truth to his words.

"I am here now," she said.

He pulled back and smiled down at her. "Yes, you are." He ran his gaze over her simple dress. "This gown does you little justice, love."

"Do let me change, Marcus." She pulled away and headed for the screen. "I will not be long."

He shook his head and grasped her hand, tugging her closer. He began to work the buttons marching down the front of her dress. "You played valet for me the other evening, Annie. Do allow me to play lady's maid tonight?"

She saw the heat in his eyes, along with a playfulness decidedly absent on their ride yesterday morning. The combination was compelling. "As you wish."

His fingers brushed over her breasts as he unfastened her buttons. He slid the dress down her body, nuzzling her throat as she stepped out of the garment. Tossing the dress over the nearest chair, he drew her closer and placed his hands on her waist. "Stays?"

Cursing inwardly, she nodded. "I was in a bit of a hurry."

He grinned and spun her away from him. "I haven't yet had the opportunity to unlace you." He lifted her hair away from her neck and dropped a kiss on her skin. "In truth, I have never unlaced a lady before."

At his words, her heart skipped. He thought of her as a lady, at least in his chamber. She felt his fingers work over her laces, easing the stays slightly. They gapped a bit in front of her bosom. He slid her chemise down her arms and turned her to face him again. Studying the front of her, he pushed down on the loosened stays and chemise, causing a delicious friction on her nipples before freeing them.

"Now that is a lovely display," he said.

He held her waist and pulled her close, edging the stays upward to lift her breasts. He flicked his thumbs over her exposed nipples and she gasped.

Bending his head to her, he closed his mouth over one nipple. Closing her eyes, she focused on the heat of his mouth, the moist suction as he suckled her. The rasp of his tongue as he teased her flesh. He urged her back toward the bed, running his hands up her legs. Her chemise was soon up around her waist when he paused.

"Marcus?" she asked softly.

"These are a surprise," he said.

She opened her eyes to find him staring at her

stockings, a smile teasing his lips. She'd had no time to shuck them earlier for the coarser ones she wore on her nightly sojourns. These, however, were quite fine. Quite fitting for an earl's great-granddaughter surely, and paid for with Marcus' money. Embarrassment flooded her with heat of a different kind now.

"I know they are a bit too fine, but his lordship pays me well," she explained.

He caught her gaze. "They suit you, love." Running his hands over her legs, he made a sound of masculine appreciation. "Indeed, they suit you."

Lifting her, he set her on the edge of his bed, stepping closer between her legs. "Lean back, Annie."

She did so, her elbows sinking into the sumptuous featherbed, as he continued to stroke his big hands over her legs. His fingers soon teased her inner thighs very close to her center.

"Yes, these stockings are soft." He tickled her on the back of her thigh, easing a finger beneath her drawers. "Ah, but not as soft as your skin."

He removed her drawers and placed both hands on her thighs, spreading them wider. "I have thought about tasting you all night." He stroked his thumb over her center and she felt herself pulse inside. "Of putting my mouth on you and giving you pleasure."

She watched his golden head as he nuzzled her inner thigh. "You enjoy that, Marcus?" she had to know.

"Very much so." His green eyes sparkled as he gazed up at her. "You taste incredible, and the little sounds you make… Do you not enjoy giving pleasure that way?"

She thought for a moment. "I never found it truly unpleasant." Her cheeks heated. "I admit I did enjoy giving you pleasure in that manner."

He grinned and bent his head once more, flicking his tongue over her flesh. "You are incredible." She sucked in a breath as he licked her deeply. "I could taste you all night."

In the next moment he placed his mouth directly on her. He fairly devoured her as he held her still, his mouth covering her sex as his tongue flicked over her nub of pleasure. Again and again he teased her, sucking gently as she felt herself swell. "Oh, Marcus! Oh!"

He murmured something or other, then resumed his

efforts. She was lost in the sensation of his mouth on her, of his strong hands on the tender flesh of her inner thighs, of the sounds he made as he drove her nearer to the edge of release.

She could scarcely draw a deep enough breath to cry out, the soft restraint of her stays heightening her awareness of everything he did to her. She gasped as her climax took her, sinking into the bed as he kept feasting long after the first wave crested.

Her breaths were shallow as she tried to collect her scattered thoughts. He came up and kissed her open mouth and she tasted herself on him, salt and musk and a hint of the vanilla she favored. It was a heady mix, taken with his own unique flavor.

She sensed him straighten from the bed as it bounced slightly upward. "Believe me, I received almost as much pleasure from that as you did."

She managed at last to breathe a bit and she opened her eyes and glanced at him. He was still fully clothed but she could not miss his arousal straining in his fine evening breeches. He laughed softly and she brought her gaze to his face.

"Almost, love." He began to disrobe, tossing his clothes on the floor. "Almost."

Chapter 10

Marcus read the passion on her face as he took off his blasted clothing. Her breasts were pushed up high by her stays, their nipples begging for his lips. Her chemise was bunched around her slender waist. Her hair fanned out on the coverlet beneath her, her legs dangled over the edge of the bed. Her thighs were still spread, her flesh wet and beautiful framed between the silken stockings she wore. He could look at her all night, and would have if his cock was not demanding its own satisfaction.

She would be tight. Wet and hot. Ready to find her pleasure again with him deep inside of her. He knew this instinctively. Her breath was still a bit labored and her eyes glazed with passion. The passion he had given her.

He was soon naked, watching her as he stroked his hand over himself. "Do you see what you do to me, Annie? What tasting you does to me?"

She stared at the head, at the bead of moisture gathered there, and nodded. "Take me, Marcus."

He needed no further encouragement. He stepped closer to the bed, sliding deep into her pussy as she contracted around his shaft. Her legs were up around his waist now, her hands on his upper arms as he thrust into her heat again and again. This was hotter, more intense, than the last time he had taken her. She began to cry out again, his name and those sweet, intelligible sounds she made at climax, and he pulled her closer still. Writhing against him, she closed her eyes and surrendered to their passion.

He could not stop moving within her, keeping her at the crest of her pleasure as he fought to hold on to his own control. When she let out a keening sound and shuddered around him he finally pulled himself free to spill on her belly.

Taking in great gulps of air, he braced his arms on the bed and dropped kisses on her sweat-dewed breasts. He could not resist tasting those nipples again, licking each in turn as she moaned her pleasure the simple act gave her. She was so responsive now, her entire body made for his loving for the rest of the night.

Lifting his head, he ran his gaze slowly over her. Her color was high, her breathing rapid, as her breasts rose and fell. He saw that she had twisted and her stays were constricting her.

"Damn." He eased her up and quickly unlaced her. "I did not realize you were having trouble breathing, love."

She shook her head and smiled up at him. "Oh, it was not the stays, I am certain." She took in a deep breath and let it out slowly. "Not completely."

Her words filled him with masculine pride. He had caused her such sweet discomfort, then.

"Nevertheless, allow me to get you out of those clothes."

She eased to a sitting position and he removed her stays and chemise. Taking his time, he drew those lovely stockings down her lovelier legs. He dropped a kiss on each knee and joined her on the bed. Drawing her into his arms, he began to kiss her, feeling her come alive in his arms as her passion rose to meet his. Stroking her, he found her wet. Hot. He was soon as ready as she was.

Pinning her beneath him, he entered her. Slowly this time, each stroke bringing him closer to climax as he felt every inch of her. A fine sheen of sweat covered her brow, curling the golden tendrils framing her face. Her lips were a temptation he could not deny and he covered her mouth with his.

Their tongues touched, the action seeming more intimate than what they had just shared. His cock twitched with a heat deep inside of him begging for release. As she began to come around him again he withdrew and spent into the sheets.

Cuddling her close to him, he turned and she rested her head on his chest. He could feel her breath on his sweat-dampened skin, sense her breathing begin to slow beneath his hand resting on her supple back. Contentment flooded him. More than sexual satisfaction, there was a sense of peace he seldom felt out in Society.

"I am going to miss this," he murmured. He dropped a kiss on her hair, stroking the long curls and twining them in his fingers. "I am going to miss you."

She sighed, rubbing her cheek against him. "It is as it should be," she whispered. Her face was turned from his, her fingers absently caressing him. "Just for the Season."

He nearly changed their arrangement then and there. Why couldn't they continue after he took a wife? Other gentlemen of his acquaintance did it all the time.

He did not make such an offer now, however. Instead, he just nodded.

The time-constraint had been imposed by her, after all. Perhaps she had obligations outside of their connection. She had to be somewhere all day, in all those hours while he was thinking about her and anticipating their time together.

"How did you start on this course, Annie?" he asked softly.

She lifted her head, a sad smile on her face. "Certain circumstances forced me to consider another way to survive, Marcus. There are others to consider besides myself."

There it was again, the hint of more than met the eye. Her manner of speaking, of carrying herself when not lost to their passion, struck him anew.

"You do not owe me any sort of explanation. I am just grateful to be the only gentleman for you at present."

A darkness flickered in her eyes as her mouth turned down. The expression was gone in the next moment.

She sat up, gathering the sheets around herself and

toying with her hair until it lay in a thick coil against her breast. Her eyes were sad now, the expression a different sort of darkness than had been on her face moments before.

"It was a death in the family. We were left with nothing. I had no other recourse left to me."

He simply let her speak, suspecting that she needed to voice this even if there was nothing he could do to alleviate her distress then or now.

"This particular avenue unveiled itself to me and I was fortunate enough to have some success at it," she said.

"Had you no other relatives, then?" He shifted to a sitting position. "No man to take care of you and your family?"

Her lips grew thin, her brow furrowed, as she obviously recalled someone decidedly distasteful. In that moment she did not look quite like herself. No, she appeared almost a different person. Frightened and ill at once.

"I will not speak of him." Even her voice was different. Halting and cold.

He knew then that man had taken advantage and given her nothing but pain in return. Anger filled him. "Who was it?"

Her expression cleared and she looked beseechingly at him. "You must not concern yourself. It is in the past, and there it shall remain."

He stared at her. She was so young, so new to this life, that it could not be very far in the past. "Annie, perhaps if you tell me, I can—"

"No!" She turned from him. "You may have paid for my body, Marcus. You have no claim on my heart."

"Your heart?" He edged closer to her. "I have made no demands in that regard."

She waved a hand. "Oh, I was being poetic." She faced him. "It is my concern and mine alone."

There was much more to the mystery, then. She was obviously more than a simple country miss who fell into the business of pleasure. She had an air of culture, of gentility. He had seen than almost immediately and tonight it was as clear as crystal. She would not share the rest of it at the moment, and he was loath to prolong the pain the recollection obviously caused her.

"As you wish it." He forced himself to ease, leaning once more upon the pillows. "I shall respect your privacy."

She offered him a small smile, pretty and sweet, and he felt his heart twist in response.

"Thank you," she said.

"You, however, may ask anything you wish of me."

She arched a golden brow. "The Earl of Lacey will divulge his secrets?"

He laughed. "I am an open book."

She settled down on her side, the sheets still swaddling her, and propped her head on one hand. "I believe I know a bit about you already."

"Oh?"

"You were betrothed but the girl broke your heart."

"She jilted me, Annie. I assure you, my heart was not engaged."

She nodded. "You have some pressing need to marry, however. And soon. It is said you are once more on the hunt for a bride."

He stiffened. "How the devil do you know that?"

"Gossip travels, my lord." She lifted her head.

"Even in such low circles."

"Marcus," he corrected again. "I did not mean that you were beneath me, love. I admit I wondered if you had…"

"Investigated you? You are not precisely incorrect, though your personal life was not my concern."

Sourness swirled in his belly at the thought of her taking such mercenary actions, necessary though they might have been. "My finances, then."

"No," she said simply. "Your reputation as a gentleman. Your habits, any particular proclivities. I had to be certain."

He felt relief at her words. "For your safety, then. You are a wise girl."

She shrugged one bare shoulder. "I have more than myself to protect. It would never do to put myself in a dangerous situation."

He longed to question her further. She had investigated him before their initial tryst? How? What had truly driven her to this life? There had to be more to it than what she had stated in such veiled terms.

She would never let him provide for her beyond the

Season. He knew that was a certainty now. She was proud and resourceful, and his respect for her grew nearly as strong as his desire for her.

If he did not have his own obligations to fulfill this Season perhaps he could have had the luxury of unraveling the pleasing puzzle she made over the autumn and winter. There was nothing else for it, however. He was as set on his course as she was on hers.

Once again he forced his mind to the present. This proved no hardship, as reclining in bed with her was as pleasant a situation as any he could envision.

"Come, love." He beckoned her over to his side and after a brief hesitation she complied. "Let us put both the past and the future aside and get some rest."

A sound of contentment slipped past her rosy lips as she cuddled closer. "Just for a while, Marcus."

Her eyes drifted closed and he watched her for a long moment.

Just for a while.

* * *

Marianne woke before Marcus, and was vastly relieved to see the sky was still dark. Their conversation had been astounding, and more painful than she could have imagined. It was almost as if he wanted to help her. To keep her after the Season. That, she could never allow. By then Bree would be betrothed and their worries would be over. Surely it was only a matter of time before even this exclusive arrangement with him would be unnecessary. An unexpected twinge of regret struck her at that thought.

She studied his face, noting the worry lines eased and his lovely mouth relaxed. He appeared to be quite different than the cold Earl of Lacey he presented to Society. This Marcus, caring and gentle, bold and passionate, was a different being entirely.

He had his own demons, then. More than whatever necessitated marrying so soon. He was not hurt by the broken engagement, which for some reason put her at ease. She thought of that comment she had made, speaking of her own heart. He had no right to ask her about her past and she had no right to ask him about his future. She was bought and paid for, a willing and well-paid participant in passion. Hearts had no place in bed with them.

She closed her eyes and thought back to that first time with John. He had hurt her. Belittled her. Made her feel like less than nothing as he took his pleasure again and again. Three times that night, in positions that had shocked her. He had paid dearly for her maidenhead, he had said. He deserved to take every last bit of pleasure with her body as he desired.

It was little wonder that the prospect of her very first encounter upon coming to London had filled her with dread. George had investigated the gentleman. No rumors of violence, no tales of maids debauched in his employ. The man had been gentle with her, easing his way as if he had sensed her reticence. Such reluctance was surely unusual for a courtesan, but it had seemed to rouse a caring protectiveness. She would always be secretly grateful to him and the other man she had dallied with before Lord Devlin had engaged her services for Marcus.

She was fortunate to find such a protector. Marcus was good to her. He paid her well, though he seemed to be growing a bit too curious about her life outside of his bed. There were but a few weeks left to the Season. June was upon them already. Soon they would part ways. He would marry and she and Aunt Hattie would take up residence with Bree and the gentleman she married. If their paths crossed in the future, she was certain he would never equate Bree's spinster sister with the girl who had warmed his bed for a short time one Season.

No, he would not spare her a thought once he embarked on his predestined path. She suspected her body would long remember his however, and the heat of those memories would keep her warm.

If her heart missed him as well, she would simply have to ignore it.

Chapter 11

The day was as sunny and pleasant as any they had encountered since moving to Town. Marianne sat in the small garden of the townhouse, alone with her thoughts for the time-being. Sharing her tale with Marcus last night, even in such vague terms, had cost her more than she had expected. Surely she would never be free of the horrid memories of that night with John. He had all but raped her, though she had initially agreed to the tryst and set the monetary conditions in advance. Suddenly she felt quite cold.

She looked down at the calling card in her hand, proof that Marcus wanted her in his bed again tonight. *At midnight*, he requested in his fine, elegant hand. Thankfully, the memory of John's brutality faded as she recalled the tender passion Marcus had given to her last night.

"Three calls this morning, Marianne."

Marianne turned as her aunt stepped out onto the terrace, happy for the excuse to escape the dark memories. "All gentlemen I suppose, from the smile on your face."

Aunt Hattie nodded, settling on the bench beside her. "Lords Wilbrey and Shaston, and a Mr. Meryton."

Marianne thought for a moment, recalling what she had gleaned since coming to Town. Sitting quietly at the parties while her sister garnered attention had proven useful for gathering information. That was certain.

"The first gentleman is the second son of Baron Wilbrey," Marianne said. "Adequate finances there."

Her aunt nodded. "What of Shaston?"

Marianne shook her head. "It is rumored that his father has squandered the family fortune. I daresay his interest in Bree is fleeting."

"And of a decidedly different nature than matrimony." Her aunt sniffed. "Well, it is quite enough that you had to take your present course. I will not have Brianna turned into a courtesan."

Shame filled Marianne at her aunt's declaration. "Never."

Aunt Hattie's eyes went wide. "Oh, I did not mean to imply that you are a courtesan! What you have done for us…" She grasped Marianne's hand and brought it to her breast. "Oh, my dearest girl. Your sacrifice, now and in the future, humbles me."

"In the future?" Marianne let out a harsh little laugh, holding Marcus' card aloft. "Yes, my own prospects are quite dim beyond this Season."

Aunt Hattie blinked. "You deserve the chance to wed as well. You should have had a season of your own. Secured your own gentleman to protect and care for you." She eyed Marcus' card. "For more than the length of one Season."

The bitterness Marianne sought to ignore threatened to swamp her. "John put an end to any of that, Aunt. Though had he not, it would never have occurred to me to make our way in Town in this manner. I should be grateful."

"Hardly that." Aunt Hattie scowled. "I cannot believe he approached you with lascivious intention, Marianne. You should have come to me."

Marianne shrugged away her aunt's concerns. She would never reveal how painful that night had been. "He said afterward that he had wanted me for years. I daresay he paid well for the privilege of taking what should have gone to my husband."

Her aunt gave a slow nod. "I pray that will ease your heart going forward." She patted Marianne's hand, quiet for a moment. "Marianne, do you believe John will keep your secret?"

"Oh, he will never divulge his actions. Millicent would string him up by his manly parts should she learn of what he did to me that night. It was all she could stand when she learned he was giving us money 'out of the kindness of his heart.'"

"John's wife takes their standing quite seriously. My stepson is a bit afraid of her, I believe. I agree. You are safe on that account, then."

"Yes." She let out a breath. "On that account."

"What do you mean?"

How could she tell her aunt how difficult this charade was rapidly becoming? The woman had enough to worry her, with two girls to care for on limited funds despite Marcus' generosity.

They could not afford to engage a secretary, and the calls and invitations were coming fast and furious. There were dress fittings and entertaining and attending parties and the like. It was far different from their quiet life in

Shropshire, and in the sunlight the woman looked older to Marianne than she had but three months ago.

"It is nothing, Aunt." She stood and put on a smile. "I believe I will check on Bree now that she is alone. Measure her feelings on the gentlemen showing such marked interest."

Aunt Hattie stared out at nothing Marianne could see. "Capital notion, dear," she said absently. "Your sister needs you."

Yes, Bree needed her. Aunt Hattie as well. They both needed her to keep to her course and withstand the rest of the Season. She had come too far to lose her resolve now.

What was done was done, and if she had to live with the consequences for the rest of her lonely life, so be it.

* * *

"Joining us at the club again, Lacey?" Lord Bottom laughed. "Can't say I can recall a time when you've been out and about for a bit of leisure twice in one week."

Erlington added his snicker to the mix, leaning back and rubbing his protruding belly. His obvious indulgence over the past months was more than evident. "Lacey's holdings necessitate his hiding in his study for long hours at a time, is that not correct?"

"Some of us take our responsibilities seriously, Erlington," Marcus said.

Bottom let out a guffaw at his comment.

Marcus sat down at the table where the two of them half-heartedly played cards. "I am attempting to make full use of the Season, gentlemen. There are a few men with whom I must discuss matters."

"Your bride search, then," Erlington nodded. He let out a belch. "Saw you dancing with Stilling's sister the other night. Pleasant enough girl, if dull."

"What about one of the Prestwick sisters?" Bottom winked one drooping eyelid. "Round and plump, and no doubt jolly in the bedroom."

Marcus shook his head. Discussing prospective brides with Rob was one matter. Taking advice from these fools was another entirely. "I have a few candidates in mind, thank you."

"What of the Ellsworth girl?" Erlington asked. "A prime piece."

"Yes, she's quite pretty," Bottom put in. "She's rumored to be in need of a wealthy husband."

"She'd be no hardship in the marital bed, I'd wager," Erlington said.

Marcus nodded. "Miss Brianna is pretty, but—"

"Ha!" Erlington cut in. "Not the younger chit, Lacey. I was referring to her stellar sister." He licked his lips. "Luscious girl."

"That golden hair, that pure skin. And those dark blue eyes…"

"A man could get lost in them," Bottom said. "And in that ample bosom as well!"

Marcus puzzled over their comments. "I supposed the elder Miss Ellsworth to not be much more than passing pretty."

"Then that doxy of yours has you quite blind," Erlington said. "She's a treat, and quite pleasant if a bit shy."

"Shy?" Marcus thought for a moment. "I hadn't thought her shy, just a little remote."

"Cold, I'd say." Bottom laughed again. "Well, I'd take a hand to warm her."

Marcus shook his head. "I have no particular interest in her or any young woman at present."

"Tick tock, Lacey," Erlington said. "Less than two months remain of the Season. Jockeying for position will being in earnest, and soon. You aren't the only gent wanting to wed this year."

Marcus let out a breath. *Even a fool was right now and again.* "I suppose I must decide."

"Straight-laced must be dragging his feet for some reason, eh Bottom?" Erlington said.

"Perhaps all those nights spent with his light-o'-love has ruined him for respectable ladies."

The mention of Annie stirred something in him, something primal, and it was all he could do to keep from punching Bottom in the face. "I would thank you not to discuss my personal affairs, gentlemen."

"Quite the gallant!" Bottom said then. "Would that Devlin reveal precisely where he'd found this treasure. You'll have no need for her after the Season, I daresay."

"Straight-laced keep a mistress? Ha!" Erlington said.

Marcus flinched. He had been considering doing

just that last night as she had slept in his arms. Would she put aside this life when they parted ways, as she had told him? Or would she fall into the hands of one of these dolts? Surely her family issues would not dissipate after the Season, no matter what she might choose to believe.

"Again, my personal life is my own."

"Yes," Erlington pouted. "Devlin said as much."

Marcus silently thanked Rob for his support. Perhaps he would call on him and ask for his assistance in choosing one direction to focus his attentions.

"...Lacey?" Bottom urged.

"Hmm?" He faced the man. "Pardon?"

"Are you going to the parties again tonight?"

"Yes," Erlington crowed. "We'll be very interested to see whom you dance attendance upon as the days turn into weeks."

Marcus waved a hand. "I had not realized how very dull your own lives had become."

"I'll take dull and independent to lively and leg-shackled, thank you very much," Bottom quipped.

Marcus stood. "I believe I shall adjourn to the dining room."

He left them gaping after him. Everyone knew his business, then. Even Annie knew about his quest, though he had been a bit mean-spirited when he had asked precisely how she had gained her information. He respected her intelligence, and suspected there was more to her. Nearly from the first moment he had known her.

Her family's welfare drove her. Would they need her help after the Season? If so, would she fall into the bed of some coarse gentleman like Bottom or Erlington?

"What does it matter?" he grumbled to himself. He nodded in greeting to a few gentlemen taking advantage of the club's fine dining and settled himself at a table. He requested his meal from the waiting servant and sat back, sipping at the claret soon at his elbow. Annie would be gone from him in a matter of weeks.

"What maudlin thoughts turn that famously-handsome Lacey visage so dour?"

Marcus looked up, a genuine smile curving his mouth as he nodded at Rob. "Do join me, Rob. I need a sane dining partner, I wager."

Rob smiled and sat across from him, signaling a servant over to see to his needs. "Spent some time with

Bottom and Erlington, I wager."

"How have neither of them wandered in front of a moving carriage?" Marcus muttered.

"They have their fortunes and no need to change their lifestyles, Lacey. No stipulations or deadlines."

Marcus nodded. "I know. I am at a loss." He sat up a little straighter. "I am glad to see you this evening. I had hoped to seek your sage counsel, actually."

"Mine?" Rob thanked the servant who brought his own glass of wine and ordered his meal. When they were again alone he faced Marcus. "Surely you do not need my help running your estate. You were practically born to it, despite the series of events that dropped it into your capable hands."

"Thank you, but no. I have to settle on a young lady to court."

Rob's brows raised. "You met with Grimes this afternoon, did you not?"

"Yes. I approve of him, Rob. Thank you for the recommendation."

"My pleasure. Is he seeing to the investigations?"

"I gave him the list of names, yes."

"Then let that be your guide."

"I feel I need more to go on than cold facts."

"Truly?" Rob grinned. "You?"

"I admitted I am at a loss. I want a bride who is biddable and pleasant, but one who might not bore the life out of me."

"You want sexual attraction."

It was a bald statement, but Marcus nodded. "After setting up a certain arrangement, I come to find I enjoy those matters much more than I have in the past."

"That could be based solely on the lady in question."

Marcus nodded. "She is singularly the most beautiful creature I ever beheld."

"You need beauty, then."

"It would be a definite asset, but I find I crave affection as well."

Rob studied him for a moment, though Marcus would not ask what he looking for precisely. "She did loosen your laces, didn't she?"

"I suppose." Marcus drained his wine, requesting another glass as their meals arrived. "I cannot fathom the prospect of a cold marriage now."

"You need to consider your prospective bride's feelings, then. Have any of the girls struck you as warm enough?" Rob laughed. "I can hardly believe this is a consideration for you."

"Well, it is. If I thought I could continue to see—" He stopped himself. "I will keep myself to my wife after my wedding."

"Are you trying to convince me or yourself?"

Marcus took in a breath, letting it out slowly. "I saw the harm my father's infidelity caused my mother," he said in a low voice. "She withdrew into herself, almost from my earliest memory."

"Your father, and your brother if I might add, were not gentlemen."

"You have the right of it there." Marcus ate some of his roast pork. "I could not bear to cause that kind of pain."

"A young, pretty, warmly-affectionate bride, then." Rob chewed, his brow furrowed as he obviously considered the ladies they'd discussed previously. "Your list should begin and end with the Ellsworth chit."

"Miss Brianna is pretty enough, I grant you. What of her sister?"

"You wish to court the eldest?" Rob grinned. "I agree wholeheartedly with your choice."

"No, not the eldest. I meant that she has come close to cutting me more than once. Would her younger sister accept my suit in the face of such disapproval?"

"I still say the eldest would suit you far better."

"And I insist she would not. Perhaps I should look elsewhere for a bride, then."

"Lord Wither's niece?"

Marcus considered the suggestion for less than a moment. "There was no spark of attraction there."

"One of the Prestwicks?" At Marcus' silence he added, "Any of the Prestwicks?"

"They are warm," Marcus allowed.

"And affectionate."

"True." He gave a sharp nod. "Miss Brianna Ellsworth or one of the Prestwick sisters, then. And Stilling's sister. I cannot discount her based solely on her irksome brother."

"True. So that is your list?"

"Barring any dark secrets uncovered by Grimes, why not?"

Rob drank more of his wine. "I suppose the time has come to narrow your choices."

"That is settled, then." Marcus dug into his meal with renewed vigor. "I shall begin my courting on the morrow."

"Which one first?"

Marcus stilled, one brow arched. "Which one?"

"Polly, Patrice, Paulette or Penelope?"

Marcus shrugged. "I shall start with the eldest and work my way down."

Chapter 12

"What have you learned?" Marcus asked the solicitor.

A fortnight had passed since handing the man his list of prospective brides. Two weeks during which, barring a stretch of a few days when she declined to accept his invitation, he had made love to Annie each night. Two weeks during which he had kept his own counsel as he watched the young ladies on his list with what he hoped was nonchalance. It would not do for the gossips to get wind of his machinations. He was loath for the ladies in question to discover they were under consideration, lest they either shrink from him or feel emboldened.

Grimes, a neat man with dark hair, leaned his elbows on the desk. He peered at Marcus for a moment through his spectacles, then gave a nod. "A sound list, my lord. If I may say so."

Marcus nodded in return. "You certainly may. Please tell me what you have learned."

Grimes leaned back in his chair. "You must realize from the first that none of the young ladies you've chosen to consider will bring any real money to your marriage."

"I am aware of that, Grimes. You've read the papers I sent over. Seen that ridiculous stipulation of my father's will. By marrying me, any of those young women will secure my fortune and estate. That is more than enough compensation, in my opinion."

"Yes, yes." Grimes gazed off for a moment. "Odd stipulation, that."

"Be grateful you were not in the Lacey employ when my father was alive," Marcus said. "I have spent the time since his passing straightening out the mess my father left behind."

"Gone three years, yes?" When Marcus nodded, Grimes did as well. "You've done quite well with your estate in such a short time."

"Then you realize my desire to hold on to it."

A small smile tilted Grimes' mouth. "I do."

The man opened a file on his desk and shuffled the papers. Marcus saw his own hand in the list atop, then notes taken by Grimes over the past fortnight. Rob was right to recommend the man, then.

"In regards to the Prestwick sisters," Grimes began. He paused, arching a brow. "Is there any one of them you would consider above the others?"

Marcus thought of the bright, pleasant girls. They were nearly identical, and should he choose to marry one he prayed he would be able to refrain from calling his wife by one of her sisters' names. In or out of bed. "No."

Grimes nodded again. "All right. They are quite well-regarded in Society, my lord. Friendly and cheerful. Devoted to each other and quite close. 'In each other's pockets,' as my mother might have said. You would have an affectionate bride in any one of them, I daresay."

"And a houseful of chattering females at any given time, I would wager."

Grimes laughed softly. "There is that to consider. But if you are looking for a biddable wife, one who will be devoted to your happiness, I believe one of the Prestwicks will suit very nicely."

Suit very nicely. It lacked passion, to be certain.

"Do you know of any tendre any of them might hold for another gentleman?" Marcus asked.

Grimes shook his head. "I was unable to discover

any particular attachment of any kind among them. They make calls together, and receive gentlemen in like manner."

Marcus was quiet for a moment. "Very good. What of the next on my list?"

Grimes shuffled more papers about, setting aside the pleasing Prestwicks, and peered through his spectacles. "Lady Genevieve Stilling."

Marcus pictured the dark-haired girl. Pretty in a fashion, though not particularly remarkable. "Yes."

"She appears to be as quiet as the Prestwick ladies are boisterous. Circumspect, almost scholarly."

"I had heard she enjoys her books."

"Yes. She is known to be quite loyal to her family, however. Her youngest brother especially."

"No small feat," Marcus allowed.

"Mister Stilling has been known to irritate gentlemen of his acquaintance."

"He is rash. And lacks the circumspection his sister and older brothers seem to have in abundance."

"In any event, she appears affectionate within her family. Not a hint of intrigue or scandal."

"What of other attachments, Grimes? Has no gentleman offered for her in the three years she has been out?"

Grimes reviewed his papers once more. "It seems she had a beau her first season, but the young man did not come up to snuff. He argued with her brother over some matter and apparently she couldn't forgive him that."

Marcus thought of Stilling's famous lack of tact and penchant for evoking ire. "I daresay there is not a man in Town who has not wrestle with the desire to wring Stilling's neck."

Grimes smiled. "From what I learned in my investigations, I tend to agree with that statement. She would make you a fine countess, however. Well-mannered. Serene. You would be hard-pressed to find a lady as loyal."

"Loyal. Sounds like one of the hounds on my estate." Marcus shifted in his seat. "Still, as you say. She may prove adequate." Dismissing Genevieve Stilling from his mind, he tilted his chin toward the file once again. "What of the last young lady?"

"Ah, the Ellsworth girl." Grimes withdrew several sheets of paper and perused them for a long moment. "There is something there."

Unease flickered within him. "What do you mean?"

Grimes' brow furrowed. "Well, I received conflicting information upon my investigations."

"Pray, elaborate."

"Both girls are well-liked. Pleasing and pleasant, with the younger one possessing a very friendly manner. The eldest, however—"

"I have no interest in the eldest," Marcus cut in.

"Yes, yes. You made that clear."

Marcus had heard enough about Miss Marianne Ellsworth from Bottom and Erlington, not to mention Rob. "Then continue with your report regarding Miss Brianna."

Grimes cleared his throat. "As you wish. She and her sister and their aunt came to Town three months ago. They have no connections in London that I could ascertain, and leased their townhouse only for this Season. They dress well and appear to garner invitations to the right parties and the like."

"Yes, I seem to trip over them at every function. Though the eldest seeks to avoid my company."

Grimes stared at him for a beat. "Perhaps she is intimidated by you?"

Marcus smiled. "Lord Devlin suggested as much. While a quiet wife might suit me, a timid one would not."

"Timid? Oh, I didn't find anything about Miss Marianne Ellsworth to indicate timidity."

Marcus pinched the bridge of his nose. "Pray, continue about Miss Brianna."

Grimes nodded. "She is a friendly sort, as I stated. Several gentlemen have begun to show marked interest."

"The esteemed Mister Stilling, no doubt."

Grimes brows arched in surprise. "Yes, among others."

"She is a pretty girl."

"Yes, though according to most she doesn't approach her sister's beauty."

"I cannot say I have had the pleasure of gazing upon the elder Miss Ellsworth long enough to form my own opinion. What else did you learn? Does the girl harbor feelings for another? I will not be jilted again, Grimes. I cannot afford another delay."

"Miss Brianna seems to accept several gentlemen's regard with pleasure though no partiality has been noted. I would hazard a guess that the girl needs to marry soon and marry well, however. There appears to be no male relative seeing to their comfort at present."

Something tickled at the back of Marcus' mind. "Were you able to confirm that?"

"Not in Town. As the ladies only recently came to London, I took the liberty of traveling into Shropshire to learn more."

Marcus gave a nod. "What did you learn?"

"It seems that the young ladies were orphaned when they were quite young, then taken in by their aunt and her husband. The gentleman passed away four months ago, leaving his estate to his only child. His son from his first marriage, that is."

"That is not unusual."

"Not in the slightest. Of course, most families make provisions for the female members as well. Unofficially, at least."

"Surely the man left his wife something."

Grimes shook his head. "Nothing, and the son... Well, Mr. Filbrick is not well-regarded in the village."

"I would not want to worry over the prospect of a disgruntled or unpleasant relative's appearance on my doorstep in the future. Did you speak to him yourself?"

"Yes. I went to the man's place of residence and spoke to him. He had kind words for his stepmother, though they rang a bit false."

"What of the young ladies?"

A peculiar look crossed Grimes' face, one of confusion. "That is what I meant earlier, my lord. There is something there. He spoke fondly of Miss Brianna but his comments regarding Miss Marianne... I suppose I would call his manner boastful."

"Boastful?" Marcus straightened. "How so?"

Grimes shifted in his seat. "Well, he told me that he gave the ladies enough money to set themselves up in Town for the Season. Said that was more than should be expected of him, after they had lived off his father's largesse for most of their lives."

"He sounds like an ass, but I do not understand why

171

you consider that particularly boastful."

"He smiled in what I would call an oily manner and said he was amply rewarded for his generosity and considers any debt repaid."

"What the devil does that mean?"

Grimes shook his head. "I cannot fathom. Miss Marianne is a noted beauty, my lord. Perhaps he had designs on her and begged a kiss before sending them off?"

Marcus snorted. "A kiss for a townhouse in London for the Season? That would have had to be one remarkable kiss."

Grimes colored. "In any event, I sensed he wanted to crow upon something regarding the young lady when Mrs. Filbrick arrived home. His manner changed drastically and he seemed to shrink into himself."

Marcus offered Grimes a small smile. "I am certain that is not all that shrunk."

Grimes chuckled. "True. She is a formidable lady, to be sure. I daresay I fought the urge to check for my own, um, belongings before I took my leave of the couple."

Marcus thought for a moment. "Fending off the ardor of a man given sole control over her future might change a lady's demeanor."

"I thought as much, my lord. When I asked about in the village, all and sundry spoke of Miss Marianne as light and gay and quite a pleasure to be around."

"In Shropshire, at least." Marcus pushed the image of the prickly Marianne Ellsworth he knew aside. "And Miss Brianna?"

"Well-liked also. She is considered a bit capricious, but perhaps one can expect that in a young lady of her eighteen years."

"Yes." He stood and shook Grimes' hand. "Good work. I believe I can pursue any of the young ladies with confidence now."

"I am glad to help you put any reservations aside."

Grimes closed the folder and held it out to Marcus, who shook his head. "You may keep those with my other papers, Grimes. I have no need for the particulars now. My path is clear, if divergent."

Marcus took his leave and climbed into his carriage. Any of the four Prestwick sisters, Genevieve

Stilling or Brianna Ellsworth. Grimes' tale came back to him, however. Something had happened to alter Marianne Ellsworth before they came to Town.

If nothing else, that solidified Marcus' resolve to keep that lady from his consideration. A distasteful relative with lascivious designs would make for an unpleasant encounter should he decide to pay a call upon the Countess of Lacey. Better to keep to the light-hearted sister.

He had a long night ahead of him, then. Thankfully he had set a card out for Annie this morning. With luck it would be gone from the appointed spot and he could anticipate her in his bed tonight.

* * *

Marianne stood in the parlor and studied the card in her hand, tracing her fingers over the writing as had become her habit. Two o'clock, he had requested. His bride search began in earnest, then. There had to be no other reason he would send for her at so late an hour. He obviously planned to spend a good amount of time among the Fashionable in his quest.

"What does it matter to me?" she murmured.

She had been forced to ignore his summons for a few days the previous week, due to her monthlies' blessed arrival. In the days since he had been more than attentive, when not on his bride pursuit that was.

"Are you not ready yet, Marianne?" Bree asked, sailing into the room. "There is a long list of parties to attend."

Marianne quickly tucked the card behind a vase on the side table. "And a long list of gentlemen seeking your favor?" she asked with a smile.

Bree grinned in return. The girl was a picture of ease and excitement both. Marianne's heart lifted to see her sister so boisterous and carefree. It was the only thing keeping her going forward on her course as the Season continued, this knowledge that Bree would soon find herself a beau both worthy of her with the wherewithal to care for his bride's two female relations as well.

"Let us be off!" Bree said. "I believe I might dance with every gentleman who asks me."

"You will be quite fatigued in the morning, I daresay," Marianne teased.

A look of concern crossed Bree's beloved features.

"Pray tell me you will take the time to enjoy yourself a little tonight, Marianne? It seems it has been weeks since I've seen you take any pleasure in the evening's festivities."

"I enjoy watching you take that pleasure, Bree."

Bree grabbed her hands and kissed them loudly. "Promise me you will dance tonight."

Marianne hesitated. "Perhaps one dance."

"Three! I declare you must dance three dances tonight."

Marianne let out a breath. "As you wish."

Their aunt soon came down the stairs and together the three of them embarked on the night's entertainments.

Three dances. That was not so large a number. She could withstand a gentleman's close attentions for the length of a dance.

Then she could watch for any marked interest toward her sister and begin to steer the girl toward a worthy gentleman. That was her goal and that was what she would achieve.

Then later, at two o'clock precisely, she could set

all of this aside and focus solely on the pleasurable attention of one gentleman in particular.

Chapter 13

Marianne checked the clock on the mantle for what felt like the hundredth time. Two twenty. Marcus was late. She felt a flicker of annoyance. Very late, for a man supposedly so enamored of his mistress that he sent for her nearly every day. Perhaps he'd had enough pleasure for the evening.

"He certainly danced attendance on enough ladies tonight," she grumbled.

Stalking over to the cheval glass, she regarded herself. Her hair glowed, the curls loose and shining. Another fine night dress covered her in precisely the manner to entice his lordship. Her face wore an uncharacteristic scowl, however. She cleared her expression. Who the devil was she to take offense at Marcus' attempts to charm his future bride?

"It is no concern of mine," she told her reflection.

She settled on the chair beside the cold grate and attempted to set aside her ire. It was at that precise moment that the object of that ire strolled into the chamber.

"Ah, Annie."

He grinned at her, looking for all the world like a man well-pleased with himself. His attire was impeccable, his face and form as handsome as ever, and she fought the desire to launch herself into his arms.

Coming to her feet, she nodded. "My lord."

He arched a brow and shut the door. "I am sorry to be so late, love."

Marianne shrugged a shoulder. "I am at your disposal, Marcus. Who am I to make demands?"

He blinked at her, then smiled. "You missed me."

"Perhaps." She lifted her chin. "But I am certain his lordship was quite occupied this evening with his debutantes."

He nodded, his smile gone. "Yes. I danced more tonight than I have in years."

She had taken note of every step, too. With all four of the Prestwick girls. With Genevieve Stilling. And with Bree. That last one caused her heart to clench in a way she fought hard to ignore even now.

"Have you arrived at your choice, then?" she asked, giving him her back.

He came closer, wrapping his strong arms around

her. She held herself stiffly, fighting the urge to melt against him. He smelled so good, of soap and spice, and she could not resist breathing in deeply.

"I have a few ladies in mind, though I have yet to make my decision."

She swallowed, her heart giving a forlorn beat. "Do you desire any of them?"

He stilled, then let out a breath. "You are jealous!"

She shook her head but he hugged her close.

"Ah, Annie." His lips brushed her ear, her neck. "I could never desire another woman like I do you."

His words sent a stab of wanting through her. "Marcus…"

He ran his hands over her through the sinful night dress, teasing her breasts before pinching her nipples with his fingers. She let out a gasp as sharp pleasure flooded her.

"God, you feel so good," he said. His arousal pressed against her backside as he began to move against her. His breath fanned across her cheek. "I have thought about holding you, Annie. All night, I have thought about taking you again."

He held on to her waist, grinding against her. He felt quite large now, and hot through the thin fabric of his breeches.

"Do you remember that first night, love?" He bent her over slightly, placing her hands on the arm of the chair she had just vacated. "You were bent over like this, your lovely backside in the air."

Of course she remembered. She had been unable to focus on anything but him as he had climbed onto the bed behind her.

His hands ran over her bottom now as they had then, clutching and kneading, until he lifted her night dress. She wore nothing beneath, as she knew he had come to expect.

"Your very lovely backside." His hand stole between her legs, widening her stance as he shifted her night dress to her waist. "I could see your flesh that night, love. So pretty and pink." He stroked her as he had that first night. "So hot and wet."

"Marcus," she sighed, easing toward his touch.

"You are wet tonight." He stroked her deeply. Slowly. "Soaking wet."

His words, his touch, roused her and she squeezed her eyes shut. "Take me, Marcus."

He laughed softly, teasing and flicking his fingers over her nub of pleasure. "Oh, I shall."

She felt him lean away from her and nearly cried out in frustration, but the rustle of fabric, the grunt of relief as he obviously freed himself, set her on fire. Like that first night, he brought his staff close to her, starting a friction that nearly sent her over the edge. She had to rise up nearly on her toes to meet him.

His manhood was hard and hot and he felt positively marvelous against her swollen flesh. Its broad head brushed her opening again and again, nearly entering her, and she trembled. "Oh!"

"I have thought of taking you like this again," he said. "Of holding on to your waist, your backside pressed up against my belly." His motions punctuated every word, his breath hot on her cheek as he ran his tongue over her ear. "Driving into your soft, wet flesh."

"Marcus, please…"

"As you wish," he rasped. He reared back and drove inside her. She clutched the arm of the chair, barely maintaining her footing as he thrust and withdrew again and again. The sounds he made were guttural, and unbelievably arousing to her ears.

"Annie, love…" he growled.

He brought her closer to the brink, each long stroke taking her out of herself as she keened with pleasure and want. She began to crest, feeling every magnificent inch of him as her climax started. Suddenly, he withdrew.

"No," he bit out.

"W-what?" she panted.

Turning her to face him, he perched her on the chair. "I need to see your beautiful face as you come."

She could say nothing, could hardly move, her body was so tense. Nodding, she opened her legs to him and he entered her. Deep, close, his movements became wild now. In the next instant she climaxed, shouting his name as he continued to ride her. Again, she crested, clutching at his arms as if to keep from falling off the earth. His shout of completion filled her ears as he somehow managed to withdraw and spill on her belly.

As she struggled to catch her breath, she opened one eye to peer up at him. Satisfaction was stamped on his face, a carnal glint still in those gorgeous green eyes, as he cleaned her belly with the edge of his shirt. Aside from the open fall of his breeches and the hem of his shirt, he was still dressed like the titled gentleman she had watched all evening at the parties. For this moment in time however, he was her lover.

"You are a beautiful girl, Annie." He dropped a kiss on her lips. "But when I give you your pleasure? You are utterly breathtaking."

She felt herself blush at his praise. He took her hand and led her into the bedchamber. "Climb into bed, love. Let me undress and I shall join you."

She removed her night dress and got into his bed, reveling in his hot gaze on her body as he quickly disrobed. He was soon beside her, seemingly content for the moment to simply hold her in his arms.

She stroked her fingers over his warm, wide chest. He was the most beautiful man she had ever seen, and even relaxed he possessed a sensual power. She might have had scant experience before Marcus bought her for the Season, but it was clear to her that he was a singular gentleman. Again she recalled the pleasure he had so easily roused in her.

"Your bride will be most fortunate," she whispered.

He stiffened, then let out a breath. "I daresay I will not share with her what I do with you, whomever she turns out to be."

Because she was his whore. Shame churned in her belly at that realization. She had his passion but not his respect. Never his respect. That was saved for his future bride. She lifted her head to face him. "I suppose that will surely be her loss."

He shook his head at her. "You misunderstand me. I have never known passion like this, Annie. I am quite certain it does not await me in the marriage bed."

That was something, then. Once again the image of Bree in his arms filled her mind. Her heart gave a lurch as she imagined Bree in his bed as well.

"What is it?" he asked.

She forced a brightness she didn't feel to form her expression. "Nothing." Trailing her fingers over his flat belly, she found his manhood. Stroking him, she watched his eyes darken as his shaft grew hard in her hand. "Love me again, Marcus?"

He let out a shout as he pinned her beneath him. "All night, Annie." He kissed her, burying his face in her neck as his hands seemed to be everywhere at once. "All night."

* * *

"You look exhausted."

Marcus looked up from his breakfast to regard Rob. "What brings you out and about so early?"

Rob shrugged and settled across from him, nodding his thanks as a servant set a cup of tea in front of him. "I have some calls to make." He drank and peered at Marcus over the rim. "On a few ladies of your acquaintance."

Marcus lifted a brow. "Have some breakfast, then."

"I've eaten." Rob smiled at him. "You were in rare form last evening."

"How so?"

"I have never seen you dance so much."

"I am running out of time." Marcus set his dish aside and drank his tea. "Thank you again for recommending Grimes. The man's investigations were most thorough."

186

Rob nodded. "Good. Have you settled on your bride, then?"

"No. And I do not plan to for at least a fortnight."

"Dancing is all well and good, Lacey. But you must begin to make calls as well."

"I suppose." Marcus leaned back. "I find I am just too tired and relaxed to withstand that particular ritual today."

Rob's eyes narrowed. "Spent another night with your dove, I take it?"

"Until the dawn," Marcus admitted. "I believe the girl will be the death of me."

Rob laughed. "Ah, but what a way you would go. It is a pity that…" He shook his head.

"What?"

"Perhaps you will change your mind about keeping her after your marriage."

How much he wanted to do just that! "I will not, though I am sorely tempted."

"Has she secured your affections, then?"

Marcus was quiet for a moment. "Of that, I am uncertain. I know I am beginning to crave more than just her beautiful face and form."

Rob shook his head again. "Careful, Lacey. You need to convince any prospective bride that she will be the only one on your mind, if not in your heart."

"My heart remains my own, Rob. I do not see a change in that circumstance once I wed."

"I do believe I am a bit sad for your wife, then."

"She will be taken care of and I will keep myself to her. That is all that is necessary to make a sound marriage."

"A sound marriage?" Rob scoffed. "A dull marriage, more like."

Marcus shrugged. "I have no desire for a love match. I have seen little evidence of any in existence among the *ton*, your parents' union aside."

"They are disgustingly happy, I am afraid," Rob grinned. "Unfortunately that is all the more reason my mother is after me to wed."

"Grimes has investigated the young ladies on my short list and they have all been found suitable. Perhaps after I make my choice you can choose from the remainder."

"What an enticing offer," Rob drawled. "I believe I shall discover my own young lady, thank you all the same. Are you making any calls today?"

Marcus stared out the window toward the back garden, weighing his options. "I find I do not have the energy today for a call upon the Prestwicks. Perhaps I shall send a note round to Lady Genevieve."

Rob's eyes rounded. "Stinky Stilling's sister?"

"She is a viable candidate, Rob."

"I suppose. What of the Ellsworth chit?"

"I danced with her last evening and found her pleasant enough."

"Pleasant? Quite the glowing endorsement."

"Her sister shot me daggers, however."

"Miss Marianne? I scarce believe it."

"Well, not quite daggers. She was watching us closely, however."

"She is very protective of her sister. I sensed that on our ride through the park."

Marcus thought for a moment. "Grimes had some interesting information on the elder Miss Ellsworth."

Rob leaned forward. "Surely no scandal dogs the

family?"

"No, but it seems her personality is much altered since leaving the country."

Rob scratched his chin. "The girl does seem ill-at-ease now and again." He smiled at Marcus. "Usually when you are nearby."

"I tell you the chit has no strong feelings about me. Should I declare for her sister that might change, however."

"It most definitely will change. I would not do so unless you are completely certain in your intentions."

"As I said, I shall give myself a fortnight."

"That long?" Rob quipped.

"Rob, I have to decide and soon. There are but six weeks left to the Season. Surely a month affianced is required before setting a date to wed by Christmas."

"What of your dove?"

Marcus thought of Annie then, of the jealousy pouting her luscious lips and sparking her remarkable deep blue eyes. "We shall part ways, as per our agreement."

"I cannot see you forgetting her."

He had seen a complex mix of emotions on her face, there in his bed. Jealousy and hurt as he mentioned his marriage bed. Heat and affection as she took his words to heart. He would never feel for another woman what he did for her.

"You may count on this, Rob. I shall never forget her."

Chapter 14

Marcus was quite sick of the sound of his own voice. The call on Genevieve Stilling was not going as he might have hoped, and the past thirty minutes felt like three hours at least. The girl held herself so still, she could have been one of the statues dotting the Stilling townhouse's gardens around them.

"I enjoyed our dance last evening," he said again. Lord, he sounded like a dolt. "I thank you again for the pleasure."

She nodded, her dark hair peeking from beneath her bonnet. "Thank you, my lord."

He folded his hands in his lap. "Have you seen any exhibits of late?"

This apparently, at long last, sparked her interest. "Oh, yes!" She turned to face him, her brown eyes opened wide as she warmed to her topic. "We went to the gardens, they are just lovely this time of year, and there was an arrangement of Oriental plantings and fruit trees. I daresay I have never seen anything like it."

He nodded, silently urging her to continue.

"There were flowers so delicate they resembled

humming birds! I do not recall their scientific name. Perhaps Percy will." She turned toward the terrace doors, open to the parlor within.

Marcus cringed inwardly. *Please, do not let her call her brother out here.*

"Percy, dear!" she called, her face alight.

Shuffling footsteps sounded on the terrace stones as her brother stepped out to join them. "Yes, sister?"

"The plantings, dear brother. The flowers that looked like tiny birds. Do you recall their name?"

Stilling scoffed, a pout on his face. "Hardly. I merely took you there after you pestered me all weekend."

Genevieve colored at her brother's insensitive comment. "Forgive me, then."

Any animation was leeched from her features in that instant. Once again, Marcus fought the urge to wring Stilling's neck.

"Lacey," Stilling sniffed, giving an obviously reluctant nod. "I trust you are well."

"Quite," Marcus returned flatly.

The other man stared at him for a long moment,

then turned to his sister. "I am off to make a call of my own, sister." He flicked his gaze toward Marcus. "At the Ellsworth townhouse."

Marcus arched a brow at his statement. The gauntlet was thrown, then? Insolent pup. Very well, then. "Do give the ladies my regards, Stilling. Miss Brianna has promised me another dance this evening."

Stilling scowled. It was not nicely done of him, but Marcus did not note any response from the man's sister. That was indeed telling. No, she seemed more vexed that her brother was going out to pay a call on a young lady than the notion that Marcus would dance with another. He would most certainly not find an affectionate wife in Genevieve Stilling.

Resisting the urge to check his watch, he turned back to Genevieve and watched as her expression of irritation eased into her more-familiar one of disinterest.

Splendid.

* * *

Marianne watched Bree for any affectionate regard toward today's caller. Mister Stilling was his usual smiling, jovial self this afternoon, the petulant little boy she had glimpsed several times before gone from his countenance as he now basked in Bree's rapt attentions.

They sat in the parlor, Bree and Mister Stilling on the settee with Marianne facing them. The room was decorated with bouquets of flowers from several of Bree's admirers which had not escaped Mister Stilling's notice, hence the irritation that had flashed in his dark eyes upon entering fifteen minutes earlier.

"Why, the gardens are simply remarkable this time of year," he said. "I would be most honored to escort you and your sister one afternoon."

"That would be lovely," Bree said. "What say you, Marianne? Wouldn't it be lovely to visit the gardens with Mister Stilling?"

"Indeed," Marianne agreed. "And Mister Stilling is most gracious to extend the invitation."

"How could I not?" He bowed his head in her direction. "Miss Ellsworth, there is little beauty I encounter without thinking of you and your sister."

Marianne hid her smile. That was nicely done.

"Such pretty speeches!" Bree laughed. "I daresay, Mister Stilling, you will turn our heads with such talk."

He held a hand over his chest, the gesture self-deprecating. Marianne hid her own answering smirk. If only the smug expression on his face did not clearly contradict the motion.

"I assure you," he went on. "I have yet to see two more beautiful ladies in three Seasons."

"Only three?" Marianne could not resist asking.

Mister Stilling's face flushed a bit, but he soon recovered. "I have been escorting my sister to the parties for that long, I am afraid."

Marianne stiffened at what his words implied. It was poorly done of him, intimating that his sister was nearing the shelf.

"Your sister seems a lovely girl, Mister Stilling," she said. "How did you leave her today?"

His eyes rounded, then he nodded. "Quite well, Miss Ellsworth. In fact, perhaps she will end this Season in a different manner than the one in which she began it."

"Oh?" Bree asked. "Pray tell me, does she plan to wed?"

"Hmm, perhaps it is too soon to tell." He preened a bit, leaning against the back of the settee. "She does have what appears to be a serious suitor at long last."

Marianne bristled at his tone. The subject was a sore one indeed for Marianne, knowing that after this Season she herself would be firmly on the shelf despite her age.

"Perhaps your sister would not appreciate your discussing such a matter in company?" Marianne asked.

He waved a hand. "My sister and I have no secrets, Miss Ellsworth. I am certain she would not mind my crowing over her accomplishments."

"Accomplishments?" Bree asked. "Then it would be an advantageous match?"

"Brianna," Marianne said in warning. "It is not our place to delve into such matters."

Mister Stilling had the temerity to reach for Bree's hand, letting his touch linger a bit too long in Marianne's opinion. "I take no offense, Miss Brianna. Yes, I believe becoming the Countess of Lacey would be most advantageous for my sister."

Marianne's breath seized. Marcus was Genevieve Stilling's suitor! The prospect chilled her, though she should have expected it. He said that he would renew his bride search in earnest, and last night's performance at the parties surely bore out that truth. The jealousy she could not fight last evening came back in a rush.

She recalled the sight of Genevieve Stilling receiving his smiles and attentions. Envisioned them dancing in full view of the *ton* and all that implied. She closed her eyes for a moment, picturing Marcus making love to Genevieve as he had to her last night.

"Miss Ellsworth?" Mister Stilling's voice reached her. "What think you of that?"

She opened her eyes to find him and Bree staring at her. "D-do you believe she will accept his suit?"

Mister Stilling sneered a bit. "Oh, I find him insufferably dull myself. Straight-laced Lacey, he's called." He laughed. "My sister just might be the perfect woman for him."

Bree fell silent at his statement, her expression of distaste no doubt mimicking Marianne's at his harsh description of Marcus and Stilling's sister.

"I daresay we have another appointment, Mister Stilling," Bree said suddenly.

Marianne took her sister's cue and nodded, coming

to her feet. "Do forgive us, but we must get ready."

Mister Stilling blinked, then stood. "I had thought to…" He looked down at Bree. "May I count on the honor of a dance this evening, Miss Brianna?"

The look in Bree's blue eyes was chilling. "I am not at all certain, Mister Stilling."

He recovered and turned to Marianne. "I bid you and your sister a lovely afternoon, Miss Ellsworth." He took her hand and bowed over it. "I look forward to seeing you both this evening."

Bree remained still, her face a picture of the disinterest Marianne often affected when out in Society. The man bowed to her and took his leave. At the sound of the front door closing, Bree visibly relaxed.

"What a horrid man, speaking of his sister in such a manner," she said.

Marianne sat beside her. "It was very poorly done of him, to be sure."

"Genevieve Stilling might not be as effervescent as some of the ladies," Bree nodded. "But she surely does not deserve such censure."

"No." Marianne thought of Mister Stilling's

comment about Marcus. "Nor does Lord Lacey."

"I should say not! He has been most pleasant to me of late." Bree's brow furrowed for a moment. "Do you believe his interest in Mister Stilling's sister is sincere?"

The prospect hurt more than Marianne was wont to acknowledge. "How can one judge such a matter, Bree?"

"True. I wonder if his pursuit of me is then."

Marianne froze. "What?"

"He is most eligible, Marianne. And handsome. If he is a little stiff in company, what does it matter?"

Marianne blinked, her eyes suddenly stinging. "It does not matter in the least. He is respectable and wealthy. He would make any woman a fine husband."

"Me, Countess of Lacey." Bree raised her chin in a haughty manner, then fell back laughing. "Oh, I daresay that would not suit me in the least!"

Marianne swallowed past the lump in her throat. "I did not detect any abundance of attention toward you than toward any of the other ladies he has danced with over the past few evenings."

Bree's eyes narrowed. "You have watched him, then?"

"I… I am an interested observer, Bree. A man's demeanor among Society can be quite the opposite of the way he comports himself outside of the ballroom." *Or inside the bedroom.* "It would not do to only judge a man by the way he presents himself directly to you."

Bree tilted her head. "I suppose. Lord Devlin has been just as attentive to me, however. And to you, if I may say so."

Lord Devlin was indeed most attentive to her. She had found his gaze on her quite frequently over the past week. That shrewdness she had seen the morning of their ride had been evident as well. He did not seem to remember her as the courtesan he had hired for Marcus' pleasure, but he had gotten quite a close look at Annie that night. He had spent more than a little time with her in that guest chamber's bed.

"I have not heard that Lord Devlin is looking for a bride," Bree went on.

"He is most charming," Marianne said. "Perhaps he takes true enjoyment in the parties. Dancing and chatting with many ladies."

"Perhaps." Bree seemed to be envisioning

something quite pleasant, for her smile was wide. "Or perhaps he thinks to court the Ellsworth sister who is by far the most beautiful."

Marianne managed a smile at the compliment, as she fought the urge to vomit on the carpet. The very last thing she needed was a public courtship coming from a gentleman who had once arranged her purchase!

"Let us not get ahead of ourselves," she choked out. "You are the one to marry, Bree. I am not a concern."

"But why? You are far and away the prettiest. In fact, I have not seen a prettier girl all Season, Mister Stilling's words aside. Why can you not consider marrying?"

Marianne fought tears in earnest now. Bree could never know the real reason she could never marry: she was not pure.

"I want to see you wed, Bree. Should I find a gentleman in the future, after you are safely settled, I will reconsider."

"Safely settled?"

"You know we lack adequate funds to continue on as we are."

"I do." Bree studied her face for a long moment, finally letting out a sigh of irritation. "There is something more to this, Marianne. For some reason you see no need to share your burden with me."

"Come, now."

"I have come upon you and Aunt Hattie in close conversation. More than once. There is something more to this. Something driving you."

"Bree, I do not want you to fret about this."

Bree took her hands. Marianne was grateful for the gesture, as her own felt as cold as the grate beside her.

"When you wish to share your worries, I am here." Bree squared her shoulders. "Until then, I will seriously consider any suitable gentleman who shows interest in marrying me."

Marianne hugged her tight. "Thank you, Bree. It is what I want for you." *And what we need.*

Bree nodded against her neck. "I pray this will make you happy."

Happy? She sincerely doubted she would ever be happy. "I shall be content."

Her sister said nothing more, apparently taking

Marianne's words at face value.

Chapter 15

Marcus checked his pocket watch, an absent smile on his face as Genevieve Stilling went on about her brother's new gelding. The room was close, the parlor too small for those assembled. His cravat rubbed his neck as he nodded at her. He watched her face, seeing the animation lighting her brown eyes and coloring her smooth cheeks. She was a pretty girl, really. Adequate mouth, delicate chin. It was a pity that she only showed this side of herself when either in her brother's company or discussing the dolt.

As she went on to tell him about the bookshop she had encountered on their trip back from Stilling's purchase in the country, he studied her. Her hair was dressed simply, pulled straight back from a center part. Thin braids circled her crown, unadorned. Her dress was of quality, as he could judge by those worn by the other ladies in the room. A dark purple, it made her skin look quite pale. He could not help but compare it to Annie's complexion. Warmed by candlelight or passion, her skin was smooth and incredible to touch. And her hair, thick and lustrous even in the low light of his chambers.

Genevieve gestured with her hands, putting Marcus in mind of the delicate touch Annie employed to drive him quite mad.

Shaking his head, he forced his mind on the one-sided conversation. "I trust you found something to please you there?"

"What?" She blinked up at him, then smiled shyly. "Percy helped me reach a particularly large tome on a high shelf, one illustrated with flowers and nature. He told me it was a silly expense but he bought it for me in any event."

Dolt. "That was very generous of him."

"Oh, he is the best brother. My older brothers never had time for me, or for Percy for that matter. I do not know what I would do without him."

"And what of when he weds?"

Alarm flitted across her face and her hand-fluttering increased. "Oh, I suppose it is inevitable. He is so handsome and well-regarded."

"He is courting Miss Brianna Ellsworth, I believe?"

She nodded. "Yes. Though I believe he feels a tendre toward the eldest."

His gaze sought out the sisters, and he found them with their aunt across the narrow room. Miss Brianna was surrounded by young gentlemen, Rob among them. Miss Marianne Ellsworth, however, kept herself slightly apart from the throng. That did not stop the gentlemen around them from looking at her with blatant interest. Perhaps there was something about a lady of mystery? She did seem to draw his attention time and again despite any overtures to the contrary on her part.

He saw that her eyes were on her sister, and concern and affection was clear from his vantage point. They were a dark blue, putting him in mind of Annie's lovely gaze. Her hair appeared golden in the many candles above, catching the light as she tilted her head to listen to the conversations around her. She did look quite pretty sitting so still there, her hands held in her lap. Nearly beautiful, save for her pinched expression. Would her lips appear full if she did not purse them all the time?

"I daresay I shall be quite lost when Percy weds," Genevieve finished.

Marcus shook his head and looked away from the Ellsworth sisters and their court of admirers. He smiled at

Genevieve. "But what of your future? Surely you wish to wed?"

Her eyes took on a faraway look. "I suppose I must, though I should like to find someone who lives not far from my family home." She started and looked back at Marcus. "Our home has such an extensive library, Lord Lacey. I should hate to be parted from it."

He gave a nod in answer. The library? Not likely the reason. He guessed the lady would never willingly wed anyone who would not allow her continue to see her idiot of a brother every day. That thought doused any hopes that she was the bride for him.

As she went on about the library and the latest book she had read to her brother, Marcus continued to watch the Ellsworth girls. Miss Brianna was pretty, and she had no irksome brother to come between them time and again. As prickly as her sister was in him company, he was not seized with the urge to throttle her as he was with Genevieve's sibling. That was a point in the girl's favor, in his estimation.

"Oh, there is Percy now!" Genevieve's voice rose in excitement. "I must go see how his evening progresses. I believe he danced with both sisters earlier this evening, though now he seems put out by the other gentlemen seeking their attention."

Marcus arched a brow at the girl's astute observation. "Would you like to join the group across the way?" he asked, holding out his arm.

She nodded and fled, leaving him standing there. He lowered his arm then watched her slide close to her brother as the Ellsworths rose, clearly readying for their departure. He sighed. That was it, then. On to the other ladies on his list.

He glanced at his watch again. Half-past twelve. In thirty minutes he would be home and Annie would be in his arms. Two nights in a row, though he had not been that fortunate since they had begun this arrangement. His body twitched in anticipation and he shifted on his feet. Would he ever cease craving her company? Her touch, her voice. Her beautiful face and her sweet body? No.

Perhaps he was being too harsh on Genevieve. After she wed she would not be able to separate from her brother, true. After he himself wed, he would not be able to give himself completely to his bride with Annie still in his heart.

After calling for his carriage he turned to go, brushing close to Marianne Ellsworth in the entry as she trailed after her sister and aunt. She did not see him, keeping her head bowed as he had noticed she tended to in company. He stilled as he caught a bit of her scent, one he had not noticed on her before. The room was quite warm, and perhaps that explained its evidence now. He breathed her in. Vanilla. Just the hint of it, but his body hardened in an instant. Watching as the three of them boarded their carriage, he saw her turn her head to look over her shoulder. That graceful neck, that smooth cheek, those dark eyes.

"Beautiful," he breathed.

Shaking his head, he laughed to himself. He was thinking of Annie. That was all. Desiring her to such an extreme that he saw her in every girl he encountered tonight. Boarding his own carriage, he set the Ellsworth girl from his mind and focused fully on his Annie and every delicious thing he would do to her.

* * *

By a quarter past one he had her naked and spread

beneath him. Her glorious hair was fanned out on his pillows, her smooth thighs open. "I have thought of you all night."

She laughed softly, the sound a bit husky. "You always say that."

He quickly stripped off his own clothes and settled down beside her, stroking her smooth cheek. "And it is always true."

She tilted him a look. "I am quite certain you thought of many other things this evening, Marcus. Did you not attend the parties on your bride quest?"

He shrugged a shoulder. "Yes, but I still could not stop thinking about you." He kissed her delectable lips. "I swear, I saw you in nearly every woman I spoke with tonight." He kissed her cheek, her throat, breathing in her vanilla scent. "In fact, I even started to…" He stopped himself from revealing that the mere scent of Marianne Ellsworth had him wanting.

She ran her fingers through his hair, urging his face to hers. "Started to…what, pray?"

Shaking his head, he laughed. "It is nothing. It was surely deprivation stiffening my cock."

"Deprivation?" She smiled now, her full lips very pink. "Why, just last evening I thought you had had your fill?"

"Never, Annie." He kissed her again. "I daresay I shall crave you forever."

An inscrutable look crossed her face. "Your future wife would surely object."

"I do not wish to discuss that particular subject. You are inside me now, love. There is no denying it."

Her gaze grew so soft then, affection clear in their dark-blue depths. Was she coming to care for him too?

"Marcus, do not say such things to me. It is not sporting of you to ape a courtship. Pray, save those words for your intended."

He shook his head. "You have not been with me in company Annie, but I assure you I am not known for making pretty speeches. I have never told another lady such a thing."

"A lady," she murmured. A pout turned her mouth down, then she visibly brightened. "You may not have a skillful tongue when it comes to such speeches, Marcus." She arched her breast into his eager hand. "But as a lover? Oh, there you are quite well-favored."

He grinned and brought his mouth to her breast. Her taste filled his senses, her soft moans of pleasure filled his ears. Circling one nipple with his tongue, he began to suckle.

Settling between her thighs, his cock stroked her belly. "Ah, love." He switched to the other breast, dragging his tongue over its nipple and earning a gasp of pleasure from her. "Allow me to remind you of all my tongue can do."

Nodding, she placed her hands on his head and held him close. "Yes, please."

He made his way down her body, anticipation nearly making him come into the sheets. "Vanilla." He spread her wide, drinking in her scent before stroking her deeply with his tongue. "I cannot tell you what that scent does to me now."

She tilted herself toward him, urging him to take her. It was all the invitation he needed. Covering her sex with his mouth, he began to suck gently. His tongue found her nub and teased and tormented it until she screamed his name. Holding her tight, her taste intoxicating, he felt her climax start.

Nothing felt like the sensation of her flesh growing tight against his mouth. He lifted her slightly to plunge his tongue deep inside of her. Again and again he thrust into her, mimicking what his body would enjoy before the night was out.

She rode his tongue, arching wildly beneath him as her passions rose to their peak. He could not seem to get enough of her. So soft, so hot. So sweet he felt his own climax start. He would come in the sheets as he had feared earlier, but at this moment he didn't care a wit. He continued to tongue her as he held himself rigid against the bed. He had never felt such intensity outside of a woman's body, save for the time she had taken him in her mouth.

Shuddering as he barely held back his own release, he finally lifted his head. She was still lost in her rapture. That he could see. Her arms were thrown over her head, her face turned slightly away into the pillows. Graceful neck, smooth cheek, full parted lips. She was everything beautiful.

"That was a very close thing." He came up and

kissed her cheek. "I have to admit that your pleasure nearly brought mine prematurely."

She sucked in a breath and turned to face him, her eyes slowly opening. They were glazed, passion softening their color to nearly black. Placing a hand in the center of his chest, she eased him upward. "Then let me offer my assistance."

He sat back on his heels as, in one smooth motion, she came to her knees and took him in her mouth. Squeezing his eyes shut, he gave himself over to her as his climax roared through him.

"Is that better, Marcus?" he heard her ask as if from far away.

He could barely put two thoughts together let alone enough words to let her know just how much better it had been. He simply nodded and fell down beside her. After taking in a few bracing breaths, he opened his eyes to find her smiling at him.

"I promise you, I shall make it up to you."

"Of that, I have no doubt."

They were quiet for long moments, their breathing in sync as passion ebbed and comfort grew. She was amazing, his Annie. He had never felt this before. This connection. He knew she'd had other lovers, and the thought that she had shared any of this with them caused jealousy to curdle in his belly.

"How many have there been?" he couldn't help but ask.

Her breath stilled, then she shifted to meet his gaze. Her eyes grew shuttered. "Enough."

"I pass no judgment, Annie. I am merely curious." He gave her a small smile. "And a bit jealous, I admit."

She took a breath and nodded. "Just a handful. I… Just a handful."

"Are you saying—?"

"You can count on one hand the men I have been with, my lord. And have a few fingers left over."

If her words set his mind at ease, her tone did not. He arched a brow, tracing his finger over her cheek. "Oh, we are back to 'my lord'?"

That garnered a small smile in return. "Marcus."

"You can count on one hand?" he repeated. He lifted her hand in his. "This hand?"

She nodded.

He gently opened her hand and kiss the center of her palm before facing her again. "Was it terrible?"

Her brow furrowed. "I do not wish to talk about this."

"I just want to know if you were safe, love. That is all." It was not quite true, but the thought of her in danger caused something different than jealousy to rise within him.

"They were kind, Marcus. They simply wanted to see to their pleasure." She pulled her hand from his, fisting it on his chest as she lowered her gaze. "They made sure of my comfort. I was never hurt."

"That eases my mind. But what of your pleasure?"

She raised her head and looked at him. "I never felt any pleasure with them."

Something inside him shifted. He was right, then. From the beginning. She was new to pleasure and it was as amazing to her as it was to him.

"Tonight then," he said. "Tonight you can take your pleasure."

She leaned into him as he rolled onto his back. "There is nothing lacking there, Marcus. You have given me more pleasure than I ever knew existed."

He stretched out, folding his hands behind his head. "Ah, but tonight you may take your pleasure. From me."

Her eyes sparkled as she ran her gaze over him. She trailed her fingers over his chest. "But what of you?" She smiled slyly and, amazingly, his cock began to fill. "If I take my pleasure, what will that leave you?"

He laughed, quite comfortable with the motion now. "I daresay I will find as much or more before the night is out."

Chapter 16

Marianne studied the incredible male specimen before her, completely hers to command. Marcus was beautiful, from his golden hair to his finely-chiseled face and well-muscled form. The heat in his green eyes threatened to make her swoon. As a smile curved his lovely mouth she recalled the pleasure he had just given her. Her scent, he had said, his tone almost reverent. She could now smell herself on him. Satisfaction of a different kind suddenly filled her. He desired her, so much that he had nearly spent in the sheets as he had brought her to climax again and again with his skillful tongue.

"I watched you sleep that first night," she said softly.

He arched a brow. "Did you? I admit Rob and I had imbibed quite a bit that night, though I rarely drink so. I was unaware of your presence until you placed your delicate hand on my cock."

She shivered at the memory of rousing him as he had slept. Stroking his chest, she let out a purr of desire. "You are so beautiful, Marcus. Your body is magnificent."

"Hardly out of the ordinary, I imagine. Surely you have seen the like before."

She searched his face for any censure. There was none, thank goodness. After their recent conversation she could not bear it if he thought she had found any of the other men attractive.

"None," she said honestly. "If they were at all like you, I did not notice. I was bought and paid for. There to perform a service. That was all."

For some reason that made him smile. "And that first night with me, love? As you watched me sleep?"

"I felt something different entirely," she admitted, her cheeks heating. "I had never felt desire before."

He lifted his head slightly. "And you wanted me?"

She shrugged a shoulder. "How could I not? I did not realize it at the time but it seems that my body was meant for yours."

Lowering her gaze, she saw his manhood swell. "You reacted in your sleep to my touch, Marcus. Your shaft grew hard beneath my fingers." She trailed her fingers over his flesh, marveling anew at its heat and smoothness. "And when you came into that guest chamber, I found I could not look away from you."

"From my body, you mean," he teased.

She smiled. "That. And your eyes."

He closed his eyes then, flexing his hips as she began to stroke his manhood. Its broad head was swollen, and a drop of moisture gathered at the tip. Emboldened by his passivity, she brought her mouth to it and tasted him. His saltiness danced on the tip of her tongue.

"Ah, Annie," he groaned. He stilled, reaching down to lift her mouth from him. "You are to take your pleasure, love. Not give me mine."

She considered his words, then came to a wicked notion. It was something she had never done before, though one of the other gentlemen had asked her to. "May I ride you, Marcus?"

His member twitched in her hand. "God, yes."

She stretched out on top of him, rubbing her breasts against his hard chest. His hair tickled her, causing her nipples to ache. "You feel so good beneath me," she breathed.

He murmured something in answer as she spread

her legs over his belly. His arousal was at her bottom, and she rubbed up against it. Her body swelled at the close contact. Lifting up, she reached down to put the broad head at her entrance. She could not quite make it fit from this angle, and she soon cried out in frustration.

"Lean back," he ground out. "Take in all of me."

She did so, settling down over him in one motion. Oh, she felt so full! Bracing her hands on his chest, she tentatively began to move. Up and down she slowly stroked him, feeling every inch of his shaft deep inside. He began to thrust beneath her, his hips arching off of the bed as she rode him. It was too much! Surely she would be torn in two at any moment, but the pleasure was so intense she did not care.

Quickening her movements, she felt herself grow wet around him. He slipped deeper inside, and it was impossible for her to cease. Sobbing his name, she began to clench around his shaft. He was so hard, so hot, she began to come. His hands were on her breasts then, his strong fingers teasing her nipples as she cried out. "Marcus, my love!"

He groaned in encouragement, his hands tight on

her hips now as he ground up against her. She grasped his wrists, afraid of falling. Afraid of tumbling into the abyss. It was so intense, so freeing. Throwing her head back, she found her pleasure.

He began to burst inside of her, his seed shooting so deep she felt it to her core. He did not withdraw, but she did not care. This was so right, the two of them so close. It did not matter. Their moans shook the bed as she collapsed on his chest.

"Oh, my," she sighed.

Again he groaned. "That was…" He let out a breath. "There are no words."

She leaned up, their sweat-soaked bodies sliding pleasurably against each other, and smiled. "Thank you."

He cupped her cheek with one hand, his eyes holding a tenderness she knew she would remember forever. "Any time." As he eased out of her, a look of regret crossed his face. "I stayed inside you, love. I am sorry."

Waving a hand, she settled against his side. "There should be no consequence, I am certain." Her monthlies had arrived on schedule but a week ago and passed as usual. Marcus had spent inside of her twice before that, so apparently her special balm did its work.

"I am sorry all the same. I had promised you."

She gazed at him and smiled. "Pray, do not worry over me. Trust me, I will not have any reminder of this time when you are wed, Marcus."

His eyes darkened, then he nodded. "Save for memories, dare I hope?"

She shivered, an echo of pleasure dancing across her flesh. "Oh, yes. Only memories, but I shall cherish them."

His face took on a brooding cast. "Annie, I know we have discussed this before."

She stiffened, certain of what was coming. "Marcus, do not."

"Forgive me, but I must. Can we not continue this beyond the Season?"

"Absolutely not. You will have chosen a bride and I will not be the cause of another woman's distress."

That tenderness once more filled his gaze. "I have no intentions of making a love match."

"What should you do if your wife were to fall in

love with you?"

He laughed, a harsh sound. "I have no worries that will ever happen. Don't you know that Straight-laced Lacey is too cold to elicit such tender feelings in a female?"

"What do you mean?"

His eyes took on a sad expression. "My mother was cold, Annie. Reserved. I am cut from the same cloth."

Her heart broke at the conviction on his face. She knew she was revealing too much, but she could not bear to see such pain. "You are quite worthy of being loved, Marcus."

"Do you love me, Annie?"

She shook her head. "That is not a matter to discuss. I have told you before."

"You called me your love, you know." He stroked her hair, freeing the damp strands from her brow. "Before. As you rode me."

She looked away, studying the whirls of hair on his chest. "Gentlemen use the endearment all the time, Marcus. You yourself call me such."

"That may be so, but I have never called another

woman 'love.'"

Trepidation filled her and she brought her gaze to his. "What are you saying?"

His face took on a contemplative air, then he shook his head. "Nothing of import. Forgive me. It seems two orgasms so close together have turned my brain to mush."

She took the solace his quip afforded, settling down in his arms once more. If he thought he held tender feelings toward his courtesan, perhaps that was only natural. She was beginning to love him, damn her foolish heart.

It would never do for either of them to expect more of this relationship that what it was purported to be. An exchange of passion for pounds, really. Their hearts had no place in their arrangement.

If it killed her a little bit each time she let herself go in his arms, that was her own misfortune.

* * *

Marcus had not spoken one word in the past forty-five minutes. He sat in an arm chair, flanked on either side by two Prestwick sisters. They sat in pairs on matching gold settees, the very pictures of genteel womanhood. They gestured and chattered, at him and around him, each as lively and animated as the next.

They wore dresses the color of summer, in pink and yellow and green and blue. Their golden hair was dressed identically, upswept and coiled in braids at their crowns. There was little to differentiate among them, but Marcus attempted to. If he intended to court one of the sisters, he should settle on one today.

"Isn't that so, Lord Lacey?" the one closest to his right asked.

He searched his mind for her name, coming up blank. "Pardon?"

She giggled, jostling her sister who joined in the sound. "The gardens, Lord Lacey. They are simply beautiful this time of year."

The gardens. Genevieve Stilling had gone on about them the other day, so Marcus assumed they were indeed quite something. "Yes."

The one closest to his left began to talk about the musicale they had attended last evening, and they soon took turns naming different pieces played. As they spoke he considered each of them in turn. The closest to his right, Polly or Patrice, had skin that fairly glowed with good health. Her eyes sparkled, and were a pleasing shade of blue. Not quite the dark blue that he might have preferred, but quite pretty in their way. The girl beside her, perhaps Patrice, had hair a bit lighter than her sister. It was rich-looking and shining, though not as lustrous a shade as he much favored.

Turning his attention to his left, he eyed the pair seated there. Penelope and Paulette, perhaps? One had eyes a bit darker, more like the shade he had come to desire. Her lips were not quite as full or rosy as he would like, however. Her sister's lips were plump and sweet-looking. It was a pity he could not take something from each girl to make one perfect bride for himself.

He sighed inwardly as the truth struck him. He compared each girl to Annie and they could not help but fall short. He needed more time with them to discover which one might suit. He ran his gaze over them once more. Now if he could only remember which was which.

"Miss Prestwick, will you attend the parties tonight?"

He directed his question toward the fireplace in front of him, loathe to single out any one of the girls. They nodded, their mouths curved in smiles.

"May I ask the honor of a dance, then?" he asked.

He would choose the first to answer. In the next moment all four of them began to voice their assent. His shoulders slumped. At least this evening they would be forced to separate. Even they surely deemed it unusual for a gentleman to dance with all four of them at once.

He stood. "What say you to a turn about your own garden?"

They stood and, in a flurry of skirts, he was whisked out the terrace doors and onto a stone path. Four hands gripped each of his arms, a feat he could not have imagined possible. Voices droned in his ears, making him suddenly long for Genevieve Stilling's stoicism. Tonight he would dance with each one of them.

It was going to be a long night.

* * *

"How goes your bride search?" Rob asked.

Marcus stood on the fringe of the dance floor, discreetly wiping perspiration from his brow. He had danced with each Prestwick in their turn, his ears fairly ringing from their continued discourse throughout the endeavor.

"I am at a loss," he admitted. "I cannot tell you the strange experience I encountered this afternoon."

"You called on the Prestwick sisters?"

"Yes."

"On which one?"

Marcus shook his head. "All of them, apparently."

Rob was quiet for a moment. "You shall need a larger bed."

Marcus laughed despite himself. "Trying to separate one from the others? I admit I felt like a wolf attempting to lure one sheep away from the flock."

"And have you?"

He watched them where they danced with other gentlemen in attendance. "I am afraid not."

"They are quite pretty, Lacey. Any one of them would make you happy."

"I have no illusions about the happiness to be found in marriage, Rob. At best, I would like to be content."

"What of your dove?"

Marcus shot him a look. "She makes me happier than I have ever been, but it will soon end."

"It doesn't have to."

"I told you, I will not keep a mistress."

"Marry her, then."

Marcus thought for a heart-stopping moment of what it would be like to come home to Annie every night. To spend every day in her company as well.

"You are mad," he told Rob.

Rob shrugged. "Have Grimes investigate her. You said yourself that she doesn't seem quite like a seasoned courtesan. Perhaps she is not as low-born as you suspected."

"She is not," Marcus bit out. "I do not know the circumstances that brought her to her particular line of work but she is far from what I would expect a well-used girl to be."

Rob was quiet again, his eyes settled on a spot across the room. "If there is indeed more to her, you deserve to know what that might be."

Marcus looked at his friend, reading contemplation on his usually-affable face. "What are you saying?"

Rob grinned, his eyes bright once more. "Nothing." He tilted his head toward the Prestwicks, who had once more gathered together. "Go. Attempt to distinguish one from the others and let me know how you progress."

Marcus left his side and, with little enthusiasm, headed for the flock of potential brides.

Chapter 17

Marianne watched as Marcus danced with first one then another of the Prestwick girls. Any one of them would make a fine countess, and the notion caused her stomach to clench. His talk of affection last evening had stayed with her all day. When George had reported that no card awaited her in the appointed spot, she'd felt acute relief that she would not have to go to Marcus tonight. She had called him her love! Goodness knew what she would say after watching him court so many lovely ladies tonight.

Bree had a trio of suitors in front of her now, Lords Wilbrey and Shaston and Mr. Meryton. Marianne was relieved to see that Mister Stilling was keeping his distance. His disparaging remarks about his sister still rankled. Marcus did not seem to pay that woman any marked attention this evening, however. Perhaps he had somehow disqualified her from his list of candidates on his own.

"You look upset, dear," Aunt Hattie said.

Marianne started, unaware that the woman had returned from the retiring room. "Oh, I am fine."

"These evenings wear on you."

"I admit, I grow tired of affecting this particular expression."

Aunt Hattie smiled. "Your lips must fairly ache by the time we return home."

Marianne laughed, drawing the gaze of the three men in front of Bree. She quickly schooled her expression once more. "Just a few more weeks. Until the end of the Season."

"I pray it will be so." Her aunt smiled. "Then you can be the carefree girl you once were."

"Yes, Aunt." Although she knew in her heart she would never be that girl again.

"May I have this dance, Miss Ellsworth?"

Marianne looked up to find Mister Stilling before her. So much for his keeping his distance. "Oh, I had not thought to dance."

He smiled, the expression attractive yet somehow false. "I am confident I can change your mind."

The strains of a country dance could be heard, so she slipped her hand in his. Letting him lead her out on the dance floor, she could not help but notice Marcus escorting one of the Prestwicks. Polly, perhaps. At least they were well down the line and she would not have to step close to the pair.

"Hello, Miss Ellsworth," she heard a gentleman say.

Turning her head, she saw Lord Devlin escorting Bree into the dance. He stared at her and she shakily returned the expression. Those eyes of his, so dark and assessing, ran over her for a long moment before congeniality reappeared on his countenance.

The steps were complicated, and she was thankful for that. She was forced to attend to her movements and not to Lord Devlin's continued attention. He and Bree passed close to her and her partner in the dance, causing her to lose her footing. Mister Stilling caught her swiftly, causing a startled laugh to escape her. Lord Devlin suddenly stilled and looked at her again, his eyes wide and his mouth agape. A chill washed over her.

"Mister Stilling," she said. "I must beg to rest."

He glanced over at Lord Devlin, who had resumed his steps while his gaze remained fixed on her. Scowling, he took her hand. "Of course, Miss Ellsworth."

It took long minutes to cross through the twirling dancers, but at last she reached her chair. She turned to Mister Stilling and smiled in relief. "Thank you."

He stared down at her. "My pleasure, Miss Ellsworth. You may count on me at any time."

He continued to hold her hand, stroking his thumb over her palm. She needed an escape and, from the intensity of his gaze and Lord Devlin's continued attention, she suspected she would not get any peace out here. Extricating herself, she curtseyed and escaped to the retiring room.

What had Lord Devlin thought, staring at her like that? Had he recognized her? She had laughed, letting down her guard but for a moment. Was he astute enough to see through her guise?

Suddenly queasy, she sank down on the couch. The most horrid thoughts accosted her and she shut her eyes as if to keep them at bay.

What if he did recognize her? Would he tell Marcus? Would he reveal her secret to the *ton* and destroy any hope of Bree making a worthy marriage?

"That cannot happen."

"What is that, Miss Ellsworth?"

Marianne opened her eyes to find a Prestwick girl in front of her. "Nothing of import."

The girl plopped herself down beside Marianne, letting out a breathy sigh. "Oh, I daresay I could use a rest as well."

"Are you enjoying the evening, then? Polly, is it?"

The girl's eyes went round. "Yes! How lovely you guessed my name. Lord Lacey cannot seem to get us straight in his mind."

"I saw you and your sisters dancing with him."

"He is most handsome. He is usually so stiff in company, I was surprised to discover that he is an adequate dancer."

Marianne thought of the graceful way he moved with her, the sensual slide of his hands, the tenderness of his lips. "I am not."

"Have you dance with him, then?"

"No," she rushed out. "I have seen him dance with my sister, however. He moves quite well."

Polly nodded and then scrunched her face in thought, the expression adorable. "I do not think he is the man for us, though." She seemed to realize what she said and dissolved into more giggles. "I mean, for me!"

"Does one of your sisters favor him?"

Polly shook her head. "I daresay not. He is too stiff and formal for us."

"I am sorry to hear that."

"Yes, you and my father both. He wants the Lacey fortune to go to one of us."

Marianne nodded. The truth of it was that money was the only reason she was with Marcus nearly every night. She should not be surprised to learn that it factored into every decision made in the ballroom as well as the bedroom. Wasn't that why Bree was marched before her prospective beaux every night?

"Perhaps your sister will be the one," Polly said.

"My sister? Oh, Lord Lacey has not indicated such an interest."

"Hasn't he? It is said she is on his short list of prospective brides."

Marianne felt her nausea rise again. "Is that so?"

"They would make a pretty couple, though I believe she is too lively for him as well." Polly stood and brushed her hands over her skirts. "It was lovely talking with you, Miss Ellsworth. Perhaps we shall see you at the Ralston musicale?"

Marianne nodded once more, her thoughts a muddle. Marcus was seriously considering Bree? This situation was growing more tangled by the moment. She came to her feet. There was no way she would ever let Bree marry Marcus. Or let Marcus marry Bree. It was untenable.

She might be able to deny her love for him now, but should he offer for her sister? Surely her resolve would melt like Shropshire honey in July and she would blubber the truth to all and sundry.

Her head pounding, she stood and left the sanctuary of the retiring room. As she passed by a grouping of potted plants she felt a hand brush her shoulder.

"Miss Ellsworth," she heard a man whisper.

Startled, she turned. Mister Stilling stood behind one of the plants. She blinked, still too surprised by his incongruous presence among the greenery.

"Mister Stilling, whatever are you—?"

He grasped her hand and tugged her into an alcove

she had not known was behind the plants. "I had to speak with you, Miss Ellsworth."

She shook off his hand and stepped back, quickly taking in his appearance. His face was flushed, his eyes bright. Had he imbibed too much spirits?

"Mister Stilling, this is not proper."

"Who are we to speak of propriety?" he countered.

She froze. Had he somehow found out about her other life? "State your meaning."

"I know you feel it, Miss Ellsworth." He came closer. "This attraction between us."

She blinked. "I assure you, I do not."

He did not touch her, just leaned in until she was forced to flatten herself against the wall at her back.

"Mmm, you smell heavenly," he said. "I caught your scent out on the dance floor, sweet and warm."

"Mister Stilling, please."

"Percy, love." He breathed in again. "Call me Percy."

She shook her head.

"Ah, Marianne."

"I did not give you leave to call me such, Mister

Stilling!"

He pulled back, a dazed look on his face. Once more she wondered about his intake of spirits this evening.

"That may be but I assure you, you shall." He smiled, the expression full of the boastful confidence she had seen on his face often over the past weeks. He took her hand once more. "Dearest Marianne."

Her heart began to trip. "Mister Stilling, pray cease!"

"Will you do me the honor of becoming—?"

"What ho, Stilling!" a masculine voice called.

She looked up as Lord Devlin entered the alcove, the plants swaying behind him as if he had pushed his way through them. He smiled at her, then turned toward Mister Stilling. "Making an offer, Percy? Here, in the dark?" He stepped between them. "One would question your intentions toward the lady."

Mister Stilling bristled. "My intentions are honorable, I assure you."

Devlin arched a dark brow. "Then whyever are you accosting the lady here, away from the watchful eye of her aunt?"

Stilling's face flushed. "I do not seduce innocents, Devlin."

Devlin narrowed his gaze on her and she felt her own cheeks heat. If he had realized she was Annie, he knew she was no innocent. She could not decipher his expression, however.

He faced Mister Stilling. "You would not be impugning my honor here in front of Miss Ellsworth, would you Stinky? Surely you are not asking to meet me at dawn?"

Stilling paled now, shaking his head. "I am not! I have a serious regard toward Miss Ellsworth."

"Then present it in a formal fashion, you dolt."

Stilling turned to her, wearing an expression she could only attribute to misplaced affection. "May I call upon you, Miss Ellsworth?"

"No, you may not!"

He smiled indulgently. "I see you attempt to test my faithfulness. I shall call upon you soon."

He left the alcove, but only after shooting a dark look at Devlin.

"Insolent pup," Devlin grumbled.

She picked up her skirts and attempted to move past him. "Good evening, Lord Devlin."

He moved swiftly, blocking her exit. "Are you not going to reward me for preserving your honor?"

His tone was teasing, on the surface at least, and she met his gaze. "Thank you."

"Brr, such coldness." He grinned. "I had found you to be quite warm. Before."

Her breath caught as he ran his gaze over every inch of her. He had seen her up close, and nearly as naked as the day she had been born.

She could not withstand another moment in his close company. "Excuse me, Lord Devlin."

He finally stepped aside and let her pass, laughing softly. Rushing headlong into the ballroom, she searched for a sign of her aunt or sister. They were near the entrance, obviously waiting for their wraps. Aunt Hattie must have seen something of her troubling exchange with the two gentlemen, for her manner appeared impatient. Taking a breath, she hurried toward them. She crashed into a solid mass of man, and knew in an instant upon whose chest she now leaned.

"Oh, Marc—!" She gasped. "M-my lord," she swiftly corrected herself.

"Miss Ellsworth?"

She splayed her hands on him, her elbows tucked close as he gripped her arms. Studying the buttons of his waistcoat, she attempted to form some sort of reply. "Lord Lacey, do forgive me."

He was silent, as she so often saw him in company. The position was so much like last night's, she feared he would soon recall it as well. Cautiously lifting her head, she gazed up into his handsome face. His expression was one of concern but not recognition, to her acute relief. Her lips parted as she let out the breath she had been holding.

"Nothing to forgive," he said, his voice deep. She felt every utterance vibrate beneath her palms.

He released her, and she nearly sank to the floor. What if he saw through her ruse now? All would be lost.

"Good night," she murmured, stepping around him and hurrying to join her family.

"Marianne, are you all right?" Aunt Hattie asked as

she handed her wrap to her.

"I am fine, Aunt," she managed to say.

Bree eyed her for a moment, then smiled. "Come, then. We shall have several callers on the morrow, so I suppose it is fitting that Aunt Hattie drag us away from the festivities."

Marianne nodded and followed them out to the carriage. She would not look behind her. She would not catch one last glimpse of Marcus' face. Thank goodness she would not be in his bed tonight.

No doubt she would reveal herself for certain.

* * *

Marcus stared after Miss Ellsworth, his gut twisting. There was indeed something about the girl. It was little wonder so many gentlemen who had been courting Miss Brianna were now turning their attention toward the eldest.

"Seen her beauty at long last, I take it?" Rob said.

Marcus turned his focus on Rob. "She seems different somehow. What the devil happened in that alcove?"

Rob smirked. "Stilling was about to offer for her."

"There in the dark? Surely she deserves to be courted in the proper manner."

"I believe the fool thinks himself in love."

In a flash Marcus recalled her flushed and beautiful face staring up at him. Her tender touch on his chest. Perhaps Stilling had the right of it.

"Does she return the sentiment?" he asked Rob.

"Not at all, from what I saw. She looked terrified at the notion."

"And what of you?"

"I find the prospect chilling myself."

"That is not what I meant. Why did you follow them into the alcove?"

"I thought someone should see to the preservation of the girl's honor."

"I heartily doubt that, though you have never been known to debauch virgins in full view of the ton."

"Nor at all, thank you," Rob said. "I saw her in *your* arms, Lacey. Considering my suggestion at long last?"

"Not seriously. But for a moment there, she nearly looked like…" He couldn't give voice to the thought.

"Never mind."

Rob laughed. "Perhaps when you pay a call on her sister you can gaze in rapture upon Miss Ellsworth's lovely visage as well."

Marcus dismissed Rob's teasing comment with a shake of his head. "Come to the card room with me. I believe I need a diversion."

Rob led the way as Marcus pushed aside his confusion regarding the mysterious Marianne Ellsworth.

Chapter 18

His bed was lonely tonight. At least the solitude afforded Marcus the luxury of contemplation as the long hours limped toward sunrise. It was clear now that he could not seriously court one of the Prestwick sisters. He had actually managed to distinguish one from the others in his mind, each in their turn, yet he still could not envision marrying one of them. While they were attractive and affectionate, he felt little regard for any of the sisters.

True, bits and parts taken from each one would surely construct the perfect bride for him. There was no separating them in his mind however, and each girl deserved a suitor who desired her for herself.

He would pay a call on Miss Brianna Ellsworth on the morrow. Rob had agreed to accompany him, lest the girl grab hold of the notion that he would offer for her in certainty. He still was unsure. She seemed quite young, and far too gay for his sensibilities.

The girl's sister would surely be there. Again the stunning image she had made this evening came back to him.

"Marianne," he said to himself.

The name sounded foreign to his ears. She had always been "Miss Ellsworth" in his mind. She had felt curiously right pressed against him for that brief moment, however. Her face tilted up to his. She had so resembled Annie then that he toyed with the idea of offering for her instead of any of the candidates on his blasted list.

She had been soft there in his arms. Almost vulnerable. Her every curve had pressed close to him. Her lovely eyes had appeared so deep. Her manner had been quite different from what he had come to expect. And her intoxicating vanilla scent had filled his head.

His cock grew hard at the memory, as it had after that brief contact with her several days ago. She was indeed quite beautiful. Nearly the same in stature as his Annie. Same tiny waist, same strong, slender arms. As she had hurried to join her family he'd glimpsed her well-turned ankles. It took little imagination to visualize how shapely her legs were.

He closed his eyes to block out the image, choosing instead to turn his mind to the last time Annie had shared his bed. She had ridden him hard, taken her pleasure as he had come high and deep inside of her. Clasping his hand around his cock, he began to stroke himself.

She had been so hot. So amazing in her release. Her perfect breasts had filled his hands, her delicate hands holding strong to his wrists as she had shuddered and cried out. His fist moved faster, his thumb grazing the head and spreading the moisture there. He was close to release, thrusting against his palm, when another image inexplicably came into his mind.

It was an image of Marianne Ellsworth, her legs spread wide as he buried his face between them. Her face was free from its customary pinched expression, wearing instead one of pure ecstasy as he licked and sucked as if he could not get enough of her.

What would she look like naked? Would her flesh be as pretty as Annie's? Would she taste of vanilla as well? Both women suddenly filled his mind, one riding his aching cock while the other straddled his mouth to find her pleasure from his eager tongue. His mind went blank at the incredible notion. He came so hard he had to bite his lip to keep from crying out.

Long minutes passed as his heartbeat slowed to

The Courtesan Countess ~ JoMarie DeGioia

normal. "What the devil…?" he murmured.

In his mind they were identical, which was preposterous. Marianne Ellsworth was not his Annie.

"I am simply lust-drunk, that is all. I miss having Annie in my bed tonight." He rose and cleaned himself up before splashing his face with the cool water. "I do not want Marianne Ellsworth any more than I want any of the Prestwicks."

He would scarcely be able to face the girl tomorrow, after the sizzling scene his mind had conjured up in the wee hours. As for Annie, he could imagine her reaction should he share this with her. She had been jealous of the ladies he courted. Imagine if he told her he got hard thinking of one in particular? He smiled for a moment. Her ire had urged both of them to new heights of passion. Perhaps he just might share this particular vision with her.

He got back into bed and buried his face in the pillow. Annie's scent lingered there, the vanilla that surely must be to blame for his odd fantasy. Breathing in deeply, he welcomed the recollections when they came and fell asleep with a smile on his face.

* * *

"Lady Genevieve Stilling," George announced from the doorway.

Marianne exchanged looks of surprise with Bree and Aunt Hattie before they rose to greet their guest. "Lady Genevieve, you pay us an honor with your visit."

"It is my pleasure, I assure you." Lady Genevieve waved a hand, urging them to sit. "Oh, I thought that after last evening a call was in order."

Marianne swallowed. Had the lady's brother poured out his foolish heart to her today? "I am afraid I do not understand."

Lady Genevieve's lips curved into a smile and she turned to Bree. "Hello, Miss Brianna. How does today find you?"

"Well," Bree answered, sitting once more. "It is a lovely day."

"Indeed," Lady Genevieve said. "Mrs. Filbrick, how are you?"

"Very well, Lady Genevieve," Aunt Hattie said.

"Have you had many callers?" she asked then, directing the question toward Marianne.

Marianne blinked. What, precisely, was the woman after? "A few, yes."

"There were several ladies here earlier, Lady Genevieve," Bree said.

"A few friends of mine came to call as well," Aunt Hattie put in.

"Oh?" Lady Genevieve said. "What of gentlemen? Have any gentlemen called today?" She laughed, the sound hesitant and uncomfortable. "Forgive me. I believe I ask too much?"

"Not at all," Marianne said quickly. "Several gentlemen did call this afternoon."

Lady Genevieve studied Marianne for a long moment, her eyes holding some sort of secret. "I am not surprised. I believe many gentlemen find you…" She smiled toward Bree. "Find both of you ladies quite interesting."

"Both of my nieces have indeed received attention of late," Aunt Hattie said.

"As it should be," Lady Genevieve said. "I believe one gentleman in particular has all but declared for one of your lovely nieces."

Again, Marianne was at a loss. Aunt Hattie's eyes were bright as she obviously considered Lady Genevieve's words. Oh, if only Bree was the girl to whom Lady Genevieve referred. Their troubles would be over then. Marianne knew full well what the lady meant by her cryptic statement.

An awkward silence fell upon the parlor, blessedly interrupted when George once more came to the doorway.

"Miss?"

Marianne met his gaze. "Yes, George?"

"Viscount Devlin and the Earl of Lacey, Miss."

Marianne's heart dropped to her toes. George had brought Marcus' card to her but an hour earlier, and no doubt worried about the ramifications of the man himself coming into their home again.

Schooling her expression into one of serenity and detachment, she nodded to him. "Please show them in, George."

Lord Devlin stepped into the parlor, his face wearing its usual smile. "Miss Ellsworth, Miss Brianna, Mrs. Filbrick. How lovely you all look today."

Aunt Hattie somehow managed a nod and a smile in return while Bree gushed her delight at seeing him again. Marianne could do neither, however. She kept her face averted, though she was unable to stop from searching the doorway for Marcus' appearance. She was not disappointed when he followed behind Lord Devlin.

He looked delicious, dressed impeccably and so tall and broad. She recalled the first time she had seen him framed in such a manner, wearing nothing but his luxurious dressing gown. Her cheeks heated but she could not look away from those deep green eyes.

"Ladies," he said with a bow. He studied her for a long moment, his brow slightly furrowed. Turning, he saw their other visitor. "Lady Genevieve, this is a surprise."

Lady Genevieve's face wore an expression of disinterest Marianne doubted she herself would ever perfect. "Lord Lacey. Lord Devlin."

Unable to stop herself, Marianne watched for evidence of any affection toward Lady Genevieve on Marcus' face. None was present, and she chided herself for the relief that afforded. He continued to watch her, however, a strange combination of confusion and contemplation on his face.

Conversation began in earnest, with Bree and Lord Devlin enthusiastically leading the way. Aunt Hattie contributed but Marianne could not bring herself to say more than a word or two. Lady Genevieve appeared to suffer from the same malady, as she fell silent after a few minutes in the gentlemen's company.

Soon tired from mentally tracing the pattern of intertwined leaves dotting her day dress, Marianne stood. "If you will excuse me, I find I need a bit of fresh air. I believe I shall take a turn in the garden."

Lord Devlin and Marcus rose, the latter wearing that odd expression again as he ran his gaze over her. His lips parted and if she was not mistaken his cheeks were burnished red.

"Would you like some company?" he asked.

She began to shake her head when Lady Genevieve stood. "I shall join you, Miss Ellsworth."

There was nothing for it but to let the lady join her. Better her than Marcus. That was certain. Whatever was he thinking, offering to accompany her? Surely he was simply being polite in front of the girl he considered a potential bride. It was no secret that she and Bree were close. She bristled. As if she would ever let false attention lure her sister into a betrothal.

"That would be lovely, Lady Genevieve," she said, turning to go.

Once outside, Marianne breathed a sigh. "I appreciate your company, Lady Genevieve."

"Please call me Genevieve."

Marianne sat, warily watching Lady Genevieve sit herself beside her on the bench. "That is quite generous of you."

"It is only fitting, seeing as we may be connected in the future." The lady smiled. "The very near future, I wager."

Oh, Mister Stilling had told her about his aborted proposal of last evening. "Lady Genevieve—"

"Genevieve," she cut in.

Marianne managed a smile. "Genevieve. Forgive me, but I cannot fathom what your meaning might be."

"Percy told me about last evening, Miss Ellsworth. Of the depth of his feelings for you."

"I am sure Mister Stilling is quite mistaken."

Lady Genevieve grasped her hands. "Please, Miss Ellsworth. Percy has never been so flummoxed over a young lady. He could speak of nothing but you this morning. Of your face, your eyes. He is quite determined to make you his wife."

Then she had not been mistaken last evening. She had never been grateful for Lord Devlin's interference in the past but she secretly thanked him now.

"I assure you, I have done nothing to encourage him."

Lady Genevieve's eyes went round. "I do not blame you. Nor give any censure. I am delighted that he has at long last found a woman worthy of his heart."

Marianne shook her head. "I do not know what to say."

Lady Genevieve squeezed her hands, no doubt attempting to give reassurance. "You must accept his suit, Miss Ellsworth. Percy is everything wonderful. Kind and generous. Devilishly handsome. He would make you a perfect husband."

Who, pray, was this perfect creature the lady

described? Surely not the petulant boy she herself had observed over the past weeks.

"Genevieve, I do not believe I am the woman to make your brother happy." This was the truth, though she would never disclose the true reason she was unable to marry any gentleman now. "I am certain he will find another lady better suited to him."

Lady Genevieve shook her head, her expression a bit frantic. "No! I like you, Miss Ellsworth. Very much. You are quiet in company. Circumspect." A nervous smile broke over the lady's features. "You and I are quite alike, I daresay. I would be delighted should Percy find a wife with whom I could get along so famously."

It struck Marianne in that instant that Lady Genevieve wished to reside with her brother and his wife in the future should she never marry. Well, she was not the woman for the position and the sooner Lady Genevieve accepted that the sooner she could look for another lady for her brother.

"I am afraid I do not care for your brother as his bride should."

Lady Genevieve laughed. "How could that be?

Percy is everything a lady would want in a husband."

Marianne seriously doubted that, but she gave a small nod. "Nevertheless, please do not trouble yourself over me. I am certain that your brother will have little trouble securing the affections of another."

Her face fell as she appeared to finally take Marianne's words to heart. "But not yours?"

"I am sorry, but no."

Tears filled the lady's eyes. "It is I who is sorry. I thought that if Percy found a bride it would allow me the freedom to… Never mind."

It was Marianne's turn to pat her hand. "Do not trouble yourself, Genevieve. Your brother is a fine man, and you are a fine sister to care so much for his welfare."

Lady Genevieve offered her a watery smile and stood. "Thank you, Miss Ellsworth. I do apologize if I presumed too much."

"That is unnecessary, believe me. You are everything kind and I shall treasure our connection, brief though it was."

Lady Genevieve nodded. "I shall leave you to your solitude, then. Perhaps we shall speak at the parties tonight?"

"I look forward to it," Marianne said with genuine warmth.

Lady Genevieve stood and returned to the parlor. By the murmurs of conversation she caught, it was obvious the lady took her leave of them as well. Marianne was at last blessedly alone in the garden, but how long would her solitude last?

She needed time to unravel the tangled mess she had made, though through no fault of her own. What capricious animals were men, that polite disinterest should inflame their desires?

What if Mister Stilling approached her again this evening? Her heart went out to the man's poor sister. Lady Genevieve obviously believed that she would never marry. Well, Marianne could certainly sympathize with that. She herself could never marry.

Even if Mister Stilling was the paragon of masculine virtue his sister believed him to be, she could never marry him. Her lack of virginity, her brief life as a courtesan, were only the tiniest reasons why she would refuse any man who offered for her. Her heart was no longer hers to give away. She loved Marcus.

He was the man she longed to spend every night with, in and out of bed. To him she was merely his temporary mistress, to be set aside when he married despite his occasional words to the contrary. It was apparently her lot to love a man she could never have.

She could hardly stand being so close to Marcus there in the parlor, even when he was not looking at her in that strange fashion. Seeing his contemplative interest in Bree, however? She did not sense any tender regard there. Surely no more than politeness as he had shown to Lady Genevieve. But he was considering making her his wife. Polly Prestwick had confirmed that Bree was on his "short list" of ladies.

The thought of Bree being able to openly enjoy his company, to be escorted on his arm to events, to bear his children, cut her deeply. She had suspected that she was coming to love him, but with evidence of his upcoming marriage so close under her nose she could no longer ignore the implications. How would she keep Bree from accepting his suit when it inevitably came?

Leaning back against the bench, she let out a long

sigh.

"Ah, I knew it," a masculine voice said to her left.

She turned to find Lord Devlin standing on the terrace, a smile curving his mouth. Trepidation shivered across her skin. "Lord Devlin!"

"Marianne Ellsworth." He came closer, a conspiratorial gleam in his eyes. "You are Lacey's dove."

Chapter 19

"I knew you were familiar," Lord Devlin said. "From that first morning I saw you in the park. The sound of your sigh confirmed it for me today. You are *her*. Lacey's dove."

Her heart pounding, she shook her head. "I assure you, I do not know to what you are referring."

He winked. "Come now, Annie."

Alarm trilled through her. "Do hush!"

His brows arched. "That is telling, my dear."

She closed her eyes, grateful for the bench beneath her as she felt herself grow lightheaded. "It is all over," she whispered to herself. "I have longed for this, in truth. But not in this manner."

Lord Devlin sat beside her, running his fingers over the line of his trouser leg as he apparently allowed her some time to recover. "I cannot fathom how you kept your secret for so long." He leaned closer. "I remember that night quite clearly, my dear. Despite the amount of spirits I drank with Lacey prior to your arrival, I remember. The sounds you made as I kissed you."

Mortification pooled in her belly, churning until she

nearly vomited on him. "Please. Do not."

He shifted, resting his back against the bench. "I remember how soft your skin was." He studied her lips, then met her gaze. "And how sweet. How could I forget?"

Oh, what she had nearly done with him. No one must find out. Desperation clawed at her. She stared into his eyes, her hands clasped before her. "Please, Lord Devlin," she implored, her voice low. "You must not divulge what you know."

He cocked a brow. "I have no plans to."

Breath whooshed out of her lungs. "I do not understand."

"There must be some reason you took to such an occupation, dove." He shrugged. "Who am I to presume to know your secrets, let alone reveal them?"

She read no malice evident in his dark eyes, just a frankness she now knew to be unusual for one of his class. He was not only the pampered son of an earl. That was evident. He was indeed as shrewd as she had feared since that first morning.

"Brianna knows nothing of this, Lord Devlin," she

rushed out. "We had no money and this was the only avenue open to me to keep us safe. Once she weds, I can end this."

Concern flitted over his features. "What do you think will happen should Lacey marry your sister? How would you be in his company each day and not reveal yourself as his light-o'-love?"

Her heart shuddered. "I had not thought he would seriously consider her as a potential bride. He never showed any marked interest in her."

"No, he would not." Again his gaze took her in. "I believe his regard is secured elsewhere."

She stilled. She would not entertain the notion despite the rush of warmth she felt at the possibility. It was nonsense, what he implied. Marcus' love words in the heat of passion were of no consideration.

"He cannot offer for her," she said. "My life would be over."

He touched her hand, the gesture gentle and comforting. "That is a telling statement as well, my dear."

She stared down at his fingers on hers,

remembering how he and the other two men had touched her since John despoiled her. Shame threatened to sicken her once more. "You must keep my secret. Please, Lord Devlin."

"I have no intention of telling Lacey what I know."

She risked a glance at him, holding her breath. "Truly?"

He nodded, lifting his hand from hers and giving her a pat. "For now, that is. You have to do something for me, however."

She raised her chin as the implication struck her. "I will not pleasure you," she hissed.

He pulled back in response. "I would not expect you to." He waved a hand. "I have no need to blackmail young ladies to entice them into my bed, I assure you."

His countenance appeared clear, earnest, and she relaxed a bit.

"Then what do you wish me to do?"

"Keep yourself to Lacey. No matter what happens."

"I have no intention of laying with another man. Ever."

He smiled then, that crooked expression she had

seen often enough on his face, and the carefree gentleman was again evident. "I thought as much. You care for him."

"I love him." It felt like freedom to say it aloud, foolish as it was to admit. "God, I love him."

"Good. I will do what I can to divert his attention from your sister. His heart is not engaged there, I am certain."

"I thank you for that. This cannot go on forever, my lord. The end of the Season is nearly upon us. Bree has to wed and I have to end this. Someone else will surely learn of my secret life. My family would not survive the scandal, let alone the hardship, should that happen."

His brow furrowed as he considered her words. "Sadly, that is all true. Then I suppose it is time for you to divulge your identity to him yourself."

Fear gripped her, cold and sharp. "I cannot. The weeks of deception aside, I have been with other men. He will hate me for what I have been, once he knows I am not a true courtesan. It is inevitable."

"That risk might be worth taking." Lord Devlin stood, that same fond expression he had bestowed on her that first night on his face. "You must decide for yourself, my dear."

She just stared up at him, at this gentleman who was so much more than he presented to the world. "Marcus has a great friend in you."

He nodded. "And I in him."

* * *

Marcus once more perused those assembled at the party. This was a smaller residence than that which had housed other such parties of late, and one with far too many people in attendance. He had given brief consideration to the notion of foregoing tonight's event, but time was fleeting. He had to make a decision to court Miss Brianna Ellsworth or find another young woman to add to his list.

This afternoon had left his mind muddled, and it did not seem that this evening would prove any different. The space was too confining, and the company of both Ellsworth sisters unavoidable. Marianne sat there with her aunt, watching over her younger sister from several seats away and looking for the world like the proper young woman she was. He, however, could not stop revisiting his fantasy from last night. His body twitched. What would she sound like in her release? Would she shout his name?

He had somehow managed to keep from revealing his lascivious interest during their short discussion in the Ellsworth parlor, and acute relief had flooded him when she had taken herself out to the garden. He had offered to accompany her! What the devil had ailed him?

Thank goodness Genevieve Stilling apparently had no more desire to be in his company than Marianne Ellsworth did. That lady had quickly stepped in to cover his idiocy, effectively taking this strange new temptation out of his range of vision. It was a pity that the girl's sweet scent had remained, however.

"Pray, what has you so contemplative this evening?" a feminine voice said near his ear.

He shot Lasking's widow a passing glance. "Lady Lasking, I believe you would find yourself in better company on the other side of the room."

She laughed, the sound sharp and artificial. "Lacey, you are quite diverting. And far and away the most compelling gentleman in attendance this evening."

He said nothing, but simply waited for her to tire of her game and search out new prey.

She pouted and sighed beside him, edging closer. "Having little success with your bride search, I take it? That is a pity. I seem to remember that the Lacey men were more than adequately endowed, with money and prestige, that is, to attract the opposite sex."

His stomach lurched. He knew she had been with both his father and brother, but for her to state as much in company nearly made him cast up his accounts.

"I have no interest in your experience with the Lacey men," he stated.

She arched her brows in mock-innocence. "Forgive me. I have been indelicate." She obviously followed his line of vision and saw that the Ellsworth sisters were in his sights. "Casting your net toward the young one? I daresay you might have more in common with her cold sister."

He grunted in response.

"She is quite beautiful, however. And sometimes the way she moves…" She tilted her head toward Marianne. "It is little wonder the other gentlemen have all seemed to have turned their attentions toward her."

He watched as Stilling approached Marianne, a lovesick expression fixed on his face. The girl shook her golden head in answer to whatever nonsense the pup uttered, but when he sat beside her she seemed to acquiesce. Her posture remained rigid, however. Again, the images of her that his mind had conjured up last night returned in a rush.

"Excuse me," he said to Lady Lasking, heading for the sisters.

Keeping his attention diverted from the compelling older sister, he stopped in front of Miss Brianna and bowed.

"Good evening, Miss Brianna. How are you?"

The girl's eyes widened, then she smiled. "Well, Lord Lacey. And yourself?"

"Quite well, thank you. Are you enjoying yourself?"

"Oh, yes. It seems a bit of a crush but that is to be expected, is it not?"

He nodded. The music rose to signal the start of the next dance and he took that as his cue. "May I beg the honor of this dance?"

She laughed lightly. "But Lord Lacey, this is the supper dance. Surely you understand the implication?"

"I shall have to escort you into supper as well then." He smiled. "I believe I should enjoy that."

She took his offered hand and stood, her eyes bright. He once more acknowledged that she was a pretty girl. None of the heat that plagued him when he gazed at her sister was evident. Good. He had no desire for his wife to be a substitute for Annie. When he married he would say farewell to her and what they had shared. He would not wish for displaced passion to reside in the marriage bed. He and his bride would each do their duty and that would serve.

They joined the other dancers on the floor and went through the steps. She moved well, possessing grace and lightness. There seemed to be no physical impediment to his selection, then. Her conversation was light as well, which suited him fine. Heavier topics of discussion, such as those he'd had with Annie over the past weeks, would have no place in his marriage in any event.

Movement out of the corner of his eye drew his

notice. Miss Marianne Ellsworth took to the dance with Stilling. She appeared ill-at-ease for a moment, then a serene expression settled over her features. He watched her move through the steps, graceful and sensuous at once. Lady Lasking had said something about the way the girl moved, hadn't she? He had no choice but to admire her figure now.

The dance ended, thank the Lord, and he took Miss Brianna's hand. She smiled up at him, the expression open and artless, and he led her off the floor and into the supper room.

It was crowded here as well, though he was relieved to note that the girl's sister and aunt were seated at the other end of the room.

"How is your Season progressing, Miss Brianna?" he asked.

"Oh, it has been quite a surprise. Marianne and my aunt have assured me that it is to be expected, however."

"What is that?"

She blinked at him. "The interest, my lord."

"Ah. And how do you receive this interest?"

"It depends on the direction from which it comes, I

daresay. And how does your Season progress?"

She had heard of his search, then. Little wonder, that.

"I believe it goes on well enough."

"And will you end this Season in a different manner than that in which you began it?"

"I should hope so. Is that not your goal as well?"

She shrugged. "I suppose. Marianne wishes for me to wed and I do not want to disappoint her."

He spared a glance at Marianne only to find her watching them. Nodding in her direction, he watched her flush yet she met his gaze. Heat scorched his body as if she touched him and he cleared his throat.

"What of you?" he asked, forcing his attention back to Brianna. "Are your wishes to the contrary?"

"Not at all! Marianne says that soon one of my suitors will come up to snuff." She giggled. "I suppose I am not to speak of such in company."

"I take no offense, Miss Brianna."

The girl studied him for a long moment, then nodded. "That is a relief. I admit I will be glad when the Season is over."

"Will you stay in Town?"

Her brow knit. "I do not know. Marianne says that all will be well but I know that we cannot return to Shropshire."

"Is that so?"

"Our uncle has passed and there is nothing there for us," she concluded.

Marcus thought for a moment. Grimes had said something had happened after the uncle's death, something that urged the three women to come to Town. From the way the man had described the uncle's son, this was not surprising.

"You have my sympathy," he said.

She nodded, giving a sniff. "I have to be strong. Marianne cannot bear all of it."

Again he sought out Marianne Ellsworth. She had evidently left the supper room at some point, and he could not help but peer out the door for another glimpse of her.

"I should not speak of it," he heard Miss Brianna whisper.

Facing her once more, he gave a shake of his head.

"Do not trouble yourself. If there comes a time when I may be of service, please do not hesitate to ask."

Her eyes rounded. "Truly?"

What, exactly, was this family's trouble? "Of course."

Her relief was visible, and the smile she gave him was bright. "Thank you, Lord Lacey."

He stood, holding his arm out to her. "What say you to another dance?"

Her fingers were light on his sleeve as she allowed him to lead her out of the supper room. He managed to move through the steps, even as he kept an eye out for the girl's sister. Grimes had not indicated there was anything plaguing them save for a selfish relative, but if they had no place to go after the Season his choice was made for him. He would marry Brianna Ellsworth.

She was in as much of a hurry as he was, and she was all things pleasant and affable. Surely his lustful leanings toward Brianna's sister would abate once he ended his liaison with Annie. It was only Marianne's passing resemblance to his mistress that caused these odd thoughts. His marriage would be sound and he would satisfy his father's damnable will.

There would be no heat between him and his wife. A man could only endure so much passion before he began to crave it. Lord knew he would never attempt upon a wife the many delicious and decadent things he had done with Annie. He smiled to himself. And would again tonight.

The dance ended and he returned the girl to her seat.

"May I call upon you tomorrow, Miss Brianna?"

"Of course, Lord Lacey. I enjoy your visits."

He inclined his head. "I look forward to speaking with your aunt and sister as well."

The implication was there, all but stated aloud. Her head bobbed in agreement. No affection was evident, only mild pleasure. That was as he wished. His mother had given everything to his father, who left her with no heart at all. She had turned cold, even toward her children. No, he would never wish his wife to love him.

He would tighten the laces once more and be content.

Chapter 20

Marianne brushed her hair, now free of the many pins that had secured her coiffure for the party. The motion soothed her, allowing her to turn her mind from the events of the evening and toward her night with Marcus.

It had cut her deeply to see him dance with Brianna. To escort her into the supper room as if an agreement had already been settled. His beautiful green eyes had watched her all night, however. She had indulged herself but once, looking her fill at his fine face and form. She had not needed him in front of her, however. He was firmly ensconced in her memory and there he would remain. Soon she would have to separate from him, when he wed. He would not marry her sister, however. On that, she was unmovable.

A soft knock came. Her eyes went to the small clock on the mantle and she rose to open the door. Aunt Hattie stood there, her face flushed.

"Aunt, whatever is the matter?" she whispered. "I do not have much time."

"Do not go, Marianne," Aunt Hattie rushed out.

Marianne urged her into the chamber and shut the door quietly. "What are you saying? Lord Lacey is expecting me."

"Disappoint him, then."

Marianne blinked. "What? This is nonsense. It is already a quarter-past two. I have to meet George around back in a matter of minutes."

Her aunt grasped her hands and pulled her to the bed. "Sit, dear. I have to speak my piece."

"But I am expected at half-past two!"

"I am certain the randy earl can easily bear the deprivation."

"He has paid for the week," Marianne said. "I gave the packet of money to you. I am obligated."

Her aunt's lips thinned to a line. "You can end this, Marianne. Tonight."

Marianne withdrew her hands from Aunt Hattie's tight grip. "What are you saying?"

"Accept Mister Stilling's offer when it comes."

"I will not!" Marianne came to her feet. "Is this what you are about? Telling me to wed? Now, after all that has transpired?"

"I never should have let you take to this life."

"I gave you no choice," Marianne put in. "You seemed quite resigned to it thus far."

Tears filled her aunt's eyes. "It was all a ruse. I did not want to add to your burden."

Marianne froze. "What?"

"How could I be fine with my dearest girl giving herself to men for money? You must end this tonight."

Marianne sank back down on the bed beside her. "You know I can never wed."

"Mister Stilling is besotted with you. Do you think I have missed the looks he gives you? The devotion clear on his face?"

"He is delusional," Marianne muttered.

Aunt Hattie waved a hand. "Nevertheless, his sister is for the match."

"How do you know that? Ah, you heard her this afternoon."

Her aunt gave a shrug. "I was seated quite near the terrace doors, dear. I heard everything."

Had she overheard Lord Devlin's scandalous words as well?

"What else did you hear?"

Aunt Hattie blinked. "Nothing. Lady Genevieve took her leave upon her return to the parlor and I had to see her out." She peered closely at her. "Why, Marianne? What else happened?"

Marianne shook her head. "Nothing really. Lord Devlin knows who I am, however."

Aunt Hattie's eyes went round. "Oh! You will stay here tonight. Keep yourself from Lacey until you accept Mister Stilling's offer."

"I will not accept his offer. I cannot wed. We have discussed this."

"You can and you will! I have been passive long enough. You will marry him."

Marianne looked her square in the eye. "And what of the wedding night, Aunt? How, pray, will I explain that to him?"

"What, pray? The lack of your maidenhead?" She shook her head. "He is besotted, as I said. Make certain that he imbibes a little too much at the nuptial festivities and he shall be so happy to have you that he will scarcely notice such a trifling matter."

"Trifling matter?" Marianne snorted. "Be that as it may, what of the rest of our marriage? The truth is bound to come out. When it does, it will destroy my marriage and this family. I cannot live with that."

Aunt Hattie grabbed her close. "Please, Marianne. Marry him. I cannot bear for you to throw away this chance for happiness. You have always been like a daughter to me. From the first."

Marianne hugged her back. "And you are the only mother Bree and I can remember. You and Uncle Filbrick took such wonderful care of us."

"And now look at what I have let happen. Please, dear. Tell me you will consider my words?"

Marianne leaned back from her, cupping the woman's cheek with her hand. "I promise I shall give it some consideration."

Aunt Hattie opened her mouth, no doubt to make another entreaty, then nodded. "Very well. That will have to do. Do take care tonight?"

Marianne nodded and came to her feet. "I shall."

Her aunt grabbed her hands again, kissing each in their turn. "You are such a brave girl. I love you,

Marianne."

Marianne's throat grew thick. "And I you."

Aunt Hattie stood and quit the chamber, leaving Marianne to finish her preparations. Perhaps it was time to tell Marcus everything. She would have to choose her words very carefully, not that he would not be filled with disgust once her meaning was made clear.

"I cannot think about this now," she murmured.

He would call on Bree tomorrow. Her sister had said as much. She would have to tell him then. Tonight would be her last in Marcus' arms.

She would simply make the most of it.

* * *

Marcus arrived home and all but raced up the stairs to his chamber. He could smell Annie's intoxicating scent in the hall as he went. Little wonder, that. Parks had told him she had only just arrived. Again he wondered at her life outside of his bedchamber.

He opened the door and crossed through the empty sitting room. "Annie?"

"In here," he heard her call softy.

Immediately his body was hard with wanting. Just

the thought of the girl sent heat coursing through him. He found her seated on his bed. Her thick hair was twisted in a long tail pulled to the front, laying across one breast. She wore another of those sinful night dresses, this one nearly transparent. Her nipples were dark rose against the fabric, hard points that made his mouth water. Her shapely legs were outlined and tucked beneath her to one side, letting her pretty feet show.

"Good evening, love." He removed his jacket and began to unbutton his waistcoat. "This evening has been interminable."

She offered him a small smile, her delicate brow knit. "You went to the parties."

He shrugged out of his shirt as he nodded. "I daresay I have had my fill of them."

Annie blinked up at him. "You have made your choice, then?"

Waving a hand, he finished disrobing and joined her on the bed. She bounced a bit, causing a gay sound to escape her.

"I have no wish to discuss it." He drew her into his arms. "I have been without you for too long to think about anyone else."

Her body curved into his as he stretched out on the bed. "Hardly too long," she chuckled.

"Perhaps. It has been too long since I have kissed every inch of you, however," he clarified. He unbuttoned her night dress, trailing his lips over every bit of smooth skin he revealed as he breathed her scent deep into his lungs. "You are delicious, Annie."

She purred against him, closing her eyes as she gave herself up to him. He brought his lips to hers, tasting her as she tentatively touched her tongue to his. His body was on fire now, his cock throbbing, but he was determined to take his time. He had made his choice of bride, and no doubt would soon have to dance attendance on his betrothed going forward. Tonight, however? Tonight there was only his Annie and he was going to lick every inch of her sweet body. He was going to drive her to climax with his tongue and then plunge so deep inside her he would never want to withdraw.

He closed his lips over one nipple, sucking until she began to moan. She clutched his head, stroking his hair until her grasp became more frantic. His fingers found her flesh, slick and wet. First one then two fingers went deep, starting a rhythm that soon had her bucking on the bed beneath him. Suddenly he could not wait any longer. Releasing her succulent breast, he buried his face between her legs. His fantasy from two nights past assailed him and in his mind she was once more Marianne Ellsworth. Inexplicably, he grew harder.

What the devil…? In the next moment it did not matter as she came against his tongue, sobbing his name. "Inside me, Marcus." Her breath came in pants. "Now!"

He moved up and honored her request, letting her heat grasp his cock tight. "Yes, love," he groaned as he began to move. Bracing himself on his arms, gazing down at her he saw who she was, the woman he had craved for nearly two months now. He sucked in a deep breath and felt his own release coming on fast. When she clasped him tight in her second climax he let her ride him for one heart-stopping moment, then withdrew to spill on her smooth belly.

"Ah, that was a close thing," he groaned, shudders still wracking his body.

She made a lovely sound of satisfaction as he held

her close. "This was most fitting."

He nodded, then stilled as her words settled on him. "Fitting as what, pray?"

She lifted her head to face him, her eyes dark. "As a farewell."

"Farewell?" Irritation bit at the edges of his sexual satisfaction. "There is nearly a month left to the Season. We have an arrangement."

Her expression was inscrutable. "You have paid through the week, Marcus. The week is over tonight."

"What of the rest of the Season?" He saw her wince at his tone of voice and forced himself to settle. "I cannot bear to go without you."

"Bear it, you shall." Looking away from him, she toyed with the sheets beneath her. "You will soon be betrothed."

"That does not signify."

She came up on one elbow and faced him again. "Your bride will not wish to learn of our arrangement."

"Who shall tell her? None of those dolts at my club know the particulars. They have their own tales to keep close, I daresay. No one shall tell her."

Her brow knit again. "Do you care for her, then?"

"Not in the least."

She narrowed her gaze. "That is plain speaking."

"She is a pleasant girl. Passing pretty, though nothing to you." He kissed the tip of her nose. "She will suit, Annie. That is all that matters."

She blinked, then nodded. "Then you will offer for her."

"I believe so. She is apparently in as much of a hurry to wed as I." He held her closer. "It has no bearing on our arrangement, however. I shall double your weekly stipend and you shall keep your end of the bargain."

Obvious outrage colored her cheeks. "Do you think I speak of money tonight?"

"Not at all. I wish only to make certain that you will be cared for after the Season."

"I trust my troubles will be over by the end of the Season."

"How?"

Her eyes held a pain he had never seen there before and his heart twisted in response.

"Come, love," he said. "Promise me you will not let

this end. Not yet."

She worried her plump lower lip, then nodded. "You are not to pay me any extra, Marcus."

She was a strange creature, his Annie. "If you wish it so."

Giving a nod, she cuddled closer. He breathed in her scent again, closing his eyes and feeling that odd sense of contentment he had felt with her from the start.

A month left to the Season. Less than five weeks. Her troubles would be over once the Season ended? Rob's suggestion edged into his consciousness. Perhaps he should have Grimes investigate her. What if money once more became an issue? What would stop her from taking up this life again?

A chill washed over him. Grimes was on retainer. After they said their farewells, after he had his full Season with her, Marcus would keep apprised of her comings and goings. He would make certain that circumstances never forced her to take another lover.

She might not really be his ever again but he would be damned if she sold herself to another gentleman.

* * *

Marianne awoke in the dark, Marcus' strong body at her back. Apparently she had turned in her sleep, and now his arm held her close. Far from the sense of confinement this ought to instill, she felt undeniably safe and secure. Content as she knew she never would be again. Squeezing her eyes shut, she let the tears seep from beneath her lashes.

Marcus would not let her end this. Not tonight. She had not anticipated his reaction. That was certain. How things would change tomorrow! He would come and speak to her aunt and to her, offering to marry Bree. That must never happen. She would speak to him first, admit all that she had been about this Season. That should effectively end any chance that he would wed her sister.

She knew now that he had no affection for her sister, and when he had admitted as much she had felt a flicker of annoyance along with relief. It was fitting somehow, as she loved him herself.

Sniffling, she twined her fingers with his. It was cold comfort, really. He did not love Bree and he most certainly did not love her. After tomorrow, he might possibly hate her.

That was the most painful realization of all.

Chapter 21

Marcus stared at his reflection as his valet finished his dress. He noted that he appeared to be precisely what he was: a titled gentleman about to offer for his future bride. He could rouse no enthusiasm for the task or its implications, just an inkling of the relief he would no doubt feel once the deed was done.

Annie's strange behavior of last evening came back to him. She was adamant to end their liaison, but he would not allow it. He had nearly fallen on his knees, begging her to keep to their original agreement. The thought of losing her, without having his fill of her until the end of the season, had reared its ugly head and caused him upset even now. In the end she had relented, but how long before she voiced her unease again?

Dismissing the valet with a nod of his head, he fiddled with his cravat and pulled on the sleeves of his jacket. The hour grew late, the afternoon waning, and he had no more excuses. He went downstairs to find that Parks had called for the carriage as he had been instructed.

"The card, Parks?" he asked the butler.

Parks shook his head. "Still in place, my lord."

Marcus swallowed a curse. No Annie tonight, then. Bloody hell!

Without much enthusiasm, he went out to the carriage and rode toward his future. Settling back against the cushions, he considered Brianna Ellsworth. She was pleasant, as he had told Annie. He had been honest about his lack of affection for her as well. He sensed no regard from her, either. That was as he wished it. It would not do to have a wife who cared for him.

His heart was closed, and it would only be a matter of time before the unfortunate woman would grow as cold and withdrawn as his mother had been. He could not condemn any children they would have to the same fate as he and his brother. Perhaps if their mother had not loved his blasted father they would have been better cared for.

Thankfully, before he could give such maudlin thoughts free rein, he arrived at the Ellsworths' townhouse. He disembarked and resolutely climbed the stairs to the front door. Seeing the place with a jaundiced eye, he saw that it was far from grand. Merely suitable, giving him a notion of his potential bride's circumstances. Well, her haste suited his needs. He was fairly certain that the family would accept his offer in any event. Rapping on the door, he awaited his fate.

Their butler answered, and today Marcus noted that his livery was a bit worse for wear. He had not paid the servant much attention on his last two visits, the import of such details irrelevant then. Now that Miss Brianna may soon be under his protection, Grimes' disclosures seemed to ring true. The Ellsworth family needed money. A quick marriage to a wealthy gentleman would suit. Once more, he was sure of his actions today.

He requested an audience with Mrs. Filbrick, Brianna's aunt and guardian. While he would most likely have to speak with the girl's older sister as well, he hoped to avoid her company until his betrothal was secured. Surely his unwanted desire for her would distract him from his purpose.

The butler showed him into the parlor to await the lady. Marcus shifted on his feet. He could not deny a touch of unease. The Lord knew he had only asked for one young woman's hand before. Joan's defection had ceased to sting weeks ago, really. He timed its cessation to the very moment he had decided to accept Rob's gift of Annie's company.

Walking about the room, he spied the corner of what looked like a calling card behind a vase set on a side table. No doubt it was left by one of the pups sniffing around the sisters. He absently picked it up and was stunned to see his own crest on it. Cold dread settled in his belly. Had Brianna saved his card as a keepsake? That would indicate that she cared for him, and that he could not withstand. So much for marrying the younger Ellsworth girl. He would have to resume the hunt this evening.

Flipping the card back down on the table he turned to go. Something caught his eye then. Writing on the back of the card. He picked it up again, recognizing his own handwriting as well as what the cryptic date and time implied. It was one of his own cards, put out for Annie to arrange a rendezvous. What the devil was it doing here?

Images crashed upon him, and his knees nearly buckled under their force. He recalled Annie's laugh, her smile. The way she tilted her head. Heat coiled within him, sharp and shocking. Gripping the edge of the table, he closed his eyes as realization struck. Marianne Ellsworth, smiling in the dance. Moving with ease. Gazing with open affection at her sister and aunt. Her expression as soft and lovely as Annie's as she had pressed close to him.

"It cannot be," he rasped. But he knew without question that it was so. Marianne Ellsworth was Annie!

He fought to remain standing as his stomach roiled. As if from far away, he heard the parlor doors open. Light footfalls met his ears, along with the familiar vanilla scent.

"My lord?" he heard a feminine voice call softly.

He whirled on her, seeing her clearly for the first time. A modest day dress hugged her figure. Her hair was done in a demure style of braids and upswept curls. There was no denying the truth, however. She was Annie. She was the same woman who had been his mistress these past weeks.

She froze before him, her eyes going wide as she apparently read his recognition. *Those eyes.* He had not really looked Marianne full in the face, save for that night she had crashed into him. He certainly had never noticed that her eyes were so like his Annie's.

"Good afternoon, Annie," he said.

She flinched and turned to shut the door tight behind her. Turning to him, she dropped her hands to her sides. "Marcus…"

"Do not address me so," he bit out. He narrowed his gaze on her. "How shocked you appear. Little wonder that, now that I have discovered your game."

She violently shook her head, her cheeks pale. "It was no game, I swear to you."

He stalked over to her. "No? Tell me why, then. Why would you take up this life? Did you really think that spreading your legs for any man who paid you would buy your sister a husband?"

"That was never my intention! We needed money, and—"

"And I was foolish enough to provide it."

Her bottom lip poked out a bit and he could tell she was attempting to hold her composure. She should have no trouble there. Hadn't she shielded her true self from him for all this time?

"Damn you," he said. "Now I know why every man is now sniffing around you instead of your sister. How many have there been, Marianne? Did you also tell them they were the only one?"

"No! It was not like that. I have never been with another man once we made our agreement."

He fought the tempting satisfaction that assertion might give. "Well, at least I got my money's worth."

She held her hands in front of her, wringing them until her knuckles showed white. "Marcus, you do not understand. My family needed money to survive the Season. My sister needs to wed to secure our future. I never wanted you to be her groom."

He held himself in check, knowing that if he said all the hateful things swirling in his mind he would shock even himself. "Consider this a withdrawal of my intentions toward your sister." He turned to go. "Thank God I never made it official," he muttered.

"Marcus, wait!"

He turned back to her and looked into those precious eyes shining with tears now. "Good day, Miss

Ellsworth."

He stalked from the room, nearly tearing the parlor doors off their hinges as he left.

* * *

The front door slammed shut, effectively severing Marianne's connection to Marcus. She clutched her arms around her middle, sobs burning in her throat. He was gone. He could not think any lower of her and now he was gone. Bree would receive no offer today, though her heart was relieved it would not be from the man she herself loved.

"Sweetheart!" Her aunt rushed in as Marianne crumpled to the floor. She helped her to the settee, handing her a handkerchief. "Easy, dear. All will be well."

"How, Aunt?" She dried her eyes. "Marcus will never see me again."

"And that troubles you?" Her aunt blinked in apparent confusion. "You told me that you were eager to end this liaison."

"Only to keep from discovery," she murmured.

"Oh." Aunt Hattie was quiet for a long moment.

"You love him."

"Yes." Marianne sucked in a breath. "He hates me, however. And now he is in possession of a secret that could ruin us all."

Fresh tears assailed her and she let her aunt hold her until they passed.

At last Marianne swiped the tears from her cheeks. "I must go to him." She sniffed. "He is a reasonable man. Usually quite even-tempered. I know I can persuade him to keep our secret."

Aunt Hattie shook her head. "He was quite angry, dear. What if he hurts you?"

Marianne thought for a moment. As strong as he was, as enthusiastic in his passions, he always took care with her. "He would never do so. I know it."

"Please be careful," her aunt implored.

Marianne nodded and stood, squaring her shoulders. She retrieved her bonnet and called for George to bring the carriage around. It would not do to let the matter sit. She had never seen Marcus angry before, and he had been positively livid. He had told her time and again that he had no heart, no emotion. She had known he was mistaken then. Today there was no question about the matter.

It was too short a ride to Marcus' townhouse, in her opinion. What she would tell him, she was unsure. There was no way she would let him divulge all the salacious details of their agreement. Whatever she had to promise, she would.

Parks looked surprised when he opened the door, recognition flitting over his features. "Miss...?"

"Miss Marianne Ellsworth for his lordship," she told him.

He schooled his expression and led her into the parlor. "I shall call for the earl."

They were the most words he had ever spoken at one time to her, and she could only manage to nod her head in answer. She removed her bonnet and gloves, then placed them on the nearest table. Her heart raced as she tried to put her scrambled thoughts into some semblance of words to give Marcus.

"Miss Ellsworth. To what do I owe this pleasure? I believe I only just escaped your presence."

She faced him. "Marcus."

He arched a brow. "Marcus, is it?" He closed the door and settled into an arm chair. "That is quite familiar. Pray, how did you gain entry? Surely not through the servants' entrance."

"I care not what your staff thinks of me. Miss Marianne Ellsworth is the sister of the woman you nearly offered for. Let them puzzle over the rest."

He ran his gaze over her, his look assessing. "Now that I see you in the bright light of day, you are indeed quite beautiful. It is strange to see you dressed so properly. Why only last evening you wore one of those delicious night dresses I have come to appreciate."

Her cheeks heated. "Please allow me to speak."

His lip curled. "There is that perfect diction once more. I should have guessed long ago, but who would ever believe that the prickly Miss Ellsworth was the wanton in my bed?"

She steeled herself against his words. "Say what you will, my lord. I had my reasons. They are why I came here to see you."

"So prim and proper."

His gaze was anything but and her traitorous body

responded. "Please."

"Yet still so beautiful," he cut in. "Pray, tell me your reasons. The Lord knows you could not share them with me before."

"How could I? You know of my family's troubles."

He shrugged and then his lips thinned, strain showing around his eyes. "Somewhat. I do not recall your giving me more than the barest details, though I asked you more than once."

"I never meant to hurt you," she said.

His brows raised. "Hurt me?" he scoffed. "Straight-laced Lacey? Haven't you heard? I am cold, Miss Ellsworth. I have no heart."

She had known the truth to be quite the opposite for weeks now but could say nothing to make him believe her. Not today.

"Get out," he bit out. "Unless you are here to service me."

She stilled, certain she must have heard him incorrectly. "What?"

"Come now," he sneered. "You must have sucked half the cocks in Mayfair."

She blanched. "No, I…"

"Even dressed as you are, you still have the ability to make me hard." He stroked himself through his breeches and she could see the bulge there. "Mmm, just the thought of your remarkable mouth on my cock… Get down on your knees and pleasure me."

She squeezed her eyes shut. The humiliation of everything she had done before with those other men crashed upon her.

"I am so ashamed."

She heard him come closer and braced herself. John had been so rough with her, twisting words of passion into cruel taunts until she begged to him to stop. He had not been angry, yet he had taken her brutally again and again. Marcus was livid. Would he hurt her now?

Though she held herself rigid Marcus drew her to him, holding her close as he murmured love words against her hair. "I am sorry, Marianne. I should not have said that. I would never force you."

She slumped against him in relief as the truth struck her. "You are nothing like him, praise God," she whispered.

Chapter 22

Marcus froze. "What did you say?"

She shook her head, burying her face against his chest. "I cannot speak of it."

Anger fled as the import of her words penetrated. "Come, love." He eased back down into the chair, holding her close to him. "Tell me."

She lifted her head and faced him. "You asked me some time ago what set me on this path, Marcus. It was my uncle's son."

Grimes' words came back to him, the lascivious glint in John Filbrick's eyes as he spoke of Marianne. Tamping down his disgust, he made himself attend her.

"He forced you," he said.

Nodding, she took a breath. "It was after our uncle's passing. We were left with nothing, even my aunt. John agreed to provide for us but he had one condition."

"Your virtue."

She gave a shiver, obviously recalling all that the foul man had done to her. "What was I to do afterward? My course was painfully clear."

He thought back to their conversation of the number of men who had her before him. "And the others? You assured me that they were gentle with you."

She nodded. "They were. There were only two others."

He gave a silent prayer of thanks for that. "Forgive me for what I said, Marianne." He took a breath. "How comfortable that name feels on my tongue."

That earned him a pretty little smile. "I have imagined hearing you say my name."

His own fantasies came back in a rush. "I have wanted you, you know."

A touch of fire lit her eyes. "Of course I know."

He shook his head. "No, love. I have wanted you as Marianne Ellsworth."

She quirked a brow at him. "You never paid me any notice in company, Marcus."

"Lately I have seen you in a different light." When she scoffed again he held a hand over his heart. "It is the truth."

Her cheeks blushed pink. "That is passing strange."

He shrugged. "I am glad to realize that the two

women of my fantasies are one and the same."

She smiled again, and then her brow puckered. "What shall we do now?"

With her a tempting bundle in his arms, her sweet scent and soft skin so close to him, he felt his passions stir. "I have a few notions."

"I have to think of my family, Marcus."

Alarm bit into him. "Our arrangement can continue."

"No. I could not bear it should the truth be known. It is only a matter of time before another learns of my double life. That would ruin you as well as my family."

He considered her words. His father and brother had done more than enough in their blighted lives to smear the family name with muck. He had worked hard to revive the Lacey reputation as well as its fortune, and had vowed to do his damnedest keep it unsullied.

"Blast, but you have the right of it," he said. "Will you let me pay you what would have been due you, then?"

"That would be taking money for nothing." She shook her head. "I will not do that."

"My brave girl." He kissed her smooth cheek. "You do not have to bear this yourself, Marianne. Not any longer."

She stared at him, affection clear in her eyes. "You need to marry, Marcus. Though not my sister, pray."

He smiled and shook his head. "No. Not your sister."

"Good," she sighed. "I need to find another man to marry her. That pressing need has not dissipated. I, however, will not continue on this path."

"That eases my mind." He held her closer. "But you will allow me to give you the funds to keep you safe."

He thought she would argue again, but she finally gave a weary nod. How had she withstood so much? Lifting her chin, he kissed her perfect mouth. He pulled back and ran his gaze over her features. She was still the most beautiful girl he had ever beheld.

"I know this cannot go on." He kissed her neck, her throat. "Let us have a proper farewell?"

"Marcus, no."

She fairly shook with apparent restraint, which

belied her words. He knew her body as well as his own. She wanted him.

"Let me love you as Marianne. Just once."

She hesitated for a mere second before throwing her arms around his neck. Grateful for his circumspect staff and the ever-faithful Parks, Marcus began to make love to his Marianne there in the parlor.

He withdrew her modest fichu from her lovely bosom, kissing every rosy inch he revealed. She made purring sounds, arousing him further as he lifted her demure day dress to reveal stocking-clad legs. He lifted his head and laughed softly. "Ah, the stockings. I should have known then."

She answered with a giggle which grew to a moan as he stroked her through her drawers. They were but a small impediment before he rid her of them. Finding her wet and ready for him, he unbuttoned his breeches and lowered her onto his cock. She let out a cry as he drew her down fully, her body contracting around him. Slow and deep, he stroked her. Closing his eyes, he sought to memorize every touch, every sound, every scent. He sucked in a great breath as he neared completion. The encounter would be seared on his brain. Heat and vanilla and Marianne.

He held her close as she found her release, coming deep inside of her moments later. He dimly realized he had not withdrawn. No surprise there. He doubted he would have been able to separate from her if someone had held a pistol to his head. "Marianne."

She sighed against his chest, her body completely limp in his arms. "Thank you, Marcus." She shifted to kiss his cheek, pulling back to gaze at him. "For taking care of me all these weeks. And for keeping my secret."

He swallowed thickly as realization struck. The knell of finality rang in her voice. "You have my word."

As he fastened his breeches he watched her rearrange herself. Gloves and bonnet, fichu tucked in place, she was the proper young lady once more. He took a sweet kiss from her lips and let her go.

If his heart ached afterward, that would be his cross to bear. And bear it he would, alone. She had enough to trouble her.

He would not add to her burden.

* * *

Marianne buried her face in her pillow, unable to rouse from the bed. Aunt Hattie had questioned her upon her return from Marcus' but all she had been able to tell her is that he would keep her secret and give her the funds needed to complete the Season. It was all that mattered, really. That she had been with him again, that she had so easily succumbed to the passion she had only ever known with him, was irrelevant. The family would be safe and that was all that mattered. At least until Bree married.

The door to her chamber opened and footfalls moved across the carpet. She recognized the light gait, the swish of skirts. Keeping herself still, she waited for her sister to think her asleep.

"Marianne, are you truly not coming tonight?"

Marianne held her breath. Bree made a sound of exasperation.

"Marianne, do answer me. I know you are not asleep."

Marianne shifted and peeped open one eye to regard Bree. She quickly saw that the girl was turned out quite well, her hair and dress suited to the evening of parties tonight. "You look lovely, Bree."

Bree waved a hand at her. "I care not, if you do not attend with us."

Marianne shifted onto her back, taking precious moments to smooth the counterpane until Bree made another sound of impatience. "I cannot."

"Yes, a headache." Bree flounced on the bed. "So our aunt has informed me. Will you tell me the true reason?"

Marianne flinched. The true reason? Bree must never find that out. "I have no desire to attend, Bree." That was a truth, for certain. Seeing Marcus again would surely cleave her heart in two. "A quiet evening is what I need."

Bree stood, placing a hand on her hip. "Then at least tell me why, after I was told Lord Lacey had called for our aunt, I arrived in the parlor to find him gone?"

Marianne stiffened. Had Bree heard her conversation with Aunt Hattie? Had she witnessed her breaking down into tears?

"I do not know what drove Lord Lacey away."

"Is that why Aunt Hattie was so upset? She would

not tell me a thing after I came to see you and found you missing as well."

"I had a call to make this afternoon," Marianne admitted. "I am sorry if I worried you. And I am sorry about Lord Lacey."

"Oh, I do not care. I know the match would have been sound but I do not believe he is the gentleman for me."

Marianne said a silent prayer of thanks for that.

"Go to the parties, Bree. You and Aunt Hattie can report back to me on any progress with the other gentlemen."

Bree narrowed her eyes, then nodded. "You will tell me all of it, Marianne. On the morrow, after your headache has abated?"

"Yes." How she hated lying to her dear sister. "Now go, and enjoy yourself. I expect a full accounting tomorrow as well."

Bree kissed her cheek and stilled, staring down at her. "You take too much on yourself. If you do indeed have a headache, it is of little wonder."

With that, Bree quit the chamber. Marianne turned

once more and let out a long sigh. Perhaps she was a coward, hiding here this evening. Marcus would be at the parties, however. Dear Marcus, who had proven to be the best man she had ever known. She should not accept his money but her stubborn pride alone would not keep them in food and clothes for this last month. They could not appear the needy women they truly were, and his money would assure their ruse could continue.

Their liaison would no doubt fade in his memory, as he would choose a bride soon and refocus his attention on his estate. She, however, would carry the memory of their last time together. How sweetly he had said her name, her given name, as he found his pleasure deep inside of her. How gently he had held her after.

"Oh, Marcus..." she sobbed.

Sometime later she turned toward the windows. She must have dozed, for the sky was light now. Her eyes felt gritty and her throat was raw. No doubt she had cried all night.

"Pitiful," she grumbled.

Once again she heard the door to her chamber open. The aroma of chocolate reached her and her stomach growled. "Ah, Suzie. That smells heavenly."

"I agree," Bree answered.

Marianne's eyes popped open and she found her sister instead of their maid. Bree held a pot of chocolate and a cup in her hands. "Good morning, sister."

Bree set the pot and cup down on a side table and faced her again. "Are you going to tell me what this is all about?"

There was nothing else for it. Coming to a sitting position, Marianne sighed. "Pour me some of that chocolate and I shall tell you whatever you wish to know."

Bree's brows arched but she did as Marianne asked.

Once she held the steaming cup of sweetness in her hands, Marianne breathed in deeply. "Thank you." She took a long sip, then patted the bed beside her. "Sit, Bree."

Her sister complied, a look of worry fixed on her face. "What has been going on since we've come to Town?"

Marianne could not tell her about the men. No doubt an innocent girl would be scandalized to learn all that she had done. It was time, however, that Bree at least knew the truth of their circumstances.

"John would give us nothing," Marianne began. "After our uncle passed."

Bree blinked. "How, then, did we come to London?"

Marianne took another sip of her chocolate, taking the time to choose her words carefully. "He had a proposition for me." She faced Bree fully. "He offered me the money we needed in exchange for something he had always wanted."

Bree glowered, her lips pursed. "You."

"You knew?"

"I knew he desired you. He was not very adept at hiding his interest, save for when Millicent was about."

"Bree, I had no other choice."

"He took you?" At Marianne's nod Bree shook her head. "And that is why you feel you can no longer marry."

It was as fine an excuse as Marianne would give right now, and all Bree needed to know. "Yes."

"And so the need for me to wed," Bree stated.

"Yes," Marianne said again. "I am sorry to force you to choose, but—"

"Do not make apologies, Marianne!" Bree stood and paced about the chamber. "After all you gave up for us? Oh, it enrages me to learn that John did this to you."

"It cannot be undone, Bree," Marianne said. "I have come to terms with my lot."

"But you can marry!" Bree's eyes were bright as she knelt on the bed. "What of Mister Stilling? He has all but offered for you!"

Marianne shook her head. "I am no longer pure. No respectable gentleman will have me."

Bree crossed her arms. "Well, that is unfair. Spending these past weeks in Society I have heard much of these so-called 'respectable' gentlemen and their exploits. Why, it is rumored that even cold Lord Lacey has kept a mistress all Season long!"

Marianne somehow managed to maintain her expression. "It is different for gentlemen, Bree. As you well know."

"Oh, I realize that." She pouted for a moment, then stood once more. "Finish your chocolate. Once you are dressed, join me in the parlor and we will review my prospects. If I have to wed, we should settle on a gentleman directly."

Marianne gazed up at her. "I love you."

Bree hugged her, and then crossed to the door. "And I you."

When she was once more alone, Marianne considered her sister's words. While her own nuptials would never transpire, she would do well to refocus attention on getting Bree wed and soon.

After finishing her chocolate, she rose and began her morning ablutions. Gone was the time for girlish fantasies. Her heart may wish for a future with Marcus but her head knew better.

She rang for Suzie and set about her day with renewed determination.

Chapter 23

"You knew?" Marcus glared at Rob from across his desk. "For how long?"

"Just over a fortnight, I wager."

"Two weeks." Nearly as long as Marcus had been without her now. "Right before my own revelation." He drew in a breath. "Why the devil didn't you tell me?"

Rob shrugged. "It wasn't my place. The girl made you happy and that was all that mattered, wasn't it?"

He winced at Rob's simple statement. Marianne had made him more than happy. "Our liaison is over."

"Why?" Rob straightened in his seat. "You may count on my discretion, Lacey. I would never divulge her identity."

"I cannot risk it."

"Because of the potential scandal?" Rob snorted. "Surely your brother and father brought enough of that down on your family before they went toes up. Your name would no doubt survive this."

"I am not worried for myself."

He left the rest unsaid, but Rob nodded. "You care for her."

I love her. "That does not signify."

Rob stared at him for a long moment. "Then who shall you consider now, as you can no longer offer for Marianne's sister?"

He thought for a moment. A fortnight had passed since he had seriously considered any another woman for his countess. "The Prestwick sisters are far too boisterous. Lady Genevieve, I suppose."

"She is quite suitable, if staid."

"I have had passion, Rob. More than I had ever expected. I shall count myself fortunate to be content in my marriage."

"What if Stinky convinces your dove to marry him? Could you bear to be her brother?"

His stomach churned at the prospect of the Stilling pup having Marianne in his bed, but that would secure her future at least.

"I would never say or do anything that could harm her. If she chooses to wed, so be it."

Rob regarded him closely, his eyes narrowed. He suspected Rob had other thoughts on the matter, yet thankfully the man kept his silence.

"The parties tonight, then?"

He inwardly cursed. "Last night was a trial to be sure. Marianne looked so bloody beautiful. And her aunt stared daggers at me whenever her nieces' attentions were focused elsewhere."

"The aunt was aware of this?" Rob's eyes grew wide. "I cannot fathom how she allowed such to continue."

"Marianne is very strong-willed. And devoted to her family. I daresay no one could dissuade her from her course."

"Apparently." Rob stood. "Come to the club, Lacey. Play some cards. I promise it will prove diverting."

He grunted in ascent and Rob left him. Over the long weeks past, he had considered making Marianne his countess. She would never agree and he could never withstand the scandal should the truth come to the surface. She would be vulnerable to every kind of hateful cut and comment, and his own reputation's tenuous hold on propriety would be of little help to prevent that. No, it was better to go their separate ways now.

He had told Rob that she was strong-willed. She was that, and loving and determined. He had little doubt that she would see her sister married soon and her family safely settled. She herself would never marry, of that he was also certain. No matter how many lovesick swains attempted to charm her.

Setting aside his work for the day, he rose and stretched. Perhaps Rob had the right of it. He called for his carriage. Perhaps an hour or two at the club would help clear his mind.

When he arrived he found the usual assortment of gentlemen. Older men with nothing to occupy their days now that their sons had all but taken over their titles. Young men with nothing else to engage them in the civilized hours of the day. And idle men of his own age who had no responsibilities, happy to let their sires shoulder the work of their estates.

Lords Bottom and Erlington fit squarely into this last category. They were lounging about, their cheeks already ruddy. Marcus cursed inwardly when he saw them take note of his entrance.

"Straight-laced!" Bottom called, waving from his

seat. "Do join us."

Erlington waved him over as well, yawning loudly. "Do, Lacey. It has been a fortnight since you've graced us with your presence. We are most interested in your latest exploits."

He swallowed a curse as he crossed to them. "My exploits? What the devil are you prattling on about, Erlington?"

"You offered for the Ellsworth chit!" Bottom cried.

"I am afraid your sources are incorrect," Marcus said. "I have not, nor do I plan to."

Erlington and Bottom exchanged a glance, then Erlington chuckled. "Ah, turned your sights on the other one, eh? You would not be the only one. She is a hot piece, to be sure."

"The way she moves," Bottom put in. "The heated expression in those large blue eyes. That remarkable mouth."

Marcus held his anger in check, but barely. "Miss Marianne Ellsworth does not deserve to have her virtues bandied about here. How could you speak of her so?"

Erlington shrugged. "Whyever not? Oh, it's of no

consequence, really. Stilling seems quite sure she'll reserve her considerable virtues for him alone."

Marcus took in a breath. "Has Stilling offered for her, then?"

Bottom shook his head. "Apparently the chit has been a bit cagey."

"Smart girl, I say," Erlington added. "Keep the man on a string until he's fairly begging for her hand."

"And everything else!" Bottom guffawed.

Marcus shook his head. "If I were Stilling, I would not want this story bandied about."

"If you were me," Stilling said from behind him, "you would feel very confident of your suit being accepted. I daresay you would do well to keep your eyes open at tonight's parties, Lacey."

Marcus turned to him, fighting the sudden urge to wipe the smug expression off the pup's face. "I believe you attempted an offer, Stilling. Weeks ago. The lady was less than receptive. Surely matters have not altered in that respect."

Stilling flinched, then gave him a tight smile. "Oh, I shall have her as my wife. She is everything a man could

325

ever want."

Marcus stilled. She was everything *he* could ever want. He held his tongue, glancing around the club. He could not argue with Stilling here and now, let alone bash his pretty face in. Not with Erlington and Bottom, and every other gentlemen in their vicinity no doubt, watching him.

He bowed his head to Stilling, his teeth clenched. "As you say."

Stilling's chest puffed as he nodded. His face took on a sly expression. "My sister enjoyed your attentions, Lacey. What are you intentions there?"

Marcus knew full well what Stilling was attempting. He wanted Marianne, plain and simple. Diverting attention from her and putting Marcus on the defensive was the surest way to keep him away from the prize. Well, he'd had the prize and he had let it slip through his fingers. Anger and frustration boiled inside of him.

"This is not the place to discuss such matters," Marcus growled. "Have you lost your senses?"

"Straight-laced!" Bottom crowed. "Good to see

you've warm blood in your veins after all."

"Maybe he'll plant Stilling a facer," Erlington added with a laugh. "Do it, Lacey!"

Stilling seemed to have enough sense after all, for he held up his hands in defense. "I was merely making conversation, Lacey. I know that should you decide to make an offer—"

"Stilling," Marcus said in warning.

The younger man blinked hard and fast. "Well, that is neither here nor there," he rushed out. "I, um, thought to make my own interests known."

"We are all aware of your interests, Stilling," Bottom laughed. "Your breeches were awfully tight last evening."

Erlington's laughter joined Bottom's as Stilling colored.

"Really," Stilling sniffed. "I have the most noble intentions toward Miss Marianne Ellsworth."

Her name sent a fresh stab of hurt through Marcus.

"Enough," he said. "Go have a drink or play a hand of cards, Stilling. Your mouth has once more gotten away from you."

With a pout fixed on his face, Stilling took himself away from them. Marcus took a breath and turned to find Bottom's gaze fixed on him, and it was sharper than he'd seen in a long while.

"You seem changed, Lacey. On edge." His eyes went round. "Do not tell us you've set your little dove free?"

"Not the one Devlin purchased for him?" Erlington clicked his tongue. "Pity, that. I suppose you've decided you should focus on your bride search. Noble, if unnecessary, in my opinion. Keep a dash of sweetness on the side to palate a sour marriage, I say."

"I care little for the reason," Bottom said. "Now that the girl is free tell me where I can engage her services, is all."

The mere thought of Bottom's clumsy hands clutching Marianne's perfect flesh caused his fists to clench once more. "I will do no such thing."

Bottom glanced somewhere over Marcus' shoulder, his brows raised. "Then perhaps Devlin will tell us."

"What are you prattling on about, Bottom?" Rob asked. "Good afternoon, Lacey."

Marcus felt a flood of relief as Rob stepped beside him. "Good afternoon."

"Tell us, Devlin," Erlington said. "Wherever did you find the dove you gave to Lacey?"

Rob began to shake his head when Bottom waved a hand. "No matter, Erlington. I believe I can find out."

Marcus' senses sharpened. "What?"

"It seems a certain gentleman who sampled your dove several months ago has at long last returned to Town," Bottom announced.

"Ah," Erlington said, his eyes wide.

"Yes, and it appears he is eager to find her again," Bottom went on. "Apparently his wife succumbed to the illness that called him to the country and he is now back among civilization."

Marcus' stomach churned as the import of Bottom's slurred words penetrated. A handful of men, Marianne had told him. Two before Rob purchased her services for the night. He had convinced himself that breaking ties with her would keep her safe, and now he had to worry about another who might reveal her secret?

He had to somehow find out the identity of this

man and make certain he never discovered that Annie the courtesan was Marianne Ellsworth.

"Rob, I need to speak with you," he said.

Rob nodded and followed him to a less populated corner of the club. He sat, urging Marcus to do the same.

"What is it, Lacey?"

Marcus sat, rubbing his sweating palms on his thighs. "Do you know the man they spoke of?"

"The one who had…? No. I am afraid not."

"This is most unfortunate." He thought for a moment. "What if he sees her? What if he guesses her real identity?"

"Consider how long it took you to do so." Rob smiled. "My God, Lacey. You were with the girl nearly every night yet you did not place her as Mar—" Rob glanced about, leaning toward him. "As she."

"I know." He sucked in a breath. "It cannot happen, Rob. I did not separate from her simply to see her life destroyed."

"Why did you, then?"

He met Rob's probing gaze. "What?"

"Why did you let her go?"

"I thought I knew the reason." He shook his head. "I believed it sound. Now, the devil take it, I am not so certain."

* * *

Marianne watched Bree dance with first Lord Wilbrey then Lord Shaston. Mr. Meryton rounded out the trio of smitten suitors, and for the first time in a fortnight she felt as if this Season might actually end as she wished. That was what she wanted. Bree married to a kind, wealthy gentleman who would care for her family as well. Yes, that was what she wanted.

She shifted on her chair and attempted to calm her body. Two weeks ago she had separated from Marcus for good and since then even breathing was difficult. Maintaining her composure at the parties proved hellacious.

Apparently any hope she had of making it through this particular night in peace fled as she watched him from across the room. She tried to look away, she truly did, but that proved as impossible as trying to sleep these past nights without dreaming about him.

He was so handsome tonight. So tall and strong.

Gazing at him, she could easily picture him without his fine evening attire. His broad chest, his strong legs. His capable hands and sinful tongue. Her cheeks heated and she slowly let out a painful breath. She had thought her heart would be the only casualty? Her pulse thrummed low and deep. She never would have imagined her body would miss him as well.

"Miss Ellsworth, you are exquisite this evening."

She shook herself and stared up at Mister Stilling. *Not this again.* "Good evening, Mister Stilling."

Stilling sat beside her, as close as was proper but no more. That was something, then. Over the past weeks he had made a veritable nuisance of himself but he had refrained from renewing his marital intentions. It seemed her reprieve was over this evening, however. He wore the expression of a lovesick swain as he stared at her.

"I have thought of only you these long nights, Miss Ellsworth." He flashed her what he assumed was his winning smile. "Marianne."

"Please do not call me so in company," she whispered.

He shrugged, looking every bit the carefree young

buck he was. "I pray that I may call you such forever, Miss Ellsworth. And soon."

Alarm trilled through her. Surely he would not renew his intentions here? Now? Oh, no. She jumped to her feet. "Mister Stilling, if you would—"

"A dance!" He took up her hand. "What a lovely notion."

She started to object but saw that they had begun to draw attention. Bree's suitors paid her little mind, save for a lingering perusal from Lord Shaston. She mentally scratched him off the list, then. No one considering marrying Bree should cast such lustful looks in her sister's direction.

"I would enjoy a dance," she told Stilling.

Again he beamed at her, and she allowed him to lead her onto the dance floor.

Chapter 24

As they stepped into the dance, Marianne saw more eyes watching them. Her shoulders slumped a bit. Gone were her days of being inconspicuous at the functions. Over the past weeks since leaving Marcus she had somehow managed to blend once more into the scenery, save for Mister Stilling's attentions. Tonight would apparently prove different in that respect as well.

The ballroom was large, as was this particular townhouse. Attendees numbered as many as at the other parties she had recently attended, but the space was far more accommodating. This was most unfortunate this evening, as she noted more people watching her with unobstructed views. Praying they were only curious as to Mister Stilling's intentions, she followed him through the dance.

His grip was tight, and lingering. His eyes were fairly wild on her face. Keeping her own downcast, she concentrated on the steps and attempted to put the spectators out of her mind. That last was excruciatingly impossible.

Lady Lasking numbered among them, her narrowed

gaze focused on her. What was she looking for? Her face had a sly cast to it, a calculation that could not bode well. She knew the woman had designs on Marcus, despite her vocalized distaste for him as a man. She wanted access to his money, was all.

In the next instant she saw Marcus take note of her and Mister Stilling. His green eyes grew dark, his face set in a scowl.

Frustration was clear on his beloved features, fueling her own. She wanted to dance with Marcus. To feel his tender, possessive touch as he led her through the motions. Once again her body flushed with desire. Gasping for air, she attempting to quell her desires.

"Miss Ellsworth, you are quite beautiful in the dance," Mister Stilling said softly. "I daresay I could watch you all evening."

She managed a shaky smile at his ridiculous comment. Spinning about, she watched in increments as Lady Lasking made her way to Marcus' side. As if drawn, she could not refrain from staring at that spot. Craning her neck as she went through the steps, she tried to decipher the conversation. Marcus' face changed to stone, a look she knew to mean that he was angry beyond the pale. She had seen that horrid expression just two weeks ago, when he had discovered her pretense. A revelation struck and she missed a step. This was the reason people thought him cold!

He held such tight rein on his emotions in company that the Fashionable would never guess the warmth beating in his heart. Once again, sorrow threatened to swamp her. She had seen his emotions, listened to his cares and worries. She had seen his passion, his playfulness. Oh, how she missed him.

"Miss Ellsworth?"

Mister Stilling's voice came as if from far away. Blinking back her tears, she came to a stop. "Forgive me, Mister Stilling. I believe the turning is too much for me."

It was piddling as excuses went, but it proved effective with her determined suitor. His eyes went round and he drew her to the edge of the dance floor.

"Forgive me, but I was carried away by the way you—" He stopped himself, his cheeks red. "I shall take you back to your seat."

"No, no," she rushed out. "I am certain a glass of

refreshment will restore me."

He sketched her a bow. "I shall return in a thrice."

Dragging in a breath, she turned to escape. A man blocked her progress and she skidded to a stop. "Do forgive me," she murmured as she glanced up at him. Cold tendrils choked her breath as the floor seemed to tilt beneath her. It was him, the first man to pay for her favors after John. Lord Faraday.

She had run into the other man a few times throughout the Season and he had not paid her any mind. She had not seen this man in company since their night together, however. To her knowledge, he had been absent these many months. It appeared that was not the only matter separating him from the other one. No. He stared down at her, recognition clear in his blue eyes.

"My God. Annie?" he asked.

Memories of that long-ago night slammed through her brain. He had been gentle when she had been terrified he would take her as John had. He had stroked her and taken his pleasure without hurting her. Afterward he had told her about his wife's illness and his heartbreak, and she had listened. He had paid her and she had never looked back. That was an enormous error on her part. She should have had George keep track of her past liaisons.

"I…" she stammered. "Pardon, me."

She attempted to skirt around him but he grasped her hand.

"It is you, isn't it?" He blinked rapidly. "But that cannot be."

She straightened, desperately trying to affect the air of chill politeness she had practiced this long Season. "I am afraid I do not know to whom you are referring."

A crooked smile teased his lips. "You even sound like her." He stepped closer and inhaled, letting his eyes drift closed. "Ah, vanilla."

She cursed inwardly. Whyever had she continued to wear her favorite scent?

"We have not been introduced," she said, knowing full well that as an earl he had every right to speak to someone of her lower station.

He opened his eyes and pulled back, giving a shake of his head as he dropped her hand. "Forgive me. Lord Faraday. And you are?"

"Marianne Ellsworth," she provided.

Disappointment flitted over his features. "I… It is a pleasure to make your acquaintance, Miss Ellsworth."

She bobbed a curtsey. "And I yours. If you will excuse me?"

He studied her face and once more she was transported to that night in his bed. Bought and paid for. Her cheeks hot with shame, she hurried from him. She found her aunt and all but dragged her into the retiring room.

"Marianne, what is it?"

"He is here, Aunt," she rasped. "The first gentleman."

Aunt Hattie gasped and she peered out the doorway. "Where? Oh, that brown-haired gentleman?"

"Yes. Is he still watching for me?"

"He is staring in this direction, yes." She cupped Marianne's cheek. "But he cannot see you, dear. Did he speak to you?"

"He knows." She turned and sat, clenching her hands in her skirts. "He knows who I am."

Aunt Hattie looked about the empty room and sat

close to her. "He cannot know. That was one night and it was so long ago."

She gave a shaky nod. "He seemed to believe me when I told him my name." She pulled in a breath. "Perhaps that will be the end of it."

"Be at ease, dear." Aunt Hattie covered her trembling hands with hers. "You are not that girl. Not any longer. Let him digest the evidence before him and he will arrive at the same conclusion."

"But what if he does not?" Marianne cried.

"There, now. Why borrow trouble?" Her aunt stood. "I shall get you something stronger than that punch they are serving."

"Thank you," Marianne managed to say.

"Oh!" she heard Aunt Hattie exclaim. "Forgive me, Lady Lasking. I did not see you there."

Marianne's stomach flipped. Lady Lasking? How long had she been standing outside the doorway? Had she overheard them speaking? Swiping her hands over cheeks, she attempted to right herself. The next moment Lady Lasking swept in, a false look of concern fixed on her face.

"Are you quite all right, Miss Ellsworth?" She preened in front of her. "Poor Mister Stilling has been walking about, holding a glass of punch and wearing a dazed expression. I assume he is looking for you?"

"I suppose."

"He is not the only gentleman gazing your way this evening." Her tone was acid now. "Lacey continues to watch your every move. And now Lord Faraday?"

"I have only just met Lord Faraday," Marianne said.

Lady Lasking waved a hand. "One would never guess that was true, dear girl. Not when taken with the way he was looking at you."

Marianne held herself very still. She would not give credence to the woman's words, not in speech or action.

"I cannot guess your meaning, Lady Lasking." She slowly came to her feet. "Enjoy your evening."

Keeping her steps even, she left the retiring room in search for her aunt.

* * *

Marcus watched as Marianne emerged from the retiring room. Her face was flushed, her eyes darting about the ballroom. What the devil…? Elise Lasking slid into view then, an expression of triumph on her rouged lips. What had she said to Marianne? He began to take a step toward her when Rob grabbed his arm.

"Lacey," he said in warning, his voice low.

"What?" Marcus snapped.

"Your attention has been marked," came Rob's reply. "And not only by myself."

He tilted his head toward a cluster of gentleman near the orchestra. Bottom and Erlington stood there, with a gentleman he did not recognize. The three of them were staring at him, puzzlement on their faces. Their attention then turned to Marianne and the unknown gentleman gave a nod. Lustful speculation came into their eyes as they gazed at her.

"I will kill them," Marcus growled.

"That should effectively end the rumors," Rob quipped.

His heart skittered. "Rumors?"

"That gentleman, Lacey. Bottom mentioned him today at the club, remember?"

Nausea roiled within him. "Tell me he did not have

her."

"I am afraid so," Rob said. "And he seems most taken with your Miss Ellsworth at the moment."

Marcus could read the man's interest from his vantage point. *Bastard.* "Who is he?"

"Faraday," Rob provided in answer.

As Marcus considered the gentleman, he appeared to be moving toward Marianne. She must have noticed as well, for she stiffened. Her eyes were frantic as she stood rooted to the floor. Casting aside Rob's hand, Marcus crossed to her.

"Miss Ellsworth," he said with a bow. "May we take a turn about the room?"

She gazed up at him, relief and alarm both visible on her exquisite features. "Lord Lacey, I do not believe that is wise."

"The terrace," he mouthed.

Her eyes darted about again, but she nodded and took his arm. Steering clear of Faraday and the others, he slowly made their way toward the open terrace doors. As he had hoped, the space was large and nearly unoccupied. Most of the partygoers had finished their supper and, while the men played cards or drank port, the ladies chatted in corners of the expansive ballroom.

He led Marianne to a secluded spot near a thickly-grown rose trellis. He stopped and turned her to him. She kept her gaze on her shoes so he touched her chin, lifting her face to his.

"Tell me what is wrong," he said.

She began to shake her head, then began to tremble. "There is a man here, Marcus. He was one of the two… Oh, I cannot say the words aloud."

He fought to keep his frustration in check. "He had you."

Tears glistened on her lashes as she gazed up at him. "He was the first, after John. I had not seen him in Town until now, and I… I fear he recognized me, Marcus."

"No. He cannot know you were that girl."

She gave a shaky nod. "That is what my aunt said."

"So your aunt knew what you were about."

"Of course," she said simply.

"And she allowed this?"

She dashed her fingers over her wet cheeks. "She

was in no position to deny me. My mind was set and we had no other recourse."

His anger eased and he nodded. "I realize that, love."

Her head shot up, her eyes full of pain. "Do not call me that, pray."

"Whyever not?"

"We are no longer together in that manner."

"The endearment is not solely for use in the bedchamber, Marianne."

She shrugged. "That is the only place I have ever heard it."

Jealousy stabbed at him. "Faraday called you such."

"Yes. The other did as well."

The other. There it was again, the proof of what she had done. Of what she'd had to do.

Gathering her in his arms, he gently stroked her back. "I hate to see you upset." That surprised him, for he had never given much care to others' feelings. Another trait inherited from his mother, no doubt. "Tell me you will be all right."

"I have to be, don't I?" she choked.

Leaning back, he gazed into her face. "Ah, love."

He brought his mouth to hers, tasting her tears and her sweetness as his tongue delved inside. She returned the kiss, moaning softly in her throat. In an instant desire pounded through him as she fit her curves to his body.

"How I have missed you," he said softly. He kissed her ear, her throat. Her scent filled him, hot and sweet. "Tell me you have missed me, Marianne. Even a little."

"Yes." She leaned her head back as he kissed the swell of her breasts. "Yes I have missed you, Marcus."

Her words ended on a gasp as he kissed the delicate skin between her breasts. Arching against him, she breathed his name again. Suddenly, she froze.

Lifting his head with a groan, he blinked. "Marianne, what is it?"

"There is someone out here," she whispered.

He listened, but he could hear little save for the pounding of his blood in his ears. "Who?"

She stepped out of his embrace and adjusted her dress, her movements frantic. "I do not know, but I heard footfalls."

346

He ran his fingers through his hair, straightening the tangle she had made as she had clutched his head to her breast. "Return to the ballroom, love. I shall stay behind."

She nodded, her face a picture of unease. "This cannot happen again, Marcus."

He stilled. He wanted to argue with her. He wanted to declare before all in attendance that she was his alone. He could do none of those things, however. It was best for her if he simply let her go.

"You have the right of it," he said.

A brief, lingering touch of her fingers to his cheek and she was gone. He bit back a curse. Why did everything he attempted prove so bloody difficult? Restoring his family's fortune and reputation. Satisfying his father's will. Now that he had found the one woman who made him believe in the future for the first time in his life, he could never marry her. Not if he wanted to keep her safe.

He could not return to the ballroom at present, and maintaining the illusion that he had not been out here with Marianne was only one reason. His cock was still as hard as stone, and his senses were filled with her scent. His mouth with her taste. How would he survive a lifetime without her?

"Good evening, Lacey," a feminine voice cooed.

He whipped his head around to find Elise Lasking strolling out from behind a tall hedge.

"Lady Lasking," he said.

Chapter 25

Marcus watched as Lady Lasking slid toward him, malice clear in her eyes. She threw a glance toward the direction Marianne had taken, then smiled. "Are you all alone out here?"

He spread his arms. "So you see."

Tilting her head to one side, she cast a look up at the sky. "It is truly a shame to waste such a glorious night. Look at that moon."

He waited for her to make her point. Her gaze returned to him, settling on his groin. At last his shaft began to soften.

She chuckled. "I see the moon is not all that is full this evening."

Her words further cooled his ardor. "If you will excuse me." He turned to go when she grabbed his arm in a tight grip.

"I would not be so hasty if I were you," she said.

He wrenched his arm from her grasp. "State your meaning."

She pouted. "Pooh. I thought you would want to dance around a bit first." She trailed her fingers over his sleeve. "Surely you grasp my meaning, Lacey. *Convince* me to tell you what I know?"

He swallowed, loath to hear what she had to say yet knowing full well he must. "What, pray, do you know?"

She paused a beat. "The lovely Miss Ellsworth is not quite what she pretends to be, is she?"

"What do you know?" he asked again.

"Nothing precisely." Her nails dug into his arm now. "But I shall find out. There is more to that girl than meets the eye. There must be a reason all the men are sniffing around her skirts."

She did not know the truth of it then, thank the Lord. But by the determination stamped on her features she would do anything to find out.

"Leave her alone," he growled.

Easing her grip, she stroked him once more. "Perhaps Lord Faraday will enlighten me."

He kept his expression even as the name struck a nerve deep within him. "Faraday?"

"Yes. Did you know the gentleman recently returned to Town? He appears to be quite taken with her as well." Stepping away from him, she preened. "No doubt he shall be more receptive to my charms than you are. His wife has recently passed away, I am sad to report."

Disgusted, he left her and returned to the ballroom. He found that no one took undue notice of his arrival, and his pulse slowed at last. His gaze was immediately drawn to Marianne, who once again sat safely with her aunt as she apparently tried her best to appear unaffected. He knew her so well now. Her hands were tight in her lap, her brow slightly puckered. He longed to go to her, to ease her distress, but knew he could not. Not with Lady Lasking's and who could guess what others' attentions on him.

Wrenching his gaze from her, he looked for Rob. He found him near the refreshments, appearing relaxed. Marcus had come to know his friend quite well also, and read the sharpness in Rob's gaze as he searched the room. When he spied Marcus he straightened, a look of impatience on his face.

"What is it?" Marcus asked without preamble.

"Faraday has been inquiring about Marianne and her life before coming to Town," Rob said in a hushed tone. "Elise Lasking has been fueling the flames as well."

"Bitch," Marcus bit out. "She just accosted me in the garden."

"From what I was able to ascertain, no one has linked Marianne to your dove. How long that continues, however, is anyone's guess."

"No one can find out, Rob."

"What can be done?"

He wracked his brain in an attempt to figure out that particular puzzle. He spied Stilling making his way toward Marianne, that same lovesick expression on his face. Would she be safe if she accepted Stilling's offer when next he made one? His family's reputation was unsullied.

"What a bloody mess," he muttered.

"Fix it."

He glared at Rob. "I am trying to, damn it all."

Two nearby matrons overheard his expletive and clicked their tongues at him. Their faces wore their surprise at his heated outburst. Would that he could be his usual icy self at the moment.

"I have to get out of here."

"You cannot leave," Rob said. "Elise hinted that you have chosen a bride. All eyes are on you as well as on your Marianne."

He glanced about and cursed. "You have the right of it."

"Give them something else to talk about," Rob said.

He looked back at him. "What, pray?"

"Dance with Stilling's sister."

He turned to find Genevieve Stilling seated by herself, her gaze riveted to her brother and Marianne. Hope brightened her features, taking her from plain to pretty. He doubted Stilling realized what a champion he had in her. Every care and concern for her brother's well-being was stamped on her face.

He crossed to her and bowed. "Lady Genevieve, you look lovely this evening."

She gave a light chuckle. "Thank you, Lord Lacey."

He held out his arm. "Would you like to take a turn about the room?"

"I…" She glanced over to where her brother sat, a look of deep contemplation on her face. Finally, she nodded. "Yes, Lord Lacey." She stood and placed her hand on his arm. "I believe that would be most refreshing."

Forcing his own attention from Marianne and Stilling, he smiled at Genevieve and began to slowly circumnavigate the room. All eyes were now on him, thankfully. He smiled down at something Genevieve said, something about the lovely trip she had taken to the park yesterday with her brother.

"Percy is ever so solicitous toward me, Lord Lacey." She sighed as she gazed at her beloved brother. "I should like to think I could return the favor someday."

"I am sure you are a wonderful sister to him."

"I do try so. Percy has been a bit put out of late."

He nearly snorted. Of late? "Oh? How so?"

"It seems that the object of his desire has been less than receptive."

He bit back his comment on that particular point. "Who would that be?"

Genevieve laughed now, staring up at him. "Do not dissemble with me, Lord Lacey. You know full well that my brother wishes to wed Miss Marianne Ellsworth."

"Is that so?"

"It is." Genevieve furrowed her brow. "He wants her and I find her most agreeable. I would very much like to have her as a sister, I daresay."

He gazed at Stilling and Marianne. She received his attentions with obvious politeness, but he knew her heart would not be touched by him. That was reserved for Marcus alone.

"I see how you stare at her," Genevieve said softly. "You want her for yourself."

He felt his cheeks heat. "That is not precisely true, Lady Genevieve."

"It is of no consequence. Percy shall have her."

"You seem so certain."

"You need to wed."

He blinked. "I do not see how one has to do with the other."

"I shall marry you."

He gave her a tight smile. "I do not recall asking for your hand."

"That, Lord Lacey, is truly of no consequence."

He nearly stumbled but caught himself. Smiling to

the partygoers they passed, he bent his head toward Genevieve. "Explain yourself."

"Marianne is the one for my brother." She sent a glance in Stilling's direction, fondness stamped on her features. "He can be quite tenacious when he desires something. He was quite a handful when he was small."

"I do not doubt that."

"You will convince her to marry Percy."

The hell he would! "How?" he managed to ask.

"I care not about the particulars. I will accept your suit and cease my parents' hand-wringing over my unfortunate spinster status. And you will fulfill the stipulations of your father's will."

At his raised brow she waved her free hand. "Stilling's friends never seem to notice when I am around, Lord Lacey. They speak quite freely, and you have been one of the topics of conversation more than once."

She had the right of it. He needed to marry and he needed to keep Marianne safe. It was futile to deny the benefits of her offer.

"I will do as you say," he bit out.

"You will speak to my parents and make it official?"

He nodded. "I have one condition, however."

"I am a reasonable woman. Of course I shall occasionally allow conjugal relations."

He shook his head. "That is not what I meant." He stopped near a relatively-quiet spot, gazing down at her. "I need you to make a promise to me."

She looked up at him, her expression open. "Ask me."

"You must make certain that, should your brother offer for her, he will stay by her side no matter what may arise."

Her brow puckered. "That sounds cryptic."

"Promise me, Genevieve. Your brother must keep himself to Marianne no matter what transpires."

She considered for a moment, then gave a sharp nod. "I promise." A smile curved her lips. "Percy likes to flatter himself about being a man with his own convictions, but he has always been unable to deny me anything."

He realized in that moment that dear Percy was not

the pampered younger brother he had supposed.
Genevieve just might wield the power in that particular
relationship after all. "You are a remarkable woman,
Genevieve."

"Then we have a bargain?"

"Yes."

She smiled up at him. "Capital! I shall speak to my
parents and send a card advising when you may call.
Pray see to keeping up your end of things. And soon."

Once more he was seized with the notion that
Genevieve was not the quiet spinster she presented to the
world. Determined and intelligent, she was a force to be
reckoned with. He hoped she would be able to
manipulate her brother as easily as she had this situation.

Taking her back to her seat, he bowed over her
hand. "I shall look forward to our next meeting."

"Thank you, Lord Lacey."

With that, he left her. Without another glance
toward Marianne and Stilling, he returned to Rob.

"What have you done, Lacey?" Rob asked him.

Marcus bowed his head. "I am all but betrothed,
Rob. Do congratulate me."

Rob cocked his head to the side. "You do not seem especially happy."

"I am not." He dragged in a searing breath. "No matter. I will marry Genevieve Stilling and her brother will marry Marianne."

Rob's mouth dropped open. "Lacey, what are you saying?"

"I bid you good evening. I am finished with this gathering."

"Where are you going?"

He closed his eyes for a moment, silently praying for strength. It took all of his fortitude to keep from crossing over to where Stilling fawned over Marianne and dragging her bodily from the room.

He faced his friend once more. "I am going home, Rob. Where I plan to get stinking drunk."

* * *

Marianne watched Marcus stalk from the ballroom, his face stony. Lady Lasking stepped into his path but he did not even pause.

"I daresay Lacey is not having a very good evening," Mister Stilling said.

"I had not noticed," she lied, her eyes following Marcus' exit.

"Hmm. My sister appears to be waving me over."

She looked over at Lady Genevieve. She was indeed fluttering her hands, the overt gesture seemingly out of character. "You should go to her."

Stilling waved impatiently in his sister's direction. "She will no doubt chatter incessantly on our ride home later."

She bit back a comment. How could a man speak so of his sister?

"Marianne?" her own sister said to her right.

She faced Bree. "Yes?"

"Will you accompany me to the retiring room?"

Shooting her sister a grateful look, she stood. "If you will excuse me, Mister Stilling?"

A pout crossed his face, but he nodded and stood. "Of course, Miss Ellsworth."

Marianne curtseyed and turned, coming to stop as he took her hand in his. "Mister Stilling," she said softly in admonition.

He gave her hand a squeeze then released it. "I

shall call upon you soon."

His tone brooked no disagreement, and there was little she could say in company to dissuade him. She felt the eyes of the curious on her, and had since returning to the ballroom from the garden. Bowing her head in submission, she hurried with Bree to the refuge of the retiring room.

"I cannot express how grateful I am, Bree," she breathed.

Bree crossed her arms, her chin lifted. "You will wish to kiss my slippers after I tell you what I have overheard."

Marianne clicked her tongue. "You know you should not— Oh, never mind that. Tell me."

"Lady Lasking has been talking about you, Marianne. She speculated that you were not alone in the garden."

"I knew I heard someone out there." She pressed her hand to her stomach, eager to quell the unease suddenly clenching inside.

"You were out there, then." Bree's mouth was agape. "With whom?"

She shook her head. "It does not matter. It will not happen again."

Bree scoffed. "You were not out there with Mister Stilling, pray?"

"No!"

Several ladies standing nearby turned in response to her outburst. "Bree, we cannot discuss this here."

"He is going to ask for your hand, you know," Bree said, her voice low. "It is unavoidable."

Her shoulders slumped. "I know. He shows his intentions in his manners and looks."

Bree took her hands. "Our aunt thinks you should accept."

"You spoke to Aunt Hattie about this?"

"She is so worried, Marianne. She will not tell me the whole of it but it seems that your marrying him could solve our problems as handily as would my marrying some other gentleman."

"Oh, would that it was that simple."

Bree took her arm. "Come, sister. Let us go home and plan what you will wear when your smitten swain comes to call."

Marianne smiled in spite of herself. "That is not funny in the least."

"Oh, I think it is."

She said no more, letting Bree steer her through the watchful crowd as they found their aunt and left the party.

Chapter 26

"What will you tell him?" Aunt Hattie asked. "He will want to speak to me, Marianne. What do you want *me* to tell him?"

"I cannot marry him, Aunt." Marianne paced about the parlor. "I do not know how many times I must tell you that!"

"Whyever not?" her aunt pressed. "He is more than acceptable."

"She has her reasons," Bree put in.

Aunt Hattie gasped. "What do you know of her reasons, Brianna?"

Marianne gave a tiny shake of her head. "I told Bree about what John did, Aunt."

"Oh!" Aunt Hattie's expression eased. "Oh. I still say a smitten husband will accept you."

Marianne let out a cry of frustration. "I cannot talk about this another moment! He shall come here and make some grand, romantic gesture and I shall have to refuse him."

Bree and Aunt Hattie fell blessedly silent, feigning interest in their book and needlework respectively.

Marianne took the solace they offered, mentally ticking off the time she had before Mister Stilling arrived. Within the hour, his note had read. She glanced at the clock on the mantle. Thirty-two minutes. A woefully small amount of time to devise an escape for all of them that did not include marrying a man who would grow to despise her.

All night she had gone over matters in her mind, still uneasy about how to face the coming challenges. People were talking about her. Lord Faraday had stared holes in her dress while Mister Stilling had waxed poetic about her eyes or some such. Lady Lasking, that harpy, had taunted and teased and indicated that she knew things about her. There was no denying that all and sundry would soon know that she had been in the garden with Marcus. She sucked in a breath and slowly let it out. Marcus.

It had been like heaven, kissing him again. His touch, his taste, had inflamed her senses. Wanton that she had become, she would have allowed him any liberty he desired in the moonlit paradise of his embrace.

Her cheeks flushed hot and she shot a glance at

Bree and Aunt Hattie. They still watched her surreptitiously, their bodies visibly tense, their heads turning ever so slightly to follow her as she made her way across the room. Another moment and she would burst into flames, her thoughts were so heated!

"Miss?" George said from the doorway.

"Oh!" she cried. Recovering herself, she managed a smile. "What is it, George?"

"Is Mister Stilling here, George?" Bree asked.

"Is he?" Marianne asked.

"No, Miss." He held out a folded missive. "This arrived for you, is all."

She nodded and took the note. "Thank you, George."

Turning it in her hands, she saw Marcus' crest. "George, where did you get this?"

"A servant brought it, Miss. To the house."

She studied the butler's gaze, reading his assurance. He had instructed his boys to no longer retrieve the notes and calling cards from the planter beside the servants' entrance of Marcus' house. Two weeks ago, to be precise.

"Thank you," she said again.

"What is it, Marianne?" Aunt Hattie asked.

Shaking her head in answer, she stepped out of the parlor into the relative privacy of the entryway. She opened the missive and read the contents. Marcus succinctly requested that she come to his townhouse directly, stating that he had information of import that could not wait. Another of his blasted calling cards was nested within, but this one had no date or time written on it. No, the message on the card simply read, "I must see you."

Bringing the card to her cheek, she breathed in his scent. Again her heart shuddered.

"What is it?" Aunt Hattie said, coming to the parlor doorway. Her gaze fell on the card and she scowled. "That is from Lord Lacey, no doubt. Marianne, he has not requested that you come to him?"

"Not in the manner you suspect." She tucked the card into the foolscap and refolded it. "He writes that he needs to see me to discuss an important matter."

"Now?"

She nodded. "He stated no particular time, just an

urgency I cannot ignore."

"But, Mister Stilling is sure to come."

"Marianne?" Bree said, coming to stand in beside their aunt. "What is it?"

"I have to pay a call," she rushed out.

"On whom?" Bree asked. "Aunt Hattie, what is going on?"

"Nothing to worry about, dear," Aunt Hattie said.

"Oh, pooh! The two of you have been saying as much for weeks now."

Marianne went to Bree, taking her hand in hers. "This is a matter for me alone, sister. I know that you want to help but I have to take care of this myself. Will you attend to Mister Stilling when he arrives?"

"Yes, but—"

"I promise that I shall tell you all of it, Bree." She exchanged a look with their aunt. "Someday."

"Someday soon," Bree insisted.

Marianne only nodded. "George, will you ready the carriage?"

"Yes, Miss." The faithful servant hurried to see to her request.

Suzie brought Marianne's bonnet and gloves, and soon she was on her way to Marcus' townhouse. Her mind fairly ached as she tried to ascertain the purpose of this conversation. After last evening—the talk, the stares, the kiss!—what could Marcus be thinking?

She arrived at his home, too quickly for her sanity but not quickly enough for her heart. Her palms were sweating and her pulse raced as she alighted. Parks met her at the door with a look of expectation, as if he had been watching for her arrival. That could not bode well for the coming exchange.

"His lordship is awaiting you in his study, miss."

She handed him her bonnet and gloves and nodded. "Thank you, Parks."

The butler's eyes held knowledge, but concern as well. Once more her heart tripped. Whatever was going on?

He turned and she followed him down a hallway she had never before traversed. Parks rapped sharply on a door and she heard a muttered command from within. Opening the door, the butler stepped back to allow her entrance. She stepped into the room, barely taking in the dark furnishings and large desk dominating the room. Her attention was immediately riveted to Marcus.

He stood behind the desk, his back to the door as he stared at something or other out the window. He wore no jacket and his shirt appeared rumpled. She longed to run to him, to touch his shoulders and ease his rigidity.

She cleared her throat to gain his attention, absently taking note of the click of the closed door behind her as Parks took his leave. "Marcus."

He visibly flinched and slowly turned to face her. His appearance was startling. His hair was mussed and he wore fatigue on his beloved features, sporting ashen cheeks and dark circles beneath his eyes.

She hurried over to him. "Marcus, what is wrong?"

He laughed harshly and raked his fingers through his hair. "Wrong?" He took a breath. "Oh, everything is right. Or it soon will be."

He made no move toward her, so she tamped down her own compulsions and sat in the chair before his desk. "What is this about, Marcus?" She saw three bottles of spirits on the desk, all but one of them empty. "You have been drinking?"

"My God, yes."

"But I have never seen you… That is, I cannot recall ever seeing you in such a state."

"Too true. I have never been one to imbibe more than a glass or two, Marianne. After so many years of seeing what my father's drinking did to my mother, getting deep in my own cups never held much appeal."

Something twisted inside of her. "Whatever could have caused you to indulge so?"

"I could not sleep," he said simply. His eyes ran over her face, want and need clear in his gaze. "You are quite lovely, as always."

She said nothing to that. "You called me to discuss a matter of some importance. Pray, get on with it."

Settling in the chair behind his desk, he folded his hands. "I believe I have a solution to our troubles."

"You heard the rumors, then?"

He nodded. "And they are not going to cease unless we take some action."

"I will not bring disgrace upon you. You have no worries there."

"I know that." His lips thinned, then he nodded. "I

had thought nothing would come of it. That we could end our liaison and you and your family would be safe."

Her heart beat thudded beneath her ribs. "What has happened, Marcus?"

He paused a moment. "Lord Faraday has returned to Town."

She blinked, processing the import of a statement she already knew to be true. "He saw me last evening. He appeared to believe me when I told him my name, however."

Marcus nodded. "Yes, he did. Unfortunately he is now quite smitten with you."

"He does not know me."

Sadness clouded his green eyes. "He does though, doesn't he? It is only a matter of time before he discovers that you really are that girl he dallied with at the beginning of the Season. He is determined to know everything about you."

"About me?"

"About Marianne Ellsworth, to be more precise. He has been asking all and sundry who you are, when you came to Town, and so on."

"He cannot know." She wrung her hands. "Not really."

"He will find out." His face grew flush. "He will realize that you and Annie are the same, and do you know why that is?" He slammed his hands down on the desk. "Because you are!"

She flinched at his outburst.

He cursed softly. "Forgive me, love. I have been at sixes and sevens, trying to find a way out of this predicament." He leaned back in his chair. "Devlin was here earlier. Faraday has been at our club, speaking of naught but you until other rumors began to fly."

She knew with certainty of what he spoke. "The garden?"

He nodded. "Lady Lasking has been stirring her own pot of poison over you."

"I do not understand. Whyever would she wish to harm me?"

"Jealousy, pure and simple. Tell me, did she take any particular notice of you or your family before men began to show interest in you?"

"I do not believe so."

"I thought not. Now, apparently, Elise sees you as a rival. Gentlemen speak of you in glowing terms." He paused to run his gaze over her once again. "With good reason, I will allow. And now with Faraday's immediate attraction, she has focused her venom in your direction."

"Are she and Lord Faraday connected somehow?"

Marcus shook his head. "No. She is in the market for a new lover and wants one who is wealthy and biddable. Apparently she has been on the hunt all Season, and a wealthy widower would no doubt suit her needs."

The truth struck her. "She approached you."

"Yes." His lip curled in obvious distaste. "I dismissed her offer in no uncertain terms. Did you know that she bedded both my father and my brother?"

She had suspected as much from Lady Lasking's comments one evening in the retiring room, but to hear Marcus state it so baldly she felt her stomach heave. "That is abhorrent."

He nodded. "Money, Marianne. That is what she wants. She sees you as a rival for the attention of eligible gentlemen, and is acting true to form. She has been known to skewer young girls in their first Season if they attract what she deems as too many suitors."

"I care not about Lady Lasking. Let her do her worst."

"Her worst?" His laugh was harsh. "Brave girl. But what if she should turn her vitriol on your sister?"

She gasped. "That cannot happen."

"It can and it will, if we do not do something to divert her attention from you and your family."

"What?" She leaned toward him. "Please, Marcus. Tell me what shall be done!"

"Easy, love. I have arrived at a solution to all of our troubles."

"A solution?"

He tilted his head, indicating the bottles at his elbow. "Though I daresay by the time I reached the bottom of that first bottle it occurred to me that the solution just may be worse than the predicament."

He fell silent and she nearly screamed in frustration. "Do tell me, Marcus. What is this solution?"

He stared at her, his shoulders slumped. "You will marry Percy Stilling."

"I will marry Mister Stilling?" She gripped the

chair to keep herself upright. "Are you mad?"

"It is what is best, Marianne. His lineage is impeccable, his family's reputation above reproach. Marrying him will secure your future safety. And your family's."

"But I cannot marry him. I cannot marry any man, and you should realize the reason why."

"Your virtue, yes."

"Which is nonexistent, Marcus. I surrendered that months ago."

Marcus shrugged. "So the pup will be disappointed on his wedding night. He shall rise above it, I daresay."

She stood to face him. "He would leave me, Marcus. Circumstances would then be far worse than if the truth came to light now."

"No!" He took a breath. "That cannot happen. He will keep himself to you no matter what."

"How can you be so certain? You never seemed to have much use for the man, yet now you speak so highly of his loyalty and conviction?"

"Sit, love."

She managed to do so, reading the resignation in

his eyes. "There is more to this, is there not?"

He nodded. "I know that he will keep himself to you, Marianne. I have his sister's word on it."

"His sister's word? What has Lady Genevieve to do with this?" She gasped. "Oh! Tell me she does not know of my troubles?"

"No. I have her assurance on the matter, however. She will make certain that Stilling remains by your side no matter what may arise."

"However did you achieve such a thing?"

Again, that sad expression crossed his face. "I agreed to marry her."

Chapter 27

Marcus watched Marianne's reaction as the statement settled on her. Her eyes grew shiny and she shook her head.

"You are marrying Lady Genevieve?"

He nodded. "It will solve several problems, actually." His words sounded so cold to his ears but he pressed on. "She desperately wants off the shelf and her brother wants you for a wife. I need to marry to satisfy my father's will and she wants to see her brother happy."

"Happy?" She gave a delicate huff. "I daresay that is far from the outcome we can expect."

"Stilling is a lucky bastard, Marianne. He shall have you as a bride. How can he not be happy?"

She glared at him. "Would you be, Marcus? Tell me the truth. Would you be happy to discover that your wife sold her favors to gentlemen?"

He rose. "Marianne, do not upset yourself."

"That she let herself be bought for the length of the Season?"

"Do not say that, love."

"I am not good enough for him." She wrapped her

arms around her waist, curling into herself. "For any man, in truth."

He came around the desk and drew her out of the chair. "You are everything good, Marianne. What you did… You believed you had no choice."

"I did have a choice. We… we could have moved to another part of Shropshire. Taken in sewing, perhaps. Or I could have taught some nobleman's children." She squeezed her eyes shut. "I did not have to become a whore."

Her words cut him. "Do not call yourself a whore. I have never thought of you that way."

"Didn't you? Those were your very words the day you discovered my deception." She sniffed and lifted her head a notch. "And what of that first night, Marcus? You came into that chamber as your good friend's head was buried between my breasts!"

That image came back in a rush. He had thought the jealousy he had felt that night was now gone but her words easily called it back. "Stop this."

"Did you not think of me as a whore as you lifted my night dress and took your pleasure with me?"

That encounter was seared on his memory as well. She had been so beautiful, like no other woman he had ever seen. He had been unable to resist taking her, nor had he been able to for the rest of the Season. "No."

She turned from him and he wrapped his arms around her. He could feel her every breath, could feel her trembling.

"I did not think of you that way," he said. "I saw you and I wanted you. It was that simple."

"And you had to have me for the whole of the Season," she finished, her voice quavering. "I am grateful to you for you attentions, Lord Lacey. Believe me, I am. It saved me the trouble of finding any number of other gentlemen to keep us in food and clothing."

He held her tightly until she stopped shaking. "I wish that I could be the one to marry you, love. I wish that I could make all of this go away and have you forever."

Her breath hitched but she said nothing.

"My family's reputation is abysmal," he went on. "My standing in Society is tenuous at best. Marriage to me will not save you, should the truth come to light."

"Oh, Marcus," she sighed, leaning back against him.

"And come to light, it shall." The bitter words burned as they left his throat. "There is no denying that fact."

She hung her head. "I know."

Bending his head to hers, he breathed in deeply. "I shall never forget you." He brushed his lips over her smooth skin. "I will always treasure our time together."

"That sounds so final," she whispered. "How strange, then, that we should find ourselves brother and sister by marriage? That is, if your idea comes to fruition."

The pain of it stabbed at him. "It will." He turned her to him, seeing the wet tracks of her tears on her cheeks. "You are the strongest woman I know, Marianne. I have no doubt that you will do what is best for your family. Would that you took as much care with yourself."

She waved a hand. "I will be fine. Haven't you heard, my lord? My lover has found me a wealthy, respectable husband."

Her terse acceptance of the situation was harder to

bear than her earlier refusal. Stilling would have the right to touch her. To kiss her and taste her. He would be the one to ride her again and again until she grew round with his child. That was the worst of it. Stilling would have her forever.

"I cannot bear the thought of him putting his hands on you," he rasped.

She stepped out of his grasp, turning to face him. "What did you say?"

"I still want you for myself."

Her eyes went round. "And you insist that you do not think of me as a whore?" She pounded her fists against his chest. "You arrange my marriage and then still expect me to come to you whenever you wish it?"

"God, no! I would never do that to you."

"And what of Lady Genevieve? I daresay she would have serious objections to her husband maintaining a liaison with her brother's wife!"

He caught her hands in his. "I was thinking aloud. That is all. I know you would never betray your husband."

"Husband." She let out a high-pitched laugh, her

eyes huge. "Husband! Here we came to Town to see my sister wed and it appears that I shall take home the prize."

"Marianne."

She held herself rigid, her expression the chilled one he had seen on her face so many times before in company. The one he now knew to be completely false.

"Good day, Lord Lacey," she said. "I thank you for your solicitations on my behalf and look forward to our next meeting." She turned to go. "As brother and sister only." With that, she opened his study door and left him.

He sat behind his desk once more, digging the heels of his hands into his stinging eyes. The dampness there stunned him. He had not cried in years. Not since he was a very young boy. Not when his mother died, and surely not when his father and brother followed.

How he wished he was the cold man everyone presumed. Then he could blithely marry Genevieve and simply look on as Marianne wed Stilling. He could put aside the love and desire he had never felt before and begin a life of dull contentment with his suitable bride.

He eyed the bottles on his desk, grabbing up the one still one-third full. Draining the bottle, he let the liquor burn his belly as if it could eradicate his tender feelings for Marianne. After a long moment, he knew it could not. Lifting the bottle, he threw it against the far wall. Strange, but the resounding crash soothed him.

He collapsed on the desk and closed his eyes.

* * *

"Tell him I am not receiving," Marianne shouted at the closed door of her chamber.

There was a pause, then blessed silence. Apparently Aunt Hattie would leave her in peace for the moment, and rid the house of Mister Stilling as well. She could not face the man, her nerves still so raw from her meeting with Marcus. How dare he be so high-handed! He thought he knew what was best for her? Ha!

"But then you have always had to be the one in control, haven't you?" she muttered. "First with our arrangement, with those blasted cards of yours. Then with your insistence that I wed the man of your choosing."

She fell upon the bed, punching and flailing the counterpane and pillows in a fine snit. At last she quieted, laying her aching head on the coverlet. She had not thrown a tantrum in eons, it seemed. Not since she was a girl. Oh, it felt good! It would not solve anything, however. She would have to follow through with the bargain Marcus had struck with Lady Genevieve.

She turned, flopping onto her back on the bed. "Marcus does not love her," she said. "And I have seen no marked interest from Lady Genevieve toward him. Mister Stilling, however…" She let out a sigh.

That gentleman harbored misplaced affection for herself. Time and again he had professed his love. He was the only one in their strange quartet who stood to get his heart crushed.

She sat up, rubbing her eyes. "Well, I do not have to accept his offer. Not today, in any event."

Rising, she crossed to the small vanity table and opened the drawer. There, nestled inside, were the cards Marcus had sent her over the past three months. Lifting one from the drawer, she traced her finger over the handwriting as she had so many times before. She had kept them all, knowing the folly of it should Bree happen upon them. How to explain the presence of such obvious attention from a man she purportedly barely knew?

As if summoning Bree with her thoughts, she heard her chamber door open and braced herself.

"Are you, at long last, going to tell me what is going on?"

She smiled at her sister's impatient tone. "Ah, Bree." She faced her. "I daresay you will be shocked in the least. Disgusted, more likely."

Bree closed the door and hurried over to her. "Do not say such things! Aunt Hattie told me a bit of it, Marianne. I cannot believe you did such a thing for us!"

Oh, Bree knew. She knew. "Did what? Gave myself to men for money?" She shrugged, turning to hide her flaming cheeks. "I will not lie and say it was easy, Bree. But it was not as bad as I had feared before embarking on this course."

Bree clicked her tongue, taking her hand as she led her back to the bed. "Sit, Marianne. Tell me what happened when we came to Town."

Marianne shook her head at the futility of what she had thought a perfect plan. Facing her sister, she began to tell the tale.

"We were very circumspect, our aunt and myself.

George made the arrangements and made certain that none of the gentlemen possessed any perversions or strange proclivities. He has quite a network of informants throughout the city. He proved quite invaluable." She laughed, the sound harsh to her ears. "I shall have to retain him for service when I wed Mister Stilling."

"Mister Stilling? You are to marry Mister Stilling? But you sent him away not ten minutes ago!"

"I know. Sadly, I am merely postponing the inevitable. You see, a bargain has been struck."

"A bargain." Bree stared at her incomprehensively.

"I am to marry Mister Stilling and his sister shall marry Lord Lacey," she explained.

Bree blinked. "I do not understand. This is all arranged? By whom?"

"Lord Lacey."

"What has he to do with our troubles?"

She had to tell Bree the whole of it. There was nothing else for it. "Lord Lacey and I have been involved for the past three months."

Her sister's mouth fell open. "How? I do not understand. How could you be involved with him? I have never seen you share more than a word at a time with him this whole Season."

"It was supposed to be one night but he offered to keep me until the end of the Season." She felt herself shift as she confessed this, and she was compelled to finally unburden herself. She would have to tread carefully, for Brianna was an innocent. "The arrangement was preferable to what had come before."

"You mean the other men?"

"Um, what...? What, precisely, did Aunt Hattie tell you?"

"Simply that you spent evenings with a few gentlemen when we came to Town. That they paid you well and you did not come to harm."

"Two men to be exact, Bree. Two evenings. Two different men." She let that statement settle for a moment, and when Bree did not swoon she deemed it safe to continue. "But our aunt is correct. I was not harmed. They were gentle with me and never pressed me to see them again."

"But Lord Lacey, Marianne? How could he put you in such a compromising position and then treat you as if he did not know you in the least when in company?"

"He did not."

"What?"

"He did not know that I was the same girl."

Understanding lit Bree's eyes. "That is why you were so altered at the parties! So austere and quiet. It was little wonder that he did not recognize you. I daresay I had trouble equating that dull stick with my lively sister."

Marianne allowed a small laugh. "Matters changed, however. Two weeks ago, more or less."

"The day he called to offer for me. Well, now I understand at least a bit of that." Bree leaned closer. "But Lord Lacey, Marianne? He is so cold. So distant. I cannot imagine him embarking on an… affair."

"He is not cold. He is warm and passionate. Tender and very caring. He is not the man he presents to the world. And now that the truth may come out, I fear that more than my reputation shall be shredded."

"What do you mean?"

"My heart, Bree. I can scarcely feel it beating today."

"Do you mean to say you love him?"

She nodded. "I fell in love with him, just as I had feared. The stories have begun to circulate and there will be no salvaging myself now."

"Lady Lasking intimated that you were in the garden with Lord Lacey."

"I was. That, however, is not the only fact fueling her actions."

Bree waved a hand. "She is jealous of you. That is all. Surely she does not know the truth."

"She does not, but she will learn the whole of it if she continues on her quest to discover the connection between Lord Faraday and myself."

"Lord Faraday? What can he know of us? He has only just returned to Town."

Marianne waited a beat. "He was the first."

"Oh." Bree's brow puckered, then cleared. "He has not told anyone that. I have it on good authority, well from Polly Prestwick in any event, that Lord Faraday is very much interested in getting to know you. *You*, Marianne. Not this girl he knew months ago."

"That may be true but there is little doubt that with Lady Lasking's prodding he will arrive at the truth."

Bree straightened, a determined expression on her brow. "We shall deny it."

"That will not be enough, dear. Marcus— Rather, Lord Lacey has arrived at this arrangement which shall solve all of our troubles."

"And yet you sound far from excited over the prospect of marrying Mister Stilling."

"He is a good man, Bree. A bit self-indulgent, but his family's reputation will keep us safe. I am fortunate that he will have me, so altered as I am from the woman I was before our uncle's passing. It seems I can scarcely remember that innocent."

Bree was quiet for a moment, then stood. "Two men, Marianne? Plus Lord Lacy, of course. What was it like?"

She gasped. "Do not tell me that one of your suitors has attempted more than a press of your hand?"

Bree laughed, pulling Marianne to her feet. "There, you see? You are the same, innocent girl! You remain elementally the same, Marianne!"

She searched herself for a moment, then decided her sister was correct. She was unchanged, save for her passion for one man in particular. She acknowledged Bree's words with a nod.

"Come," Bree said. "Lord Lacey paid you very well, I am certain. Let us have Cook prepare our favorite things. We shall stuff ourselves until we pop!"

Her heart a bit lighter, Marianne followed Bree from the room.

Chapter 28

"Tell her that I am not receiving," Marcus growled at the closed study door.

"Yes, my lord," came Parks' muffled answer.

Marcus slumped in his chair. A hollow ache had taken the place of the gut-sucking pain of the afternoon, though that was something. The light outside the windows was fading, and evening was well on its way. He would not go to the parties. Not tonight. Seeing Marianne on Stilling's arm would surely cause him to cast up his accounts.

A knock came at the door again, a quick and insistent tattoo.

"Parks, I have no desire to see Lady Genevieve!" Marcus shouted.

The door was pushed open, revealing Rob's grinning face. "Surely you are not speaking of your lovely intended? This does not bode well for your marriage."

"A revelation I came to myself at approximately three o'clock this afternoon."

Rob shut the door and dropped into the chair across

from him. "And what, pray, happened at three o'clock this afternoon?"

"I informed Marianne of the arrangement."

Rob let out a low whistle. "She was not pleased, I take it?"

"Hardly. She did offer her gratitude, however."

"That is something."

"That is nothing!" He raked his fingers through his hair. "I had to do it, Rob. There is no other way to see the rumors quashed."

Rob stood, crossing to the sideboard to find one lone bottle which still had liquor in it. The soles of his boots crunched through the shards of glass on the floor. "Rough evening, I take it?" He poured himself a drink. "No matter. Come, then. We will go to the club and begin to circulate this new story of yours. It is at least as interesting as Faraday's continuing infatuation with your Marianne, despite Elise Lasking's inference that there is more to that particular tale."

"I suppose."

"We shall go and profess your impending happiness with Lady Genevieve. And ascertain if Elise's poison has taken root."

Marcus slowly came to his feet. "No doubt Bottom and Erlington will be there."

Rob nodded. "Their fat fannies are probably creasing the leather chairs as we speak. They are veritable fixtures there. And an invaluable resource of gossip."

"Two clucking hens," Marcus grumbled.

"We shall feed them the story and let them circulate it tonight at the parties. One can hardly think that Stilling would marry the woman who was once entangled with his sister's betrothed."

"My God, that sounds convoluted."

"It is not. It is completely reasonable, and had you not wasted such fine spirits attempting to drown yourself last evening you would see that."

Marcus nearly managed a smile at Rob's words.

"Go, Lacey," Rob prodded. "Your poor valet will no doubt be in fits and eager to see you set to rights." Rob sat behind Marcus' desk, propping his feet on the edge as he leaned back with his drink. "I shall wait here and plan our strategy."

Marcus regarded him for a moment, this man who had somehow become his friend and confidant over the years.

"Thank you, Rob."

Rob stared at him, that sharp glint in his eye, and he knew he grasped his meaning.

Marcus left the study. He had to face what he had done and see Marianne safe. Gone was the time, though brief, of hiding in his study and in a bottle.

A scant half hour later he was clean and dressed and ready to face what was sure to be a humiliating performance. But perform it, he would. He would pour it on so thick that even Bottom and Erlington would drink it up.

He returned to the study to find Rob apparently in deep thought. His brow was creased and he wore an expression of worry he had never seen on his face before.

"Rob?"

Rob started, then grinned up at him. "You look more the thing." He stood. "Shall we be off?"

"Yes."

He took a deep breath. Soon all and sundry would

know that he was to marry Genevieve and Stilling would
have his bride in Marianne. The pain in his stomach
returned.

"Easy there, Lacey. You look as though you ate
some off kippers."

"I am fine. Merely hungry, is all. I have not eaten a
bloody thing since last night."

"We shall eat first thing, then. Let the hens come to
us for the tale."

Marcus nodded and they departed for the club. Rob
was silent in the carriage, a first in Marcus' memory.
That was a good thing. After this evening there would be
no going back. No undoing what was to happen. He
sucked in a breath. No having Marianne in his arms—
God, in his bed—ever again.

"Bloody Stilling," he grumbled.

"Do lose that scowl. You wish to appear quite
pleased with your choice of bride. And full of nothing
but good wishes for your future brother-in-law on the
choice of his."

Marcus nodded sharply. "I shall attempt to leave
little room for doubt, Rob."

"Good."

Before long they arrived and walked in. Marcus steeled himself for the coming performance. It seemed there would be plenty of gentlemen in the audience.

"As I expected, the place is full," Rob said.

"The Season is waning," Marcus said. "All will soon be decamping to the country."

Rob nodded, leaning closer. "There will no doubt be house parties and shooting parties to come, but the prospect of spending the long evenings with only their wives' company send many men into an apoplectic fit."

Again Marcus thought of his own coming nuptials. "I sympathize."

"Now, none of that," Rob admonished. He raised a hand to a servant and they were escorted to a table. "Eat something, Lacey. And do attempt to look pleased with yourself?"

Marcus grumbled but acquiesced. Their food soon arrived. The smell of roast meat caused his stomach to grumble as well and he began to devour what was on his plate. "You had the right of it. At least my stomach will be full."

"So maudlin?" Rob smiled. "Are you speaking of your heart, pray?"

Marcus kept his face impassive. "Hardly." He returned to eating, feeling Rob's gaze on him.

"Straight-laced!" Erlington's shout from across the club came as no surprise, followed shortly by Bottom's guffaw. "Speak of the devil!"

Marcus swallowed his last bit of meat and sipped his drink. "Bottom. Erlington." He ran his eyes over them. "Out of your chairs at long last?"

Bottom's eyes boggled, then he laughed. "Lacey, are you making a jest?"

"Today is the day for strange occurrences," Erlington put in. "Heard your name bandied about all day long."

"What is this, pray?" Marcus asked.

Bottom signaled to the closest servant and had two chairs dragged over. He and Erlington sat, their eyes bright. From the drink or from the tale they would no doubt soon impart, Marcus could only guess.

"Had a bit of fun in the garden last evening, Lacey?" Bottom asked.

There it was. The first tale, spread by that bitch Elise.

"Pardon?" Marcus returned.

"Took advantage of the moonlight and a willing miss, we hear," Erlington said.

"I do not know to whom you refer, gentlemen," Marcus said.

"Come now, Lacey. You were seen, you know. Elise Lasking came upon you taking certain liberties."

"Did she now?" Marcus dabbed his mouth on his napkin. "She saw me in a compromising position?"

Erlington's gaze skittered away. "Well… she presumed that was what you were about with Marianne Ellsworth."

"I told you before, you should not speak of her or any woman in such a manner." He began to rise but Rob placed a hand on his arm. He took a breath. "I would not put much stock in Lady Lasking's tales."

"Oh?" Bottom's eyes were fairly gleaming now. "What of Faraday's?"

Marcus could not form a coherent word at the man's name being mentioned. This is what he had wanted, however. The chance to rid the *ton* of the notion that Marianne was that particular courtesan.

Thankfully, Rob took up the gauntlet. "What of Faraday?" he asked. "I heard him this very afternoon, going on about the lovely young lady. Surely he is not passing tales."

Bottom leaned closer. "It seems that the little dove what warmed his bed earlier this Season—you know her well I believe, Lacey—bears a strong resemblance to the young lady in question. He is quite enamored of her and eager to see if more than their faces are alike." He winked. "And Elise Lasking has taken an interest in proving that they are one and the same woman."

"That is enough!" Marcus surged to his feet, grabbing Bottom by the throat. "I have let your nonsensical prattling about myself go on for years now, but I shall not allow you to besmirch a lady's reputation based on one besotted fool's recollections and one grasping bitch's insistence!"

"Whoa there, Lacey!" Bottom squeaked. "I am merely putting forth the tale."

Erlington grabbed on to Marcus' arm. "See here,

Lacey. One would think you had designs on the girl yourself."

Marcus dropped his hands from Bottom, letting out a curse. "You have no right to speak of Miss Ellsworth. Either one of you."

"They do not," another man said. "And neither do you, Lacey."

Marcus froze. Damn. *Stilling.* Rob began to stand but he gave a quick shake of his head and faced Marianne's intended. "Stilling."

"I am surprised to see such kind regard on your part for my intended," Stilling said.

His stomach clenched, turning the fine meat he had just eaten to churning acid. It was done, then. Stilling had asked Marianne to marry him and she had accepted.

"I nearly offered for the girl's sister, Stilling," he managed to say. "Why would I not be concerned with the lady's reputation?"

"Because she is to be mine," Stilling said.

"You are engaged," Marcus stated.

Stilling's cheeks flushed red. "I… That is to say, it is not official. I was to speak to her today, but circumstances were somehow altered."

"She turned you down?" Erlington suggested.

"She did not turn me down," Stilling snapped. "She was unable to see me when I called."

Marcus felt as if a cool hand pressed to his brow, so sharp was his relief. "That is a pity."

Stilling eyed him. "More to the point, why did you not come to my house today, Lacey?"

"Your house?" Bottom mused aloud. "Whyever would he pay a visit to… Oh! Lacey is to offer for your sister?"

"Stilling," Marcus said in warning.

"What, Lacey? Do you not wish me to tell all that you have promised to marry my sister?"

"Lady Genevieve?" Erlington pounded Marcus on the back. "Good show, Straight-laced! I daresay she will be a fine match for you."

"Do be quiet, Erlington," Rob said.

"As to Miss Ellsworth," Stilling went on, "I shall have her acceptance well in hand before the week is out."

"Miss Ellsworth?" another man said.

Marcus turned to find Faraday shouldering his way

through the growing crowd around their little table. He wore the same besotted expression usually stamped on Stilling's face whenever Marianne was mentioned.

"What do you know of her?" Faraday asked.

"Come, Faraday," Rob drawled. "Did you not sing this song earlier this afternoon?"

Faraday cleared his throat. "I merely asked after her. Lady Lasking paid a call upon me this afternoon and had some stories to impart about that particular lady. I admit I found them quite intriguing."

"Do tell!" Erlington urged.

Bottom stayed quiet for once, his hand rubbing his throat as he eyed Marcus with caution.

"Do not," Marcus growled. "I have heard quite enough about Miss Ellsworth this evening."

"She is to be mine, Lacey," Stilling said again.

"She is?" Faraday frowned for a moment, then shrugged. "If that is so, then she cannot be the girl I knew. I was beginning to think… Well, that cannot be the truth."

"No," Marcus and Rob said at the same time.

Stilling puffed up his chest. "Leave off any more

comments about my future bride, all of you."

More talk went on, escalating into ribald comments about "Annie" and Marianne.

"The resemblance is uncanny," Faraday said. "Those eyes. That remarkable mouth."

"You had her months ago, Faraday," Bottom scoffed. "Perhaps Lacey should be the one to confirm such a likeness?"

"I will not," Marcus said.

"You've had her all Season long!" Erlington said. "You must have some notion…" He fell silent and an expression of horrifying enlightenment crossed his face. "She is the one!"

"No!" Marcus shouted. "Damn it, she is not the same girl."

"Come, Lacey," Bottom said. "Tell us Marianne Ellsworth is not the wench you've been riding all Season."

Marcus punched him square in the face. The sound of smashing bone and flesh was sickening and satisfying at the same moment.

"My nose!" Bottom gurgled. He straightened and

blood coursed down his face. "You broke my nose!"

Marcus held up his fist again. "Say another thing about her and I shall do more than that."

The others gawked at him in shock. "Straight-laced," Erlington murmured.

"I suppose I should thank you for defending my intended," Stilling grumbled.

"I did not." Marcus took in a breath. Certainty filled him as the answer struck.

"W-what?" Stilling stammered.

"I did not defend your intended," Marcus said. "I defended mine."

Chapter 29

Rob grinned, evidently ready to take up the story as he stood and placed a hand on Marcus' shoulder. "Tell them, Lacey."

Marcus handed his handkerchief to the bawling, bleeding Bottom and faced Stilling. "I am sorry to inform you of this Stilling, but Miss Ellsworth will not be accepting your suit after all."

"What? The hell you say! She is mine and you will marry my sister!"

"I will not." He held up a hand. "I have not offered for your sister, and I am not free to do so."

Stilling fairly trembled with ire while the others looked on with keen interest.

"Tell them," Rob said again.

"Marianne Ellsworth and I have been secretly engaged for these past three months," Marcus declared.

Erlington's mouth dropped open. "But Devlin bought you a…" He stopped himself as he caught Marcus' glare. "We thought that you were with your dove all Season."

"You thought wrong." He gave a nod. "I was

spending time with the woman I planned to marry. Proper, if somewhat private, calls."

"Then the girl I…" Faraday shook his head. "Of course she is not the same girl. Please forgive my interest in Miss Ellsworth, Lacey. I did not know of your arrangement."

Marcus inclined his head. Perhaps he would not kill the man for being with Marianne before him after all. "Thank you."

Stilling's face was pale, and Marcus almost pitied him. Almost.

"I suppose I should have expected something like this," he muttered. "There had to be a reason she was keeping me at arm's length."

Marcus merely arched a brow in answer to that. "Do give your sister my regards, Stilling."

Stilling nodded.

"The dove, Devlin," Erlington began. "What became of her?"

Rob shrugged. "I heard through my contacts that she returned to Cornwall soon after her rendezvous with Lacey. It seems that he paid her enough to go back to her family."

Faraday clicked his tongue. "Pity, that. I had hoped to sample her considerable charms again." He smiled. "I daresay it is a good thing she is not the same girl. Had she married Stilling, the boy would have been quite out of his element."

With that, Faraday took himself from them. Stilling left as well, sulking over to a table of his own and loudly ordering a drink. Erlington led a whining Bottom away and Marcus sat once more.

"My God, that was a close thing," he muttered.

Rob laughed. "That was well done of you. Whyever did you not think of that before?"

"My family's reputation." He laughed at himself. "Hang it all, Rob. I love her. I will not stand by and let another man have her."

"Good." Rob held up his glass. "To your intended. Now you have only to get her acceptance."

He recalled her ire of the afternoon and let out a breath.

"If I have to grovel I will. She will be mine."

* * *

"Miss?" George said from the open parlor doorway.

"Yes, George?"

"A gentleman has called, Miss."

Marianne froze. Surely Mister Stilling would not come to her this evening. She had finally convinced Bree and their aunt to go to the parties without her and ascertain if any gossip was circulating. She had hoped to avoid Mister Stilling's company and his inevitable marriage proposal for as long as possible, but it seemed now that he had different ideas. There was really nothing else for it, however. She had to accept his suit and set about her future as his wife.

She could almost bear his inevitable hatred if it was not for the fact that Marcus would marry the man's sister. That caused a pain she knew would last for the rest of her life.

"Miss?" George asked again.

"I suppose you may allow him entrance," she said.

George nodded and withdrew to see to her visitor. She braced herself for his fawning and knew that she would have to endure it only until sometime in the near future when he learned the truth about her. That would surely knock the stars from his eyes where she was concerned.

She heard footfalls and the door closed once more. Presumptuous man, thinking to have her alone in her parlor!

"Mister Stilling, I do not believe that meeting with me alone is proper."

"Then it is a very good thing that I am not him."

She whirled at the sound of Marcus' voice, struck dumb at his presence. He looked far better than she had found him this afternoon, and she held herself still to keep from flying into his arms.

"Aren't you going to wish me good evening?" he asked.

She tilted her head. "Are you teasing me, my lord?"

"No 'my lord,' Marianne. Remember? I asked you to call me Marcus ages ago."

"But that was when we…" She waved that provocative memory aside. "Why are you here, Marcus?"

"I have come to tell you that the rumors are effectively quashed."

She closed her eyes. "It is done then. You and I

shall both marry."

"Indeed we shall."

His voice was gay and light, and she peeped open one eye. "You seem quite pleased with your choice of bride at present. Have things so altered since this afternoon?"

"Oh, they have." He crossed to her, taking her cold hands in his warm ones. "I am quite pleased with my choice. Quite pleased, indeed."

That heat was back in his eyes, passion and something else. He never showed any warm regard for Lady Genevieve. Something was amiss.

"What is going on?" she asked.

"I chose you," he grinned.

She blinked rapidly, trying to decipher his meaning.

"This afternoon, Marcus. You told me that you could never marry me."

"I know. However I have come to realize that, while I may not have the Stilling family's sterling reputation, I have wealth." He brought his face to hers. "You see, love? Money can excuse nearly any impropriety."

She pulled her hands from his and squared her shoulders. "Explain yourself, Marcus. Do people know that you and I were together? That we had an arrangement?"

"Yes," he said with a laugh.

She bit back a curse. "I am so pleased to see that you find amusement in my ruin."

"You are not ruined, Marianne. No one will equate you with Annie ever again."

"I do not understand."

"I have told all and sundry that you and I have been secretly engaged for the past three months."

She could only gape at him, her head fairly spinning. "What are you talking about?"

Marcus waved her to the settee. "Sit, love. I shall attempt to explain."

She did as he bade her, mainly because her legs suddenly felt unable to support her.

"Secretly engaged?"

He smiled and joined her. "I went to my club today, to put forth the story of my intention to wed Genevieve."

She winced at the unexpected pain those words

caused. "I suppose that would be the fastest way to spread such joyous news."

He barked out a laugh. "One would presume. However, once I heard the tales circulating about you I could not allow them to go unchecked. It struck me quite like lightening, Marianne. I knew what I had to do and did so. Gladly."

Her heart gave a cautious little leap. "You told your friends that you and I are engaged?"

He spread his arms. "Isn't that brilliant? The horrid tales Elise Lasking has been spreading, Faraday's insistence that there is more to your passing resemblance to Annie, could not stand up to the tale I fed them."

"It is a tale, then?" she could not help but ask.

"No, love." He drew her closer. "It is not. I plan to marry you."

She stared into those lovely green eyes of his and nearly forgot herself. When he kissed her a moment later, hot and with so much passion, she surrendered for a moment. Oh, how sweet was his kiss!

A few heartbeats later, she pulled away. "I cannot marry you, Marcus."

He nuzzled her ear, her neck, dropping soft kisses on her throat. "Yes, you can. We will have to beseech your aunt to confirm that she has been acting as chaperone this long Season, but I presume she will have no trouble there. "

She smiled as she thought of the calling cards she had held on to all these weeks. "I have your cards, Marcus. Each and every one."

He pulled back in apparent surprise, and then grinned. "More evidence of our long-standing agreement! You can, and you will, marry me."

She so longed to believe him, but she held herself away from him, separate from his beguiling touch, his intoxicating scent. "I cannot marry you," she said again. "You know what I have done. What I was."

"I may not have been your first, but I will be your last." Again he smiled that exasperating grin. "And for the rest of my days, you will be mine."

"I wish it were that simple, Marcus." She forced herself to stand. "I was with other men. You will undoubtedly come to resent that fact." Turning, she bowed her head. "Come to hate me, even."

"Never." He stood and wrapped his arms around her, hugging her close against his chest. "You will be mine. Completely and legally. Forever. You shall spend your nights with only me. You shall bear my heirs."

Forever. His insistence was so seductive. She covered his hands with hers. "I know that you say this now. But how can I believe you?"

He tensed against her, then let out a breath and dropped his arms from her. "I was a fool, Marianne. I was cold and remote." He paused. "Everywhere but in our bed. I thought I could not bear the hint of yet another scandal after enduring my father and brother's disreputable lives." He turned her to face him. "You told me once that I was worthy of love. Do you remember that?"

She nodded. Of course she remembered that long-ago conversation in his bed. "I realized then that you were not the man you presented to Society."

"I was that man, love. Cold and austere like my mother." A shadow of a smile crossed his lips. "That was, however, before you. I love you."

Her breath caught. "I have loved you for so very

long," she admitted softly.

Tenderness showed in his eyes. "I knew it."

Her cheeks flooded with heat. "But Marcus, it is not *your* character that is in question now. You cannot ignore my past."

"I took measure of your character months ago, Marianne. And did not once find you lacking. As to your past, once I listened to your explanation I understood your actions." He lifted his hand to her cheek. "Do you remember that afternoon at my townhouse? The day I learned of your deception?"

"Yes." She shivered at the memory. "You were so very angry."

"Until you told me all of it. What your vile cousin did." A flash of that anger resurfaced in his eyes, though she knew it was toward John alone.

"Please do not speak of it," she whispered.

"You gave me your reasons, Marianne. I knew then, love. Everything that drives you. I knew."

She saw it on his face, understanding and what she now knew was love. He loved her! "Oh, Marcus."

"You have done nothing shameful in my eyes. You

did everything for your family. I myself have none to speak of, but if you will let me I shall endeavor to take as good care of them as you have these past months."

His words caused that burgeoning hope to spring anew. "What are you saying?"

"I will be happy to have your sister and your aunt reside with us. I will make certain that none of you are ever put in jeopardy again."

Her mind grasped what her heart had tried to hold on to since he had walked into her parlor. He truly knew why she'd done what she had. He knew, and he accepted her for herself. He would keep her family safe.

"I will marry you, Marcus!" she cried, throwing her arms around his neck.

He buried his face in her hair, his breath tickling her. "Mmm. I do have a small stipulation, however."

"Stipulation?"

"Never stop wearing vanilla."

She giggled as he playfully licked her neck.

"We will be very happy, love." He kissed her again, drugging kisses that muddled her mind in a most delicious fashion. He lifted his mouth a hairsbreadth from hers. "Is your staff circumspect, Marianne?"

She stilled, then grasped his meaning. Her body flushed hot. "Very."

He pulled back and began to undo his cravat. "I have been without your touch far too long. Tell me I may have you today."

She watched as his strong throat was revealed, glimpsing a shadow of his gorgeous chest as his shirt gaped open a bit. He was so beautiful. And he was hers.

"You may have me forever," she answered.

He shed his jacket and unbuttoned his waistcoat as she stared hungrily. In a flash of clarity she hurried over to the door and locked it tight. Turning back to him, she removed the fichu at her throat. His eyes ran over her, causing her body to tremble.

"Those eyes of yours," she purred.

"Come here, love." He beckoned her to him. "I need to touch you. Now."

She went willingly, her body on fire as if it had been months since she had last felt his hands on her flesh.

Afterward, long moments passed with her blissfully snuggled up against him as he continued to gently stroke her cheek. It was heaven, being in his arms again, with him buried deep inside of her. Oh! Her eyes popped open. He was inside of her!

"Marcus?"

"Yes?" His voice was so full of drowsy satisfaction and she could not help but smile.

"I did not take precautions," she told him.

He raised his head, his brow furrowed. "Precautions?" Enlightenment dawned on his face and to her amazement he shrugged. "We will simply go to Gretna Green, then." He kissed her nose. "I cannot have my courtesan countess round with child before we have spoken our vows, can I?"

She arched a brow at him. "Courtesan countess?"

He cupped her face with his hands. "Yes, love."

Smiling, she hugged him close and sighed.

Epilogue

London, England 1824

"I daresay I am quite grateful we took that trip to the north," Marcus said as he entered the parlor.

Marianne looked up with a smile and a sigh. "Yes, although the wedding should be quite wonderful."

Marcus caught her mouth in a tender kiss before eyeing the pile of correspondence and the like littering his wife's dainty desk. "Why on earth are you tasked with such duties?"

She folded her hands on top of the nearest pile of cards. "Because I promised Genevieve I would assist, that is why."

Taking her hand in his, he gently urged her to her feet. "And what does Stinky Stilling have to say about his sister's upcoming nuptials?"

Marianne laughed lightly, a bright sound that never ceased to warm him. "That is not well done of you, Marcus. Mister Stilling may still be our brother one day."

Marcus gave a quick shake of his head. "I have an inkling you may be wrong on that count."

She clicked her tongue. "Nevertheless, with the

start of the Season upon us there will soon be a scurrying for position with all and sundry returned to Town. I am quite sure Bree will be in the thick of it."

He chuckled. "The true hunt begins."

Wrapping her arms around his neck, she came up on her toes and nuzzled his neck. "Will you miss the excitement, husband?" she whispered.

"Not in the least." He let his hands rest at her waist. "I was well and caught before my hunt could begin in earnest and I could not be more pleased."

"Caught, yes." She leaned back to smile up at him, her dark blue eyes sparkling. "Pleased, however? Hmm."

He growled at her. "Very pleased, my countess."

They kissed again, taking the time to taste each other before separating. The heat, the love, that he had never thought possible warmed him anew.

"Are you nearly finished?" he asked.

"Nearly, yes." She returned to the desk to straighten the cards into an order he could not quite decipher before facing him again. "We are expected to make the rounds this evening. To test the waters, as it were."

It was his turn to sigh. "At least I can expect Rob to

be there."

She slid him a look. "It truly does not vex you, Marcus? My previous, um, encounter with Lord Devlin?"

"Not overly, no. He is a good friend, most likely the best I've got. He kept our secret, after all. And there is the little matter that if not for his interference I never would have found you."

"Found me?" She laughed again as she returned to him. "As I recall, I was dropped into your lap."

"Ah, and what a lovely present you were too." He settled on one of the chairs flanking the fireplace and drew her down onto his very fortunate lap. "That night I had no notion of what awaited me in your arms, love."

"And now it falls on us to find that kind of love for my sister."

"In a far different manner, I presume?"

"Oh, yes." She snuggled into him. "We must not have another courtesan in the family, thank you very much."

He smiled at the ease in which she said that. It was still a closely guarded secret, and he would fight any man who dared to raise a shadow of impropriety in his wife's direction. That did not stop him from calling her such when they were alone and wrapped in each other's arms, however.

"You are my courtesan countess, Marianne. Always."

Her full lips curved. "I told myself that our one night, our one Season, would be enough to sustain me through the lonely years to come."

"It would never be enough for me."

Her cheeks flushed a rosy pink. "And now it does not have to be."

He nodded his agreement. "You have my passion, Marianne. And my love and respect."

"And you have all of me, Marcus. Including my heart."

Her heart. His heart, that once cold and shuttered thing, beat with hers as he held her closer still.

She would be his courtesan countess forever.

About the Author

JoMarie DeGioia is a bestselling author of Historical and Contemporary Romance. She's known Mickey Mouse from the "inside," has been a copyeditor for her tiny town's newspaper, and a bookseller. She is the author of over 40 Romances, and writes Young Adult Fantasy/Adventure stories and Paranormal Romance too. She gets lost in DIY projects around the house and works out plot ideas during long runs. She divides her time between Central Florida and New England.

Discover other books by JoMarie DeGioia

The Bridgewater Brides series, including

The Heir's Treasure

The Viscount's Vixen

The Earl's Beauty

The Gentlemen Undercover series, including

A Hero and a Gentleman

A Hero and a Rogue

The Shopgirls of Bond Street series, including

That Determined Mister Latham

The Dashing Nobles series, including

More Than Passion

Pride and Fire

Just Perfect

More Than Charming

The Cloud Canyon series, including

Chasing Dreams

The Cypress Corners series, including

Cypress Corners Boxed Set

Finding Harmony

Taming Jake

Loving Cassie

Winning Ben

Showing Jessie

Seeing Shannon (Barefoot Bay World novella)

Dreaming Eli

Giving Chase (Barefoot Bay World novella)

Kissing Bree

Wishing Joy

Bugging Nate

The Gifted YA Fantasy/Adventure Trilogy, including

Gifted

Braunachs of the Dell series, including

Luke's Gold

Patrick's Promise

The In the Castle series of Historical Novellas, including

In the Lady's Heart

In the Baron's Bed

In the Knight's Chamber

Connect with me online

Twitter: https://twitter.com/JoMarieDeGioia

Facebook:
https://www.facebook.com/JoMarie.DeGioia.Author

Website: www.jomariedegioia.com